Touch
The Great Indian
mba dream

Shiva Prakash is a writer, musician and poet. He manages global Internet products for one of the world's largest Internet companies. He has an MBA from the Indian School of Business, in Hyderabad, and a Bachelor's Degree in Computer Science and Engineering from BMS College in Bengaluru where he was selected to be a Fellow of the Melton Foundation USA. His prior writing accomplishments include poetry and short stories. He is a keen painter, guitarist and singer and has led one of the top corporate cricket teams in Bengaluru.

His interests are philosophy, spirituality, economics and humour and he lists sky-diving and hiking in Ladakh and the Pacific Coast as his most liberating experiences. *Touching Distance* is his debut work.

Touching Distance
The Great Indian
mba dream

Shiva Prakash

AMARYLLIS

AMARYLLIS

Copyright © Shiva Prakash 2011

All rights reserved. No part of this book may be used or reproduced, stored in or introduced into a retrieval system, or transmitted, in any form, or by any means, (electronic, mechanical, photocopying, recording or otherwise) without the prior written permission of the Publisher. Any person who does any unauthorised act in relation to this publication may be liable to criminal prosecution and civil claims for damages.

Shiva Prakash asserts the moral right to be identified as the author of this work

Author's Disclaimer

All characters appearing in this book are purely fictitious and are figments of my many imaginations. No character bears any resemblance to any person alive or dead. If you disagree, it could be because a misfiring synapse of cosmic energy caused the frequencies of our imaginations to collide in a transient parallel universe. This, I cannot prove, and neither can you. I may remember the collision, and I promise to say no more.

This edition first published in 2011

AMARYLLIS

An imprint of Manjul Publishing House Pvt. Ltd.

Editorial Office:
J-39, Ground Floor, Jor Bagh Lane,
New Delhi 110 003, India
Tel: 011-24642447/24652447 Fax: 011-24622448
Email: amaryllis@amaryllis.co.in
Website: www.amaryllis.co.in

Registered Office:
10 Nishat Colony, Bhopal 462 003, M.P., India

ISBN: 978-81-910673-3-0

Typeset in Warnock by
Mindways Design
1410 Chiranjiv Tower, 43 Nehru Place
New Delhi 110 019

Printed and Bound in India by
Thomson Press Ltd.

For my mother, my greatest blessing

Contents

Acknowledgements		*ix*
Prologue		*xi*
1.	The Stockholm Syndrome and an Astrologer's Prophecy	1
2.	Tailspin	15
3.	Gillette: The Best Every Man, Woman and Free-Rider Can Get	33
4.	The Fellowship of the Lost	48
5.	The Animal in J-Block	65
6.	Capt	71
7.	Satellite Attack	80
8.	The Recruit on the Rooftop	87
9.	Of Sofas and Shaktimaans	93
10.	The Smile of the Mona Lisa	101
11.	The Laws of Conservation	109
12.	Hoo Haa Hoo	118
13.	The Curse of the Minority Investor	129

14. Poolside Stimulations	138
15. The Great Mysore Sandal Soap Robbery	147
16. The Sermon on the Rock	160
17. Blink	171
18. Valentine's Day	179
19. Strategically Yours	185
20. The Roll of the Dice	191
21. The Real World	221
22. A Soul Insured	232
23. The Da Ranga Code	242
24. The Cookie Crumbles	249

Acknowledgements

This began as an attempt to rediscover a few laughs with friends. It could have evaporated into nothingness, had it not been for early encouragement, both from people who knew this context closely and from others who did not. For this I thank my dear friends, Ranjeev Babu, Ramaswamy Venkatachalam, Vijay Raghavan, Anis Ahmed, Aridaman Tripathi and Sudhir Shenoy.

I had never met Shreeniwas V. Iyer but Anis suggested Shreeni read the story, highlighting his diligence, honesty and taste. Thank you Shreeni, for your honest and kind reflections after reading every word written by a complete stranger.

Aridaman remains the only one who read the entire manuscript without a single reminder in the early days of this effort. I will remember the day you called and simply said, 'I've read it, it's good'. Curt, reliable and loyal as always.

Thanks to Ranjeev Babu and Ramaswamy Venkatachalam, the elder brothers I never had. Ranjeev—for sitting patiently through each chapter, then suggesting changes over instant messenger programs in the middle of far more interesting and challenging tasks; and Ramas—for always being there.

Thanks to Vijay Raghavan, for the many inspiring bits of advice and for walking the extra mile for me.

Thanks to the team at Amaryllis, especially Sanjana, Manoj, Shruti and Ankush, a committed group of professionals who are living their dream, creating something beautiful and worthwhile, one day at a time.

x *Acknowledgements*

Thanks to the professors, the administrators and the Deans at the Indian School of Business for creating something fantastic in India.

Special thanks to Rajat Gupta, for being such a shining example of integrity, intelligence and grace, and for having 'the idea' and making sure its 'time' came to pass.

My ISB class will always have a special place in my heart. Brilliant minds, unfettered by the world, all on their way to break the ground in their own Gachibowlis in the best traditions of the ISB.

Years ago, I was a student at the BMS College of Engineering in Bengaluru, where I was chosen to represent the institute to the Melton Foundation, spread across five countries. The Melton Foundation is the brainchild of Dr William Melton, founder of Verifone and CyberCash. Bill, as he is known to us, is a career entrepreneur, but first and foremost, a philanthropist who cares about making the world a better place. Thank you for opening new vistas to us all, and for taking the time to show people horizons beyond horizons.

I would like to thank someone special who once said, 'I wish I'd known you earlier, so you could have written at least a line about me!' To her I say, it would take a book, and a beautiful one at that. Thank you for your encouragement, love and spirit. Finally, thanks to my wonderful family and friends who make it all worthwhile.

Prologue

There is a plan bigger than yours. There has to be, when you just can't get anything right!

This book is about plans and outcomes, neither of which you control. All you can do is be true to yourself and do what your heart says. Because only the heart knows.

The rest is being planned for you by the Universe.

1

The Stockholm Syndrome and an Astrologer's Prophecy

A stone's throw from Jerusalem,
I walked a lonely mile in the moonlight
And though a million stars were shining,
My heart was lost on a distant planet

—STING

I stood before Sri Srinivasan Ramachandran—octogenarian, former corporate law expert, and now resident-astrologer to those in and around Vijayanagar in Bangalore—full of hope and reverence. I had made a long, slow trip from my corner of Bangalore to this suburb, fighting the teeming millions engaged in their struggle for existence, from the ubiquitous autorickshaw-drivers to cart-pullers, vegetable vendors, to pretty much everyone in every trade of every supply-chain in this city. All of them moving towards fusing with the 'One', cleansing their karmas in the process.

On previous visits, I had had several questions in my mind, but never ever had the courage to ask them. For example: 'Why wasn't I born in a rich, homogenous Scandinavian country full of beautiful women and sensible ratios of gender, population, and

2 Touching Distance: The Great Indian MBA Dream

economy? Mind you, I never asked to be a Shah Rukh Khan or a Rahul Gandhi; I'm just happy being the average Joe, except that an average Joe in a rich, First World country probably has it better than Shah Rukh Khan in India, and certainly has it better than any politician. But an existentialist I am, so let's move on.

I hadn't asked that question because I already knew the answer. I was born in the mother of all karma-bhoomis because I had a lot of karmic debt. We all know that, don't we? What else could explain this geographic lottery India—one billion souls getting rid of their cumulative karmas? One big densely populated country. What a concept! Done with creating India, the One must have said, 'Pretty extreme; I hope it works'. More debt, anyone? Ahem . . . one for me, please.

Why? Coming up: Born into a traditional middle-class, God-fearing south Indian family, and brought up on the knowledge contained in the holy books, full of legend, *shastras* and learning—not to mention a healthy dose of academic obsession—I had got to where most people in this country want to get to at my age. I was on the threshold of wresting a seat at the ISB, a top business school in the country, in the classical zero-sum game, from someone else. I had been invited; all I had to do was give them rupees nine-lakhs sixty-thousand, and I would move further up on the ladder to wealth, where countless devotees worshipped and kept worshipping every year, irrespective of the outcome.

Nine-lakhs sixty-thousand . . . steep, isn't it? Takes your breath away. There's a lot you could do with that kind of money in 2002: buy an apartment or a large piece of land near the city; finance a B-grade movie; or take a couple of years off to 'find yourself'. Almost ten-lakhs versus an education . . . with a tradeoff like this, there's not much else you can do besides think yourself into the ground.

All you ever knew was that as an academic achiever, you never had to pay more than what was asked of a meritorious student in India—the so-called 'merit fee'—a reasonable fee at colleges run or supported by the government, charged students who had studied

The Stockholm Syndrome and an Astrologer's Prophecy **3**

their way to the top of the pile. My entire engineering education had cost me not more than rupees twenty thousand or so, at approximately five thousand a year. What's more, an education at the Indian Institutes of Management cost no more than two- or three-lakhs for a two-year course, subsidised heavily, thanks to the other tax-paying people of this country.

Here was this new upstart college, ISB, decorated with bedazzling ornamentation in the form of international affiliations with Wharton, Kellogg and the London Business School, glittering in all its power, much like the Lord of the Seven Hills in Tirupati on an auspicious day—adorned with more gold than the self-manifested idol may want to wear. These thoughts had carved their own deep paths in my mind, down which flowed a constant stream of stress and worry. I had to get this river to stop, and the time had come to gaze at the stars and read a suitable prophecy that might be written among the many constellations of my future. And so, there I was, standing before Sri Srinivasan Ramachandran. When all else fails, talk to an astrologer; another inescapable south Indian trait.

'Namaskaram, sir', I said, with palms joined together in a deep, heartfelt reverence. Sri Srinivasan Ramachandran had this effect on you, and so did the room, which served as bedroom, puja room and visiting chamber for souls like me who were forever intrigued by their call to don a human body for a fixed amount of time. Murals of Vishnu's conch and *chakra* adorned the walls on either side of his visage, while a sacred wheel, signifying time, faced east, affixed atop his recliner. On a table were kept photos of Vishnu and Krishna, and a four-foot statue of Krishna looked over the astrologer and all who came to visit him.

Incense burned, indicating that his morning prayers had just been completed. As always, a penetrating look of cheerful gravity greeted me. Yes, to the world he was an astrologer who seemed like he had realised the full weight of what that meant to him and to everyone who walked away with his interpretation of the time-space continuum. A continuum wrapping itself tantalisingly around

4 *Touching Distance: The Great Indian MBA Dream*

their lives, constricting their options and opportunities while they fought the python-like grip to believe they were really free.

There are several kinds of astrologers in this world, and I, for one, have seen a few, more out of curiosity than faith. Several are palpably phoney, bedecked with affectations and effects ranging from soft devotional music and psychedelic lighting, to the tarot, talking parrots, large posters of the human palm and anything else you could install to communicate your prowess in the art of clairvoyance. In a less stressed-out country, these themes might well make for the interior of a rather popular pub!

But I have to say that Srinivasan Ramachandran was different. He had lived in the real world, like most of us, and astrology, in all its science and art, had been inherited in his genealogy through three generations. Educated and erudite, he was as softspoken as the next Tamil senior citizen, yet as honest to his calling as someone committed to carefully snipping at a bonsai or tending meticulously to their aquariums.

Incense rose in the air and the *sricharanam*—the vermilion tilak on his forehead signifying his obeisance to Vishnu—was now creased, signifying his happiness and soft surprise as he watched me enter. The lack of ostensible trappings created an aura of hope and reverence, causing you to prostrate immediately and completely, to implore Lord Vishnu himself to oversee this interaction.

So there I was, prostrating in all my devotional immediacy like a giant tree falling silently in the forest. He blessed me with a long life and happiness. As always, he wore a white shirt and a white *veshti*. At six feet, he was imposing, but his high forehead and aquiline features communicated intellect and wisdom, which is what I had come to seek today.

'Namaskaram. *Ungal paatu romba naal aachi,*' he said in Tamil, referring to how long it had been since I'd last seen him. We exchanged a few more typical pleasantries, asking about each other's health, general disposition and the weather, and thanked God for his benevolence upon our lives.

The Stockholm Syndrome and an Astrologer's Prophecy **5**

'Tell me *saar*, how can I help you?' he said. His accented mispronunciation was effusive in its humility.

'Firstly, sir, it is so nice to see you again. Hope you've been well?' I asked, and waited for the words to manifest themselves. I knew exactly what they would be, more from experience rather than my ability to divine his thoughts.

'Manageable,' came the succinct reply, and a big smile, as always.

'Sir, I have been offered admission, as you had predicted. But the fee is very high. I would only be able to manage it if I get a scholarship . . .'

'Oh-ho, very good, *saar*,' he said, then reached across to the books predicting the movements of stars and constellations and stared seriously at them. On a cue, I pulled out my computer-generated horoscope and handed it over. He studied the papers for a while and I watched him like the tricolour painted guy in the crowd watching Sachin bat at just six runs short of his century.

'*Saar*, in the next few months, *guru* moves into fourth house. At the same time, *sani* is in retrograde. There shall be problems, but you shall overcome them,' he said and smiled. I smiled and wrote down the prophecy, deliberately ignoring my happy thoughts which were now banging on the door asking to be let out to their newly found playground. This was a time to focus on questions, not be distracted.

He proceeded to count, his right thumb touching each finger on the hand starting with the smallest, muttering names of planets in Tamil to himself, his mind pondering the effulgence or malignancy of their relative positions. Finally, he muttered a mantra, seeking Vishnu's permission, and said, 'Yes, *saar*, you may proceed. You shall get the scholarship.'

The incense, which I had tuned out, now returned, sweeter than ever, as my spirit felt at ease.

❖

6 *Touching Distance: The Great Indian MBA Dream*

3.00 am. I sit staring at the wall beyond my desktop computer. On my desk is Yogananda Paramahansa's *Man's Eternal Quest*. This was the day I needed to communicate my decision to the folks at the school. I had done everything possible to help make this decision: I had called friends from other B-Schools, students at the ISB, even spoken to my employer and HR about sponsorship opportunities. I surmise this is what every person throwing away a job and going back to school thinks about. The decision is never an easy one, and hangs over your head like Damocles' sword suspended by its proverbial horse hair, leaving you feeling like you might just be the stupid one taking the candle of your hope a little too close to the suspension mechanism.

My present situation had some context to it. I was responsible for a family of two sisters and my mother, and my job and income meant quite a bit to me. My father's early and untimely death and the attendant financial consequences that existed in pre-ubiquitous-insurance, pro-pension, high-inflation India had compelled me to look at financial security slightly differently when compared to my peers.

The seeds of my desire to change my status quo rested in something much more compelling, something that most people simply take for granted. It was that thing they call your 'work life', and really, at the time, I had the least idea it was meant to be an oxymoron. And I was stupid enough to believe that there was to be life in work. Goddamn television and print advertising for formal clothes.

In case you haven't guessed it already: I worked as a software programmer, which was about the most meaningless thing one could ever do for a living.

Why? Here goes. I'm certain that somehow, I had been kidnapped, and I was suffering from something that definitely was a variant of the Stockholm Syndrome.

In my case, the abductor was my employer, and I was holding on for survival. I hated the relationship, but I knew that the sooner

The Stockholm Syndrome and an Astrologer's Prophecy 7

I became comfortable with it, the easier it would get. There were many similarities to being kidnapped: I was indoors all the time; there was a limitation on expressing myself; and the abductor had strict rules curtailing my physical movement. If you don't know what I mean, ask any regular outgoing person what it means to graduate from college and then sit for ten hours a day in front of a machine, writing apathetic computer programs that have no respect for either you or your aspirations.

This is the reality of those who call themselves 'programmers', and work in large multinational companies housed in swanky glass buildings. From a social perspective, the world they live in is divided by genetics, no less. The division separates the two kinds of people that inhabit these places: born-geeks and non-geeks. If you are a born-geek, you probably salivate over the speed of the latest AMD processor and reach climax every time a computer program works. If, on the other hand, you are not a geek, and are chained to a desk for ten hours a day, pushing keys that generate code into a computer, then you are headed for physical, emotional and spiritual debilitation of the worst kind, where there is simply no liberation except for the act of leaving through the door . . . or through the window. Several times, I stared out that window, wondering whether it was high enough, and every time I saw someone else looking through it, I read their thoughts, then debated the optimal course of action – call for an ambulance or kick them through it myself?

Sometimes, sitting in that glass cage they called the office, staring at that screen they called the monitor, I'd formulate escape plans. One of them had now come to manifest itself. I'd always wanted to get a post-graduation degree, preferably an MBA.

After all, most MBAs are portrayed as always seen talking to customers, wining, dining, cracking deals or forever being interviewed by sexy journalists. Admit it, you never saw a photo of an MBA with a bad haircut and lousy clothes, sitting in front of a screen, with the most horrific expression of self-doubt on

8 *Touching Distance: The Great Indian MBA Dream*

his face. I was seduced: marketing, strategy, finance – all of it sounded so bloody appealing. If any convincing was still required, the B-School brochures were full of bright, smiling faces, flawless blue and black suits, with enough delectable females to make you want to get there on all fours. So distant from the population at software companies filled with depressed individuals who had no interest in each other's lives, and even lesser in their own.

Programming brought a lot of solitude with it, and a very pernicious one at that – the kind you slowly embrace, like a drug. Oh, I had the symptoms all right: I sent emails to the guy in the next cubicle instead of talking to him; I became good at my job and even better at hating it and being deeply unhappy. I preferred having lunch alone, and pretended to be lost gazing at the carpet when acquaintances walked past in the hallway. I began to desire a life with no human contact. Employees laughing made me suspicious, but I forgave the more attractive girls, thus observing that I was thankfully still somewhat sane. I knew I was sinking into a hole in history that would very soon be covered by the sands of time, and I almost willed that sand dune to cave in. The writing on the epitaph was clear to me, and I read it with a sardonic shrug and a masochistic smile:

> *Here lies yet another software engineer.*
> *May his frustration rot in peace!*

❖

In time, I got the better of my inertia. After toiling over GMAT books, application essays, the CAT and a few other lesser-known entrance exams, I finally got admission into a great school. The escape hatch had opened! But there were downsides a year away from my responsibilities here in Bangalore. So much money to be borrowed . . .and even more to be repaid. This is India, you see, where the risk premium in the interest rates applies to everyone alive.

The Stockholm Syndrome and an Astrologer's Prophecy **9**

It was also a decision that wasn't exactly being made in the best of times: not too long ago, two planes had flown into two tall buildings and an international war waited to be unleashed, like rabid dogs within smelling distance of slowly melting ice. With the looming war, there was a widely expected economic depression, promised to follow with the certainty of eyeballs chasing a Baywatch babe running across the screen.

I thought some more. As always, I thought myself to sleep. I needed to decide on the most expensive purchase decision within the next twenty hours or so, and communicate my acceptance to the ISB.

Back home, I leafed through *Man's Eternal Quest*. As the letters 'D-e-s-t-i-n-y' swam into focus, I dropped off to sleep.

❖

I woke up tired. Six am and the horns on the street outside were blaring away like battle sirens. I reflected upon my situation.

9:00 am. I got out of bed and composed my thoughts: I had made a decision.

I turned on my computer.

I was ready to send that letter.

I was turning down my offer of admission.

It was too scary. If I was truly meant to go, it really should not be so difficult, I reasoned. As I walked away trying to come to terms with kicking away this opportunity, the email rammed into the admissions inbox at ISB and my fate seemed sealed.

I shaved, showered and felt terribly confused, but relieved at having made that decision. I then went to work in my glass cage with the soulless machines and the soulless people who sent me emails. Would it kill them to smile once in a way? Look at what I was giving up – the least they could do was to be happy for me.

It felt like a strange sort of day. I looked listlessly at the screen, my thoughts far away, dominated by a feeling of loss.

10 *Touching Distance: The Great Indian MBA Dream*

Something even worse had happened the week before. It was one of those things that should never have bothered me, something really Dilbert-ish, but nevertheless did, because it involved a friend and colleague.

Our team had moved to a new floor with new cubicles, desks, elevators, carpets and plants. The new air smelled like a concoction of odours. It was an exciting day for everyone around. My best work-buddy, Ramesh, had been given one of the two available independent cubicles, with the other one going to another senior employee. At a software glass cage for young professionals around the age of twenty-five, an independent cubicle is the equivalent of a nice office with an expensive ficus in the corner, a nice aquarium with fish most people have no idea how to pronounce the names of, and a drop-dead gorgeous secretary who really wants to read, then discuss and realise your mental desires every time the door closes.

Ramesh was a friend, and a peer, so this meant that my manager valued him more than she did me. I didn't contest the fact that Ramesh was the more committed employee – he'd long made peace with the abductor.

Nevertheless, what hurt no end was that Ramesh had glided into the cubicle so easily, not asking me even once if I wanted it or whether I was okay with it.

As the day unfolded, I grew tired, but just sat there, like a sitting duck waiting to be shot. Much as I tried to reconcile my decision with fate, the heaviness in my heart grew more profound by the minute. I had dropped off while reading *Man's Eternal Quest* the previous night, but who's to say the book had not been reading me while I slept. At approximately 7.30 pm, it began.

A colleague, who was applying to IIM-Bangalore for a part-time course, asked whether I had accepted my admission to ISB. When I told him of my decision, he looked at me like I had just pushed someone into a gas chamber, patted them on the back and turned on the tap. 'Dude, what are you doing!' he said. 'Even if you

The Stockholm Syndrome and an Astrologer's Prophecy **11**

make it to IIM–B, you will still end up working here for the three years that it takes to finish that excuse for an MBA, and you will probably continue with this job thereafter. The degree would not make a difference.'

I stared vacantly at the pixels on the screen. He was right, and I'd made my peace with this line of reasoning. Why was he bringing it up again? Hadn't he got my telepathic back-me-up or leave-me-alone email?

'Look at me, man: there are no guarantees. I've tried the IIM–B admission before and it didn't happen. The last time, they chopped me down at the interview stage. I still have no idea why!'

It was then that he brought up something that he simply should not have.

'Where is Ramesh? He's always around here, isn't he? Oh, he moved to the independent cube? OK, tell him I said Hi.'

When you think about it, it's funny how something like that just does it.

As he walked away, oblivious, he did not see the dagger in my chest, its hilt engraved with pre-ice-age-ocean polished pebbles spelling the word 'reality'. Of course, he did not hear my fragile ego break into tiny pieces, falling silently on the newly carpeted floor. New floor, new cubes, same old me.

I packed my bag, got up and walked to the new elevator. I pushed a button, which I could barely read through the refraction in my tears. As the doors came together in closing, the first teardrop hit the floor.

Great sadness, and great relief. Someone had kicked me out the window on the tenth floor and I was finally free for a few moments. As the elevator landed on the ground floor, I had fallen to my deliverance and an after-life.

❖

Frantic calls and even more frantic emails to ISB ensured that I held my place. I told them I was coming, and that I had changed my

12 *Touching Distance: The Great Indian MBA Dream*

decision. That night, as I marked the page on *Man's Eternal Quest*, I could not sleep, but this time it was out of sheer excitement.

As my eyes grew sleepier, accepting the twilight of the passage into the subconscious, Sri Srinivasan Ramachandran came into focus. His prediction echoed in the silence of my hope.

I smiled. Somewhere in the heavens, the gods were laughing at a poor mortal's plight.

❖

Two weeks before my term at the ISB began, something strange happened.

We owned a small housing site on the outskirts of Bangalore, and were told that someone was keen on buying it. I was surprised: we'd been trying to sell it for a long time and we'd never made any headway. The location was terrible and we were quite fed up of protecting a small piece of housing land far-off, where neither law nor rule was expected to come to bear. We were only too happy to get rid of it. The transaction concluded soon and before we knew it, we had a small amount of money. My mother insisted I invest it in my tuition fee, despite my protestations and doubt. As I prepared to courier the draft to ISB, I could not help smiling at the happy timing of this sequence of events.

The words of the astrologer replayed in the stillness of my mind. Was the universe aligning itself like Paulo Coelho promised?

❖

A few days later, I made the big march to the office, my strides easily outclassing that of any of the soldiers at the Wagha border. It was my last day in the glass cage. Goodbyes were said. My colleagues gave me a gift that Ramesh had picked up. Before the ubiquity of cell phones, it was one of those fashionable, small Casio handheld digital diaries, useful for taking notes and storing phone numbers. Trust my buddy to pick out something useful and elegant. 'This

The Stockholm Syndrome and an Astrologer's Prophecy **13**

will help you,' he said with a smile tinged with sadness. The small gesture of goodwill overwhelmed me. I was walking away from strong friendships, that existed for their own sake. Would I ever make such friends again at the ISB?

Later that day, bags packed, I was again overcome with emotion as I said goodbye to my mother and sisters. My mother had done all she could to raise us all by herself for the last eight years, and now she was filled with pride. To all my doubts about quitting my job and taking on an education loan and then selling the property, she had simply said, 'It's for the education. Don't think about it; it will be worth it.'

I felt the weight of my familial responsibilities more than ever as I stood on the steps of the train pulling me away from my family. Through the city and then through the outskirts, my heart pounded with glee, like the base drum of a rock band taking you pleasantly by surprise.

As dusk fell, I felt energised like never before. I opened one of the pre-term books I had to read. Statistics. I did my best, but was too excited to read or to fall asleep. Hours passed and it was now close to midnight. I paced up and down the aisle, buying a few cups of tea from the vendor passing through, and gazing into the horizon.

Unable to sleep, I walked to the end of the compartment to the open door. I stood at the very edge, holding on to the metal supports on either side, and felt the full blast of the winds of the Deccan Plateau against my body.

The wind was cool, and I felt a chill run down my spine. Standing there, I sent a prayer heavenwards, thanking the gods for helping fulfil an aspiration. A feeling of quiet exhilaration overcame me: I was finally moving far away from the abductor, who seemed out of focus now. I had escaped! With the wind dashing against my face, I felt at one with the universe, and heard those immortal lines from Phil Collins echo from far away:

Now I, now I wish it would rain down, down on me.

14 *Touching Distance: The Great Indian MBA Dream*

I was blissfully absorbed in the moment when I heard someone cough and stumble behind me. My position wasn't exactly what you call safe, hanging outside a train in India, so I decided to postpone my moment of being-at-one-with-the-universe. Besides, I didn't want to risk a second kick in the same month.

I snapped back and turned around to see a portly guy in a vest and shorts, looking at me. His smooth developing belly peeped out of the bottom of his one-size-too-short vest. He looked about twenty-five, and his hair—gosh, yes, all of it—stood on end. His eyes gazed vacantly at me from behind gold-rimmed glasses, suggesting a combined feeling of boredom and disinterest. You see a lot of unique creatures while travelling on a train, and this was certainly one of them. Without doubt, a south Indian version of Homer Simpson.

'I mean, er . . . like, what's the time?' he asked, his index finger reaching for his navel.

'2.00 am,' I said disgusted with his finger's goal.

The wind howled behind me, and he just stood there, rocking gently back and forth, probably processing what I had just said. This guy was either very drunk or very sleepy.

2

Tailspin

Into the distance, the river all black,
Stretched to the point of no turning back
A flight of fancy, on a windswept field
Standing alone, my senses reel

—Pink Floyd

'2.00 am', I repeated, unsure whether he had heard me.
He burped in reply, and stumbled, crashing his shoulder into the walls as the train changed its angle ever so slightly. This guy wasn't exactly a circus born tightrope walker.

'I mean, like . . . 2.00 am, huh?' he grunted.

I nodded.

'*Shivaneey!*' (Oh Lord Shiva), he said in Kannada, 'I've been sleeping for six hours straight.' He rubbed his eyes.

'Shiv,' I said, introducing myself. I extended my hand but wasn't sure if I should have.

'Oh, Hi. I mean, like . . . Rangashekhar. You can call me Ranga,' he mumbled as he shook my hand.

'Are you on your way home?' I asked him.

16 *Touching Distance: The Great Indian MBA Dream*

He rubbed his eyes a little more and said, 'Gosh! Another three hours . . .'

I repeated my question.

His expression changed and assumed a lot more gravity.

'No, like . . . I mean, I'm going to study.'

'Where?' I asked, half dreading the reply.

'ISB,' he responded, with an air of intent.

'Oh really? Me too.' I said breezily, not knowing if I should match his seriousness.

'Oh, cool. I mean, like . . . that's great. Where did you work before?'

I named the glass cage.

'Oh, I used to work there. Then I joined TechPlant just when it started. I mean, like . . . I was one of the first to join the founders. It's a great company. I mean, like . . . lots of stock options. I mean, they've got great strategy. Mid-market US businesses. I mean, there was a Morgan Stanley report about them. I mean, there was a Forrester report about them. I mean, even Blackstone wanted to, like get in early and stuff. The guys are visionary. Ha! Ha! Ha! I used to drink chai with the founders, Krish and Swami, pretty often in the early days. They'd really had it slaving for that company they used to work for before.'

My head reeled from the number of names and references. What the hell were Forrester and Blackstone, and how did he know all these names? Some of them sounded like expensive whiskey brands. I felt stupid. Who was this guy? The next billionaire techie? Apparently, he'd made all the right moves: he'd joined a hot start-up; drunk pots of tea with its visionaries and maybe even peed against the same tree soon after. If I was supposed to compete with him for my post-MBA job, what chance did I stand?

'I mean . . . where did you do your engineering from?' he asked.

I named the college; it *was* one of the best. While I had been offered admission at more prestigious colleges, I'd decided to stay

Tailspin **17**

back in the city. After my father's death, I needed to be with my family.

'I went to REC Suratkal,' he said. REC Suratkal was the top college in the state.

Hmm, there it was. He looked dishevelled and unkempt and slightly lost as he conversed, but left you feeling like you were in the presence of an intellectual heavyweight. He looked like he could tear off some toilet paper, concentrate on it, then be struck by a bolt of inspiration and solve a math problem that was making a Harvard professor impotent. Heck, he seemed like the sort to just as likely to flush it down ten minutes later, too lazy to reach for a new length. Needless to say, I felt a little insecure and shallow.

'I mean, there are a few more guys in my compartment. Let's talk to them in the morning. I mean, I need to go to the loo now,' he declared and walked away.

I looked out the door. The wind now felt downright chilly. The rocks of the Deccan Plateau glistened in the moonlight, and looked like they were being critical of my expectations.

❖

The next morning began on a warmer note. I stepped out on to the platform with my belongings, and looked about. There I was, looking upon a sea of new faces. The Kacheguda railway station was crowded and dirty. Resigning myself to fate, which I was sure was laughing out loud, I trooped along in the direction of the masses, dodging coolies trying to grab my luggage and taxi and auto-drivers screaming locations and prices in my face. My fellow journeyman from last night was nowhere to be seen.

I stepped outside the station and was greeted by more filth and noise; leaving my senses attacked with the non-stop stimulus of an Indian railway station. Then, I saw a group of guys talking to the driver of a white Ambassador. And there, much to my relief, ironically, was Ranga. I walked over quickly. The discussions were soon completed amidst quick, knowing introductions and the four

18 *Touching Distance: The Great Indian MBA Dream*

of us got in. It was 5.00 am and the day was just breaking, but it was pretty stuffy already, and not in a culturally-beautiful-Chennai-kind-of-way.

In the cab we quickly slipped into a pleasant conversation. The mood was one of anticipation as we cruised on comfortably towards our destination. Everyone in the cab was an engineer, had worked in a top technology company and had approximately the same kind of education and experience. Ranga knew one of them, Praveen, and they went on and on talking about people they knew. I was surprised to know that none of the others had concerns about the high fee or any trepidation about placements, which were to come up in a few months.

I wondered what these people were like. Given that we'd all got off the train together, I concluded that we must have had pretty similar value systems arising from homogenous socio-economic bearings. To be honest, I was a little more than happy to meet people attempting to share cabs. Until that point, I had more than my fair share of the fear that my class would be filled with business scions and spoiled brats. My fears were not baseless. One of the most ludicrous things I'd seen on an email-group set up for those who had received admissions, was the following:

'Hey Arvind, are you bringing your Josh Machine to campus? I'm bringing mine. Is there covered parking available?'

An email meant for that Arvind had been sent to one-hundred fifty people. Positioning, positioning, position in . . . .

I asked the others in the cab if they were shipping cars or submarines to ISB or worrying about underwater or covered parking.

Praveen quickly said, 'Oh yeah! I need to make friends with those guys. Networking is everything, man; it's all about the money, dude!'

Phew!

Nevertheless, I felt pretty good. These people seemed driven, intelligent and even if I didn't like their opinions, independent. All

Tailspin **19**

of them sounded like they were pretty sure of success, and that its arrival was more a matter of time than chance.

We approached the institution as the light grew to a soft glow. As we turned into the gap in the median approaching the school, an impressively large Infosys office announcing its name on a large concrete structure, loomed on the left. At the aesthetically designed portal, huge electronically operated gates that held the fort swung open after we were subjected to a quick check by the security guards, and we drove into the institute. The landscape was dotted with rocks and shrubs and not much else. The odd tree had grown to a modest height, somewhat embarrassed by the lack of water in the rock below it.

'Where exactly are the buildings?' I remember wondering as we continued to drive on a road cut through an endless expanse of shrubs, wild grass and short, thick trees. I'd seen the brochure, and was hoping the structure wasn't just a product of digital imaging.

Half a kilometre on, a reddish-pink building came into the view. It stood all by itself, majestic like a colossus on the stony ground. A flawless lawn surrounded it like a huge green carpet. Talk in the car ceased as everyone soaked in the scene in awe. In the background were other buildings and hillocks, but this structure seemed to be right out of a powerful mythological tale. Given the barren land all around, it just didn't fit in.

The cab turned and entered the road that ran right around the structure, to the Student Villages located on its periphery. Student Villages – the name evokes rustic environs; but no, it was a large group of apartment buildings with a few smaller lawns in front of them. Painted alabaster white, each building comprised only two floors – ground and first. However, the buildings were not the first thing you noticed about the Student Villages. What you saw made your jaw drop.

In the centre of each Student Village, right in the middle of the cluster of apartment blocks, stood a magnificent tower. A stark square column, it rose forever and must've been at least a hundred

20 *Touching Distance: The Great Indian MBA Dream*

feet high. I couldn't help but think of the Tower of Isengard, from the *Lord of the Rings*, home of the wizard Sarumon The White. A long-stemmed chalice was cut into the column running right through the centre of the tower, giving it an element of stately art. You could almost see Sarumon looking over students with a steely cold stare, as they looked up at the tower.

When your gaze finally dropped down to earth, you saw huge boulders standing just outside the apartment blocks. The architects had left the largest of the boulders untouched. One of these rocks was almost twenty feet high. It was as if the man-made structures had sprung up from the ground wherever they could, displaced by, and at the mercy of, these fascinating living boulders that had stood their ground for millions of years.

How could one concentrate, leave alone study, in such an evocative place, I wondered. All I'd done in the past few minutes was stare unblinkingly at the magnificence all around me.

Beyond the Villages, there was more beauty to behold. The Deccan Plateau stretched on for miles together. The horizon stood watching in the distance, and there was nothing but blue time between you and eternity. Small hills with very little vegetation dotted the landscape. I had never seen anything so beautiful, so stark, so raw, so bare, so powerful, in my entire life. The place seemed surrounded by a strange energy, and some of it was mine.

In the foreground, the contrast screamed in your face when you looked at the Student Villages and the landscaping. It was man's effort to create something out of nothing.

A few words from the brochure came to mind: *An idea whose time has come.*

That idea was attributed to Rajat Gupta, the CEO of one of the most famous companies in the world, McKinsey. Any MBA student would give anything to get where Rajat was, and you knew why when you looked at what was around you. If Rajat could dream of, and then help create what you had just seen, even these timeless boulders would step aside and give way.

Tailspin **21**

Praveen and Arvind walked towards the first Student Village. They had been allotted rooms there. Ranga and I remained in the cab. Bidding good luck to each other, we decided to catch up for lunch.

The cab drove on and stopped in front of a set of shorter buildings called Executive Housing Blocks. This was to be our accommodation for the first term, until renovation was completed in Student Village 3.

By now, it was 7.30 am and already the heat was rising up from the black-top road. I turned to look back at the Atrium, the first sight I had seen as we had arrived at the ISB.

The Atrium was built on a raised patch of circular ground that covered an area as large twenty football fields. It was an enormous building clad in the same reddish-pink stone, and stood beautifully against the bright blue sky. It seemed to float effortlessly on the huge lake of grass all around it. When you saw it for the first time, you simply could not take your eyes off it. The question that thudded into your head was: 'How in the heavens did they build this?'

Ranga and I checked in at the arrival lounge, which was really a hotel lobby. Yes, the institute had a hotel within it, complete with five-star rooms and room service.

We were assured by the institute that we would be moved into Student Village 3 at the start of Term 2, and that accommodation at the Executive Housing was superior to that in the Student Villages. They were right: my room was large, and had its own television and attached bathroom. It also had room service and large French windows, which overlooked yet another manicured lawn and some of the oldest rocks on the Deccan Plateau. This had to be as close to supreme luxury as one could get on an academic campus. I left the bags in my room and for the next half hour walked outside, as if in a trance. I looked back at the Atrium, then at the Towers of Isengard in the two Student Villages, then the hills that pointed the way to the horizon. This place was beautiful, and there was no one in sight. I walked bare feet on the lawn bordering the Atrium

22 *Touching Distance: The Great Indian MBA Dream*

and took it all in: the air, the warmth, the structures, and the breeze that came from the edge of the hills where time dropped off as if on cue.

As it became hotter, I walked back to my room and took a shower. I called my mother and assured her that I was fine. Indian familial ties are strong; the pain in her voice was already tangible.

She had me in a barrage – Had I eaten? Was the room alright? Was food going to be available? Had I slept well?

I assured her that I was in the lap of luxury. She thought I was exaggerating.

❖

I walked out into the corridor and saw the door of the adjacent room lying open. Ranga was in the room next to mine, and I thought this was a good thing. In this strange place I did not understand or recognise, a Kannada speaking guy from my hometown was somewhat reassuring. I popped inside.

'Man, this place is something, huh? I mean, like . . . check out the pillows and the mattress; so soft,' he said.

'Dude, forget about the pillows. What did you think of the buildings outside?' I asked.

'Yeah, pretty cool. Hey, check out the TV and DVD player. I wonder if there are any film DVDs in the cabinet? he said.

❖

An hour or so later, I went to the cafeteria, which was roomy and plush, like everything else around.

A number of students had arrived a week earlier to attend a refresher course on MS-Excel, Basic Accounting, and Statistics. I scanned the cafeteria for some pretty girls but to my dismay, there were very few around. It amazed me to see so many serious people.

The atmospherics gave me a high. I almost talked to the girl who was dropping off her used plate on the sophisticated conveyor

Tailspin **23**

belt that ran to the back of the cafeteria, but held back. She was dressed in jeans and a t-shirt that made it hard for you to look up at her face, and she didn't make eye contact. She was heading for the door and before I could do anything close to making an advance, some guy in a loud yellow shirt put his arm around her waist and chatted her up. Moments later, she stepped outside and gave another guy a hug and talked in a chirpy, cheerful voice. Before long there were more guys around her. I half kicked myself for not opting for that refresher course.

Sometimes, it's quite humiliating to be a man in India. You can't walk up to any girl without her being surrounded by a bunch of ape-like brats, and even if she is alone, you'd have to ignore a thousand jealous stares from wolves plotting their own attack. Over a period of time, I'd simply given up trying to fight my way through the crowd. I'd resorted to a strategically different path, one that I figured had a higher chance of success. I did all those things that gave me a platform above the crowd, so I could be seen. The usual suspects – sports, music, literary activities and so on. And guess what: no show! I felt like a performing artist on the road, with no takers. The girls were just too busy lapping up the attention that was being showered upon them by salivating wolves. I learnt something else about women on academic campuses. They don't really care about the species of the animal in front of them; what matters is the quantity of attention and desperation shown.

Things were no different here. The wolves were doing their best to get closer and attack their prey. Some in their loud shirts. Some with their loud voices, and others with their loud abuses. Now this is something that genuinely baffled me. Why Hindi abuses, which serve as punctuation marks in common speech, were thrown around when trying to impress women, was beyond me. I figured it must be a regional invention, as it was simply absent in the south. If anything, we south Indians are diffident and cautious and thinking of terribly intelligent things to say, but we don't throw

24 *Touching Distance: The Great Indian MBA Dream*

caution to the winds and yell out abuses in the hope that we will look stunning.

So why do our countrymen do it? It must work at some level. Women must be thinking, 'Wow, this guy is so brave . . . he must've thrown all these abuses all over the place and never got beaten up or has at least something going for him. Maybe he's strong. I want his DNA for my child . . . NOW'. Who knows? For all I know, there could be more esoteric reasons. Anyway, whatever caused this phenomenon, I was never going to understand it.

Anyway, I loved hanging around cafeterias (a left-over habit from my days at engineering college as well) and spent time talking to a bunch of people. Most people I met seemed nice and polite, and a significant number seemed to be from a technology background. That was to be expected, I guess. One half of the class was filled with engineers, while most of the other half comprised chartered accountants. The rest was a motley group from an assortment of professions, who were as bewildered by the two dominant groups as a gaggle of Japanese tourists in India-infested England.

I was a floater; we only had five or six people from Bangalore in our class, and we were geographically distributed across different Student Villages and Executive Housing Blocks. Had we been more in number, I'm certain we would have formed our own clique, and cracked double entendres till the cows came home; or rounded up a bunch of Tamilians and watched them fight over who was better between the superstars Rajnikant and Kamal Hasan.

I noticed that there wasn't that kind of unbridled enthusiasm that you see in the first week of an engineering course, where people are just keen to make as many friends as possible. But there was this expectant flow of positive energy all around. In the evenings, at dinner time, groups of students just hung around outside the cafeteria, at the base of the Atrium, and were spellbound by the rush of the strong winds that swept into the well of the Atrium, creating a loud hum and blowing away papers, skirts and . . . fears.

Over the course of the year, the well of the Atrium would leave more memories and evoke more thoughts than any of the classrooms.

◈

The well of the Atrium housed the concrete columns upon which the ISB Atrium rose. The Atrium had all the classrooms, professors' and administrative offices, library and pretty much everything that pertained to ISB. Other than the Student Villages, this really was the heart of ISB and stood rightfully at the centre of the layout, while the Student Villages stood at four corners on its periphery.

The Atrium had four staircases leading into it, in the shape of a perfect cross. Once you took a staircase, you either went up to the first floor or descended down to the well of the Atrium that housed the cafeteria, grocery store, coffee shop, photocopying centre, meeting rooms, and elevators. Several aqueducts ran all around it in a circle. Most of the well was occupied by a very large meeting area at the centre, large enough to seat five hundred people. This open air theatre was given a living element by the four staircases, which carried a light breeze that was exponentially amplified into a swirling torrent in the well.

The whirling winds cooled the well naturally, in concert with the aqueducts that ran all around the well. These aqueducts, maybe two feet wide and four feet deep, ran all around the periphery. The water evaporated slowly, cooling the whole place and creating a dramatic environ. Walking from the Student Villages to the well of the Atrium, into a minor tornado-like swirl, was straight out of a very moving dream.

◈

It was Sunday, the day before the first classes were to begin. I'd gone for a stroll, and then took a leisurely swim in the pool. On my way back to the room, I saw people sitting in twos and threes, with their academic coursepacks open. I stopped in my tracks: were they studying? . . . Why?

26 *Touching Distance: The Great Indian MBA Dream*

Was I supposed to read up the case for tomorrow? Now, this was a first; in an engineering class, all we did was sit absentmindedly in the class, take down funny doodles rather than notes, crammed for two weeks before the exams and made sure we got a distinction. I had expected this to be different; I expected to study everyday and listen super-attentively in class to make sure I absorbed everything, but I sure as hell didn't expect to study before the very first class of the year!

I asked someone about this strange phenomenon and they confirmed that they were reading the case for the next day; it was worse than I expected.

I walked into my room and turned on the TV; I needed to relax a little before I started getting into the ISB mode. After a bit, I decided to catch up with Ranga.

I found the door to his room ajar. Inside, Ranga was hopping on one leg, playing an imaginary guitar. 'Light my Fire' by Doors blared from his laptop. He was dressed in a pair of cargo shorts and vest. His hair stood on end and he continued to hop around as I watched the repulsively engrossing performance with interest. What the hell was this guy up to? Was he drunk? I quickly scanned the room for bottles and smells, but found none.

Puzzled, I turned around and went back to my room. ISB was quickly becoming a twilight zone, full of strange sights. This guy really must be a genius, I thought to myself. The rest of the class was slaving over tomorrow's case, while he was playing an air-guitar to the Lizard King himself.

❖

The first week was unforgettable. One of the courses had a set of cases that illuminated the human side of information exchange.

The professor was a leadership expert from the London Business School, and used videos and carefully selected, recorded interviews. The purpose of the exercise was to show us that information itself was not always reliable. He illustrated this with the famous Honda A

Tailspin 27

and Honda B cases. The Honda A story suggested that Mr Honda was an amazing and insightful businessman who exploited an opportunity in a market on the other side of the earth, and provided data to support that. Honda B, on the other hand, suggested that Mr Honda merely made an effort to sell in the only growth market easily available to him and was plain lucky. Which one would you believe? It really made you ask yourself – how much of a sceptic were you?

Lesson 1: Be a sceptic.

The other memorable case was that of Apple, which blew me away. The power and talent of Steve Jobs, leading to his own downfall, and the permanence of his brilliance, which brought him back, are just amazing stories.

Lesson 2: Play to your strengths. Believe.

By far, one of the more controversial assignments towards the end of Term 1 was to force-rank any fifteen people (or ten percent of the class) you chose, into 'People you'd like to work with'; 'People you'd like to work for'; 'People you'd hate to work with'; and 'People you'd hate to work for'. The data was finally collated and it was amazing how accurate it seemed. The affable, quietly confident people were at the top of the positive lists and the loud, boorish and attention crazy ones were at the top of both negative lists. While the exercise itself drew a lot of flak when it was announced, it did end up being quite illuminating.

The other courses were not as entertaining. Statistics was powerful, and accounting was just counter-intuitive. No engineer got the obvious opposite meaning of 'debit' and 'credit' – it just didn't make sense. Why someone had picked English terms and used them in a way directly opposite to their real meanings was just beyond me. The only way to conquer accounting was to learn the rules and apply them, without a question, to balance the books. Don't think; just debit or credit if you can remember which is which.

28 *Touching Distance: The Great Indian MBA Dream*

The classes required prior preparation and reading. Students were put through a gruelling test every day. The professor would pick a name at random and have a student share impressions about the case and about what we were going to discuss. At other times, in more quantitative subjects, the professor would project a problem on the board and pick someone to embarrass.

It was amazing that people came prepared and knocked some questions right out the stadium. This was a smart, hardworking bunch; they weren't teenagers or students who did this for a living. These were people between twenty-five and thirty-five years of age who had come here and had hit the books with the seriousness they'd bring to child-rearing or financial planning.

There were a few students who answered questions calmly and then went back to trading derivatives on the National Stock Exchange; some made a tidy buck between the beginning and ending of a class if the markets were volatile. No sir, this was not your regular, insipid classroom. This was a bunch of driven people who just happened to be sitting in an MBA class. If the professors were impressive, the students matched them with their intellect, speed and energy.

However, in the beginning, sitting in a class full of strangers does wonders to your adrenaline and nothing for your concentration. As hard as I tried to listen, I was constantly distracted by the girls – so well manicured, so well turned out and so well perfumed. After hours of classes and introductions and fellow students' names you could not remember, you met in the cafeteria for lunch before you retired to your dwellings, and then came back for dinner.

❖

Before we knew it, we were three weeks into the first term. That meant there were two weeks to go before the exams. Things were moving at a furious pace, and I was still working out what time of the day it was every time I woke up. You see, in a place like this, twenty minute power naps were a great tool – well researched, propagated and practiced by the entire population.

Tailspin **29**

I sat in a lot of classes, did a lot of assignments, played some football and squash, swam a little and made some friends; now, there was one week left to go for the exams. My head started to spin. What the hell was going on? I had to prepare for tomorrow's class and also study for term exams, which included four subjects, a week from now! Which one was I expected to do first? To make matters worse, every time I sat down to study, I was overcome by some distraction or the other. A team meeting, a call to play cricket, questions on an assignment, etc, etc. And now I was neck-deep in a critical battle against time.

I decided to resort to the finely honed strategy back from my engineering days. I'd put up a nice timetable; I'd go through all my semester subjects twice, and presto! I would be ready. Engineering exams were somewhat predictable, and with my two-step preparation, I was all set to crack them; it always worked.

I figured that at the ISB, the study material was less of a problem and with my skills, I'd make it.

I was wrong.

The exams were held over three days. The first was statistics, and boy, was it difficult! None of the questions were predictable, and stress was at an all-time high. You had to know the material, understand it, apply it, and then appreciate the complexity of its nuances in order to be able to crack the test. I came back feeling drained; I'd been up nearly all night for a week, managing on four hours of daily sleep, if I was lucky.

For my second exam, which was the following morning, I woke up and was ready to leave, when sleep overcame me. I decided to make myself a pot of black coffee. I'd never had black coffee before, but had heard of its magical properties. I gulped it down, trying not to think of the bitter, scathing taste. In fifteen minutes or so, the caffeine kicked in and I was able to stay awake through my exam and do reasonably well . . . or so I thought. The questions were complicated, and although I thought the material had been

30 *Touching Distance: The Great Indian MBA Dream*

intuitive during the classes, my tired brain couldn't do too much intuiting.

On the evening before my third exam, I had more black coffee and managed to stay awake and finish studying. By the time it came to my fourth exam, my brain was becoming immune to the black concoction.

The term had ended and most people had decided to stay on in Hyderabad for the three days before the next term began. I decided to stay back as well; it was blissful, to say the least. It seemed like a huge weight had lifted off me and I was able to breathe again. The stress had been tremendous, and the thought that I had another seven terms to go before I got my MBA left me staring at the wall in my room, trying my best not to think about the nights before exams.

On the first day of the term break, I checked my email and read one from the administrative wing:

> *The students accommodated in the Executive Housing block shall soon be moved to the Student Village 2, where renovations have been completed. We are expecting the move to be completed in the first two weeks of Term 2. Please await further details.*

Oh damn! I didn't have the energy to even *think* about moving. I was tired and wanted to socialise and find a girlfriend. Anyway, this wasn't all bad. I wanted to make as many friends as I could, and my social life up to that point in the male-dominated SV2 was pretty dreadful. Also, I'd developed a serious crush on two girls, and while they were not going to be in SV2—they were in SV3 from the start—they'd still be closer than before. A fleeting consolation, but enough to let me hang by the thin thread called 'hope'.

The email continued:

> *Each quad has four rooms and two bathrooms. Please provide your preferences for roommates, if any. Each quad*

Tailspin **31**

> *shall contain students of the same gender. The Administrative office will do its best to accommodate early requests for quad sharing.*

I had made a few friends, but had no idea who I was going to share my quad with. I closed my eyes and fell fast asleep. Term 2 was going to begin and one of the big subjects was marketing – a real treat to anyone who wanted to do an MBA. The professors were Wharton stars, and I was excited that marketing may be the answer to all my career problems.

❖

She's always with him. Are they seeing each other? I wish she'd spend that much time with me. Damn, I'm so far away in this Exec Housing crap. She does like it when I call her, though. Does she know? Maybe when I call her next I'll tell her.

❖

Me: 'You know what? We're moving to SV3 next week.'
Her: 'Oh, good.'
Me: 'Yeah, I'm looking forward to it. Listen, I know we've been talking about studies and work and what not. We've known each other for a month now, right?'
Her: '. . . Yeah. It's been really nice getting to know you.'
Me: 'I had something else to ask you.'
Her: 'Ok, what?'
Me: 'Hmm . . . Maybe I'll tell you another time. It's kinda personal.'
Her: 'Come on, out with it!'
Me: 'Hmm . . . not sure. Maybe another time.'
Her: 'No, I want you to tell me this right away.'
Me: 'I'm not sure I want to tell you.'
Her: 'Look, you can't call someone and tell them you have something to say, and then not say anything.'

Me: 'Oh come on, it doesn't concern you.'

Her: 'We've been talking every day. We're friends, right? You've told me so much about yourself and you know so much about me. It scares me when you say things like this ... call and say you can't say something.'

Me: 'I need to hang up now.'

Her: 'This isn't over.'

Me: 'Sure, it isn't ... I'll talk to you soon.'
Click.

Me: 'Hey, you still there?'

❖

3

Gillette: The Best Every Man, Woman and Free-Rider Can Get

These mist covered mountains, are a home now for me,
But my home is the lowlands, and always will be,
Someday you'll return to your valleys and your farms
And you'll no longer burn to be Brothers in Arms
—Dire Straits

Nilima's heart began to race. Professor Stan Roche had just declared that he had completed the evaluation of the Gillette case write-ups. It was one of the first assignments in Term 2. In the cradle of her mounting anxiety, were born twins – one of hope and the other of fear.

Prof Stan Roche hit F5 on his laptop. That simple act set in motion the beginning of shifts in the destinies of seventy-odd people looking on with rapt attention. The dreaded bell curve appeared on the screen, separating the winners from those who would have 'better luck next time'. No one yet knew who the winners were, but the good professor was merely calling attention to some ground realities about life – the reality of the normal distribution. He had

34 *Touching Distance: The Great Indian MBA Dream*

done this for years at Wharton. Deep inside his mind he smiled, recognising the emotions he had seen all too often. The human genome project was right: people were the same everywhere – anxious, hopeful, and scared like hell in the face of competitive failure. The soul of Charles Darwin, vacillating some place ethereal, sighed. He, too, had been right: even among the strong, only the fittest would survive.

'Rajesh will hand out the evaluated assignments,' the professor announced and left, the furling of his Hawaiian shirt suddenly creating a squirm in the pits of the stomachs of those who watched him leave. Indeed, no one had expected the assignments to be handed back so quickly.

Nilima grabbed the assignment marked 'Group A5' and her face turned marble-white. Anil Nayar, Rohan Sharma, Mohit Kapoor, Sagar Rai—other members from my study group—watched the show with varying degrees of enthusiasm and anxiety. In the stillness of their anxiety, they silently began to replay the incidents of the previous week.

Nilima did the most predictable thing. She turned to people sitting on either side of her to see how they had fared. She should look at the screen, I thought. Rajesh had now projected the score distributions in descending order, so each group knew exactly how many groups stood above them and how many were below their score.

In a minute, a flushed Nilima gaped at the screen and blanked out as her accountancy trained brain noticed the score on the ladder. A few moments later, she gathered control and turned around to look for us. Mohit Kapoor, the most competitive person in our group, gesticulated. Nilima walked a couple of paces towards his row and dropped the document at the end of the row he was in, not bothering to go any closer. She walked out just in time to prevent her first teardrop from soaking into the gray carpet below to meet her already fallen spirit.

Gillette: The Best Every Man, Woman and Free-Rider Can Get **35**

Twenty minutes later, only three groups remained in class, each looking equally shocked. All those in the room had at some point of their life been academic superstars, near the top of their respective classes in all the previous institutions their brains had been parked in. Suddenly, they were at the bottom of the heap, looking up in disgust. Each person scoured the sheet for valuation errors, their egos simply unable to stomach this insult. There were none to be found. The pungent smell, a newly experienced shame and defeat, hung in the room. Voices were softer, nearly choked and glances were quickly deflected onto the wall or the carpet. Eye contact suddenly seemed terrible.

Rohan was the first to accept the grim state of affairs. 'Cheers, guys,' he said, his voice utterly lacking the attempted enthusiasm, and walked out. Anil Nayar looked carefully at the answers, his brain looking for clarity and simply seeing words and numbers, unable to process either. As Mohit looked over his shoulder, Anil felt his breath on the side of his neck. This triggered a barrage of bad memories from the previous week. Anil dropped the papers on the desk and walked out. He cursed under his breath, ensuring he was out of earshot.

As I walked back to the rooms of executive housing, I felt depleted. I was thinking of making myself a cup of tea to clear my mind, when I heard a shrill cry from behind. A rather energetic Priyanka was calling out to me. Surprising, considering that she'd never made the effort to talk to me earlier. Every B-school worth its salt has its share of narcissistic wannabes, and ISB was no different. Priyanka's self-perceived superiority was seeded in her high schooling completed in the United States. She came bundled with hot outfits, a pronounced accent, a cigarette packet and no lighter. Her abuses were highly accented and louder than normal speech, so everyone could marvel at her ability to express her surprise or anguish at the most nondescript things. In her mind, these factors automatically made her superior to anything we could ever aspire to be. I had a sinking feeling. Perhaps it wasn't surprising why she

36 *Touching Distance: The Great Indian MBA Dream*

was calling out to me. She belonged, by happenstance, to a group that had exceedingly hardworking students, and had one of the better scores in class. Fortune favours the fortunate, I mused. The study groups for the first few terms had been formed and would last through the first six months while the batch completed the core courses.

I waited while she ran up to me.

'Hey, how did you guys do?' she asked with a glint in her eyes, although she had seen us all upset.

'Bottom three,' I said simply, taking it on the chin.

'Oh, don't worry . . . it will get better,' she said, and turned and half ran to her room.

Yeah, right . . . !

❖

Term 2 hadn't started so well after all. The professor really socked us right at the start. This assignment was to carry twenty-five percent of the weight in the grade. We were encouraged to approach this case with commonsense and from information gleaned from the first term and from the first few classes. From a professor's perspective, it was a clever move. Those that did well would do even better in staying ahead of the class; those that messed up would try like hell in the remainder of the term to get their grades up. The professor, as a result, would have a committed class throughout. Another early lesson – first mover advantage is a very big deal.

My aspirations of securing a Rs. 3,50,000 scholarship had taken a big dent. This scholarship was given to those at the top of the class, after the first four terms. Each exam, assignment and test was crucial. All those in our group, with the exception of Sagar, were dead keen on reducing our loan burdens. He had been blessed with a somewhat rich grandfather, whose wealth was likely to allow Sagar a life of great luxury followed by excellent healthcare on his deathbed.

Gillette: The Best Every Man, Woman and Free-Rider Can Get **37**

For me, it was lamentation in full swing. It's one thing if you are among the front runners and you then encounter some setbacks. You may begin to bleed, but you know you are in the fight. This, however, was akin to slipping on wet ground as soon as you attempted to take your launching stride in a hundred-metre dash, landing on your nose, then hearing the sound of a few broken teeth as they cracked under your body weight, then and looking up to see the rest of the contestants zoom past the finish line.

I walked into my room and took a shower. As I got dressed, I put a pot of tea to boil. The TV did nothing to distract me as I dead-stared at it, my mind blank as a foolscap sheet. I was a rabbit in the headlights, waiting for the memory laden truck to come crashing into my soul, and there wasn't a damn thing I could do about it. This room is where it had all started. There sat Nilima and Sagar. Rohan had a purposeful stare. Mohit and Anil were annoyed but somewhat buoyant. We had been in good spirits. The question was: 'What should Gillette do in Indonesia in 1995?'

Indonesia, a country with a disproportionately high concentration of bearded men. Should Gillette enter this market? If so, what should their entry strategy be? How should they get people to start shaving? These were some of the aspects of the case a scenario-rich, seat-of-the-pants, marketing classic. This was the beginning of Term 2; not the best time to get kicked in the nuts. My thoughts wandered back to the first day we actually began working on this case.

◈

Our first attempt at working as a group had been an epic failure. This was from a simulated strategy game in Term 1. The context: an airline company. We had no idea what was going on, and lost. We quickly buried that at the back of our minds, believing that we had had just too much fun guessing whether to increase fares or reduce the fleet. Whatever we did, our profits seemed to suffer. What the hell, it was a stupid simulation, anyway. We were

38 *Touching Distance: The Great Indian MBA Dream*

confident about kicking ass when it came to more traditional and more serious assignments.

All of us held the same view except Rohan. He had, in a prior team meeting, said with a sullen and matter-of-fact way that we needed to get our act together. Rohan was the oldest member of our group. At thirty-two, he had spent several years on the sea with a leading oil shipping company. Balding, well-built and handsome, Rohan exuded a quiet determination and clear thinking. I was amazed at his ability to grasp ideas and concepts after all those monotonous years navigating a humongous oil tanker through rough seas. In my opinion, he had taken a rather significant risk. He had pitched a good quantum of his savings on the ISB course and was also the only one amongst us who was married. Priti, his wife, was just as wonderful as him. During the course of the year, they were to become my virtual family on campus. 'I've taken a big risk by coming here. I just want to make sure that I don't screw up because my group can't work together,' he had said. I had wondered why he was so serious at first. Now, I was coming to appreciate his foresight.

Anil Nayar, for his own part, was as bright as they came. He had completed an MBA in his early twenties and had a glittering career in a leading FMCG company involved in processed foods. He had thrown it all away to come to ISB to re-ignite his career. He was probably one of the most reliable, hardworking and clear-thinking individuals I'd met. His problem – he was opinionated as hell! It had to be his way or the highway. Competitive to every last red blood corpuscle, he once insisted on continuing a game of squash despite a severe back strain that severely impeded his movement. When he noticed that I was feigning misses to end the game as soon as possible, he called me on it. Extremely well read, highly intelligent and very driven. I rated him a 9/10 on the smartness scale. On drive, I rated him a 10. On ease of working with, I rated him a 2 or 3!!

Gillette: The Best Every Man, Woman and Free-Rider Can Get **39**

Mohit was probably more academically accomplished. Always among the top-scorers of his IIT class, he had more quantitative talent than most individuals on campus. However, he happened to be accursed, like so many other quant-gurus. He had severe limitations when it came to relating to people and being liked, and this was to hurt him quite a bit during the year. He was abrasive as hell and had one of the worst tempers I had ever seen. He was definitely someone you would avoid for as long as you could. It also didn't help that he was completely devoid of any charisma whatsoever. He was, however, narcissistically intoxicated by his own ability to crunch numbers. He just didn't care that he wasn't likeable. Hell, it didn't affect his grades at the IIT; why should it matter now?

He was to find that out very quickly, and was to reflect upon it each night just after the whiskey drained the sadness and anger from his brain into an overworked liver.

Sagar was more of a lover than fighter. Okay, let me rephrase that: he was only a lover. I never saw him take on anything. He waded through the year, spending his time at the club for social awareness. He had a tender heart, a sensitive soul and could be a smooth talker when he wanted to; but he wasn't the one to burn the midnight oil, even to save his own ass. Having said that, I was more than a little surprised at his good grades, more so because I never saw him study or work, at anything. Lazy, hedonistic, and probably quite smart.

And then there was Nilima. A chartered accountant previously, she was also extremely driven. When wait-listed by the Admissions Office, she had picked up the phone and called them and made a case for herself, saying she should definitely have been offered a place, given the kind of people she knew were being offered a seat. Shapely and smart, she was one of those people you see in the movies – good looks and sharp brains. Dangerous. She, like the other accountants I had met, was extremely hard-working, and probably worked harder than all of us. In the first term, Nilima was the standout woman student and had just began to lose steam

40 *Touching Distance: The Great Indian MBA Dream*

as the competition began to wake up over the course of the year. However, what was still alive in her was a sharp edge, coupled with a potential for great anger. She was the sort who would simply never forgive. In many ways, she was an angry man in a woman's body. This was somewhat typical of most women at a B-School, I observed. If you collected all the adrenaline and the testosterone present in the systems of the girls and the guys on campus, you could make a bomb big enough to nuke an entire district, I reckoned.

❖

Laughter rang loud and true in my room. The occasion was the first meeting to trash out the Gillette case. Anil had arrived saying that he just hadn't read the case, but would work on it once he wet his feet during our meeting. Mohit, Rohan and I had been sensible enough to read the case. Nilima had read a few pages but she was the first to throw open her laptop and launch a blank Excel file. Years at KPMG had convinced her that God was in the spreadsheet; the same spreadsheet where the folks from Arthur Andersen had found their Satan. Sagar said he was there to provide moral support. Mohit's nostrils flared all too familiarly with undiluted anger when he heard that.

'Guys, guys! Let's try and go over the case. Why don't the ones who have read it tell us what they think?' Anil began. This was a familiar start to a case session at the school. The ones who hadn't read the case were the first to make their presence felt, the master-stroke at grabbing the judging chair and deflecting any due criticism.

'Entry strategy. Gillette in Indonesia. No one's heard of a razor there. You should look at the "educational material" that Gillette distributed in the country. It was intended at popularising hygiene and the benefits of shaving. Man, those are some print ads. They portray the local populace as cavemen or something. If I didn't know any better, I wouldn't sit in a high-rise Gillette office there for a few centuries. Hilarious!' I opened, as usual, trying to begin on a humorous note.

Gillette: The Best Every Man, Woman and Free-Rider Can Get **41**

'Yeah, it is . . . anyway, the case is about the revenue possibility in the country. It's about how many blades can be sold in the country.' True to form, Rohan wanted us to re-focus and converge.

'Hmm . . . okay. Nilima, how many blades do you usually require?' asked Anil as everyone gaped.

Nilima's face signalled murder. 'What's that supposed to mean?' she asked, cursing 'bastard' under her breath. The rest of us were in uncontrollable splits.

'I mean, I thought the case also had women as the target market . . . I mean, like . . . the Braun Silk Epil products for women,' explained Anil. Clearly, he hadn't read the case.

After more thunderous laughter, Anil was finally convinced that the case was indeed about men's razors and blades. 'Read the case, you bastard!' Nilima thundered, this time quite audibly. No sir, she could not be trifled with.

'Well, well, let's get back to the point . . . so how long does a blade last?' asked Mohit, stroking his beard.

'What do you think?' asked Anil, staring Mohit in the face. Anil specified that Mohit might well be using a razor on other hirsute areas of his anatomy.

We had heard that most teams had already put in over twenty hours of discussions on this case, while we were just into our first.

Well, to cut a long story short, after a couple more hours of joking, we all had other meetings to attend and the folks began leaving my room. Bottom line: We got no work done. One of the first lessons in group work: In general, the more fun a group has, the less work they get done. The quantity and quality of work is inversely proportional to the number of people who turn up for meetings. Towards the end of the year, this became more evident, as group meetings were usually held just to divide and distribute work. No one sat around a table to discuss a case. Rather sad, given all the laughs that were lost. Laughs that only five or six smart, desperately tired, sleep deprived people can generate.

42 *Touching Distance: The Great Indian MBA Dream*

We reconvened to meet on the evening of the day before the assignment was due. While most other teams had already done their work, the attitude of Anil Nayar had a lot to do with this decision. These were early days and people were confident and polite.

'Let's catch up in the evening. You guys don't worry. It's just about keying in the three-page report. I've read the case; we all have. We just need to put everyone's insights together. Shouldn't take more than two hours.'

'Sounds good; I'll do all the numbers,' said Mohit.

'OK . . . sounds good,' exulted Sagar, thrilled that no one expected anything from him.

'Doing the numbers' is the grunt part of assignments at B-Schools. Setting up a spreadsheet, cranking out scenarios, etc., is just stuff that needs getting done. It's not rocket science, but is painful nevertheless.

❖

8.30 pm.

We all trooped into Rohan's studio apartment. Nice one-bedroom flat with a kitchen, living area and balconies. Priti left some coke and chips out for us. She was on her way to meet the wife of another student on campus.

The evening began with Mohit bringing his laptop loaded. He was only halfway through his analysis. Anil wasn't happy, and had already cultivated a mild dislike towards Mohit.

After a short discussion, we all had agreed upon our case recommendation. What remained was just the computation of lifetime value of the customer (LTVC) and price points that should converge easily from some competitive information and other such data points. Of course, the internet was off limits as a resource for all assignments, and we were honest, so we kept it straight.

Anil said that he was going into the living room; we decided to split up. He called Nilima in to work with him as he wanted to

Gillette: The Best Every Man, Woman and Free-Rider Can Get **43**

begin writing up the case recommendation. Mohit sat elsewhere, keying in his numbers with an angry look on his face. He had secretly begun to hate Anil. Anil had the only girl around while he hadn't succeeded in his number crunching one way or another. Besides Mohit, or a part of him, had secretly begun to covet her.

Rohan and I were on the balcony. We decided that enough was enough, and began working on a set of numbers we could use, just in case the grand plans didn't work out. I had a set prepared, and we began developing those.

11.30 pm.

Mohit had told us all that his numbers indicated that Gillette should not enter the market in Indonesia. The numbers just didn't add up, quantitatively speaking. Even so, it was a ridiculous conclusion. The numbers Rohan and I had been running were fine. Secretly, Anil began to complain about Mohit and his nostrils. The personality clash that was to tear our group apart had begun in right earnest. The beginning of the end of our group.

1.30 am.

Anil had started running his own set of numbers. Mohit had seemed like he was losing it. Why didn't people believe him? He was cleverer than all of them, wasn't he? Rohan and I were almost done. Anil's document was nowhere near completion.

3.30 am.

Nilima was thoroughly disgusted by Mohit. This guy just did not work like she wanted people to. If he said he'd do the numbers, where the hell were they now? All he'd brought to the meeting was a huge ego, scowls and little else. She had lost hope in Anil as well. Sagar had run out of songs to sing to help his own nerves. He offered to put a pot of coffee on the boil. Rohan lit a cigarette and began to accept the inevitable. But I had to disagree: it was a simple goddamn write-up. There were three sets of numbers. We

44 *Touching Distance: The Great Indian MBA Dream*

just had to put them together and then write a simple three-page recommendation.

We were, however, in the middle of an ugly personality clash. Mohit was a sight with his flaming countenance, and Anil refused to speak to him anymore. A classic group situation. No one wanted to leave it to the other. No one trusted the other. Those that knew what was happening just could not push the envelope. This was a democracy and it wasn't working. No one voted. This was too early for a coup.

Nilima looked less attractive as her anger began to surface.

5.30 am.

Mohit yelled at Anil. Anil yelled back and added he had nothing more to say to anyone. I had taken up parts of the report from Anil and was nearly done. We were close to a convergence on the numbers. Rohan was through with his pack of cigarettes. Anil lit the last one. Sagar had left an hour ago. No one had complained. As usual, he had done little except offer to 'find' us the solution off the Internet.

6.30 am.

We wound up the assignment. The numbers were tied together, rather unconvincingly. Gillette must enter the market, but not with their high-end blades. They should expect to sell a greater number of their cheaper products. They should target young folks. The older ones are not going to abdicate their beliefs and start shaving now. It was too late for them.

It was too late for us.

7.30 am.

Rohan offered to walk to the office and hand in the assignment after printing a copy at 8.30 am. Anil left, disgusted. Mohit was too tired. I was relieved we had something to hand in. Rohan and I were the only two people who still had the respect and goodwill that we had earlier – for and from the others. Anil hated Mohit

Gillette: The Best Every Man, Woman and Free-Rider Can Get **45**

from the bottom of his heart, and they both hated Sagar. Nilima hated all three. Mohit was still confused about his feelings towards her. Despite the fact that they had barely talked, she had betrayed him at some level by sitting with the enemy.

I walked out of Rohan's apartment, on to the ring road that encircled the Atrium and connected the Student Villages. The hot Hyderabad sun was on the rise. It was a Saturday – no classes. The assignment had to be handed in, but Rohan had said he would take care of that. The light was harsh. I squinted and said a prayer to the Sun God. Nothing in particular; I just prayed that he stay with me. My legs each felt twenty kilos heavier. I was dog-tired. My mind was still sharp but the rest of me felt like a hundred years old. Looking around, I found that there was no one in sight. Strange. My room in the other Student Village building seemed so far away, I wondered if I could even walk the distance. I was just so exhausted. My head felt heavy, and for the first time in my life I stumbled a little out of exhaustion as I walked. The emotions, stress and fights had taken their toll on me, and I wasn't even directly involved in the conflict.

I reached my room and hit the bed. I was dead tired, but was beyond sleep. My frustration grew . . . a nap could make it all go away, but there I was, staring at the ceiling, tired in mind with my brain racing around the orbit of my anger.

I thought of the work that I needed to do. I had to prepare for classes for the following week. There were cases to be read, and more assignments to be handed in. I knew that I would have to be functioning and productive in a few hours, no matter how much of a stone I felt like at that moment. I would need to leave the bad experience of the previous night behind me instantly. The group was never to be the same again. Our grand plans for discussing cases within the group before we hand them in, would not stand. Newer ways had to be discovered.

The free-riders have to be separated from those who actually work. Those who can work together have to divide work away from those who cannot.

46 *Touching Distance: The Great Indian MBA Dream*

As I ran these thoughts in my mind, I began to put together a working model. Rohan, Anil and I were comfortable working together. Mohit was just too aggressive for his own good. He was an energy drain on the team, which was a pity. Sagar was a non-entity when it came to group work. He was happy if his name was added as part of the team that handed in the report. Nilima never bought the idea of group work in the first place. She would probably not work with us or with anyone else.

After an hour or so of trying to sleep, I gave up and walked into the bathroom to brush my teeth. I picked up my Gillette Mach 3 razor. The tag line rang in my head: 'Gillette: The best a man can get'. I had developed a new found respect for the mundane marketing folks who did this for a living. I had learnt more in the hours of the previous night than I had in many years before. Groups can go from absolute camaraderie and happiness to complete dissolution over a few lifeless numbers. The deterioration is usually quick and permanent. Like the case of a broken blade, it's very expensive, if not impossible, to repair broken friendships.

❖

It is significant that despite our terrible performance as a group, the group members excelled individually during the midway stage in the ISB year. After the CGPAs were accidentally revealed to the class by an Academic Affairs Office snafu, we learnt that when grouped GPAs were calculated (individual GPAs divided by group size), our group had the highest GPA amongst all the groups in the class of 150 students. But together, we had failed remarkably quickly. Other groups did better on group work than us because they were able to find a way to either work together or have the smartest person do the bulk of the work. By contrast, we'd all taken a sword to our meetings and cut each other dry. However, it was a small consolation that we'd still managed to get excellent grades on our own, enough to beat averages of other groups.

❖

Gillette: The Best Every Man, Woman and Free-Rider Can Get **47**

Me: 'Hey, are you all right? It's been a tough day today.'

Her: 'I'm so mad, I can't tell you. We struggled in our case, too. I heard you guys had trouble as well. I hope we do well! I had A's on all my subjects in Term 1 and I'm in line for that women's scholarship. I need to get it, I just need to . . . phew!'

Me: 'Don't worry, you will.'

Her: 'I'm not sure I will now, and I know it's tough. There are others who are catching up. Like that girl you were talking to at dinner today.'

Me: 'Oh, Janaki? My fellow south Indian? Come on, don't tell me you're jealous.'

Her: 'Please. Me, jealous? Fuck off! I didn't know her name, but she mugs like crazy. I heard she likes you . . . .'

Me: 'I still think you're somewhat jealous.'

Her: 'Think what you want. I'm not here to feel jealous. Besides . . '

Me: 'Besides what?'

Her: 'Nothing.'

Me: 'I think someone's jealous! Anyway, hmm . . '

Her: 'What hmm? Don't trail off like that. Again, don't tell me you are going to say something and not say it.'

Me: 'Forget it.'

Her: 'Fuck you.'

  Click.

Me: 'You still there?'

Her: 'Yeah.'

Me: 'Watch the language, miss.'

Her: 'That's the way I talk. If you don't like it, hang up.'

Me: 'Maybe I will.'

Her: 'Well, do it then.'

  Click.

Me:'You there? . . . Shit! Hello?'

  Click.

❖

4

The Fellowship of the Lost

Nobody said it was easy
No one ever said it could be so hard
Oh take me back to the start

—Coldplay

I woke up one afternoon to see a strange form in front of me. Blurry, thanks to my half-shut eyes. It seemed to be fairly rotund, dressed in shorts and a vest, and did not have breasts. This wasn't a woman; so, this wasn't a dream.

The form moved around slowly, looking at my table and picking up a packet of biscuits and a bag of chips. I was tired to the point of wanting to ignore this thief. I didn't have anything particularly expensive, but my survival skills overcame lethargy and I jumped up, ready to knock out this intruder with a move I'd once seen in a Jackie Chan movie.

'Gosh! What the hell are you doing here?' I screamed as I watched Ranga come into focus. He was caressing his belly as he crunched on a chip.

'Ha-ha... sorry. I mean, like... the door was open, OK?' he declared, matter-of-factly, pre-empting any precipitating reactions of surprise or outrage. He crunched another chip and spat out a few fragments as he spoke. Relieved that I didn't have to knock someone out, and somewhat repulsed by the quintessence of human degradation in front of me, I fell back on my bed, attempting to send him a hint. He turned his back to me, picked up a packet of biscuits from the table, sat down and turned on the TV.

'Dude, do you mind? I am trying to sleep here!' I yelled. This was a campus and we routinely walked into each others' rooms uninvited, but given that we were all on the other side of twenty-five, we'd usually leave the room if someone was sleeping. With the passing of youth, sleep is the only time you get to relive your life, and we all respected that.

As I tried even harder to sleep, I felt some paper under my face. It was the casebook for Competitive Strategy, one of our classes in the second ISB term. I remembered now. I'd fallen asleep after reading paragraph one, exhausted by the other two cases I'd read before for the next day's classes. Each of those had been twenty pages each, enough to knock most people out for an hour.

In the twilight of my consciousness at the moment, all three companies were completely mixed up and I could barely remember their names. One was struggling with marketing, while one had had a financial collapse; one had hired a new CEO, and the other was selling a new kind of silicon chip. I gave up, and tried to go back to sleep. Quasi-awake, I heard Ranga leave, carrying the biscuits and chips, and of course, he'd left the TV on. In my sleep, I shouted out to him, but he didn't seem to hear me.

I gave up trying to sleep. He'd left a Telugu channel playing, and it was blaring cacophonous music from a devotional film made just after Independence, it seemed. I searched for the remote but could not find it. Dejected, I dragged myself out of bed and turned off the main switch. I sank back on the sofa and felt the remote jab me in the unmentionables. Cursing under my breath, I moved slowly back to the bed and attempted to pass out.

50 *Touching Distance: The Great Indian MBA Dream*

Maybe it was from the pain of being jabbed by the remote that Ranga had shoved into the cushions, or maybe it was the smell of potato chips being circulated in the room by the air conditioner, but I slowly got up, walked to the bathroom and washed my face.

I'd just realised that I had to figure out my quad-mates, and I was late. I didn't want to be saddled with those who no one wanted.

I went to the first floor of the Exec Housing block. Most of the folks I got along well with were already settled in their rooms, and it seemed that their planning was complete.

I had been pretty popular in the term gone by. I had a reputation for a sense of humour and a non-threatening south Indian persona which people were comfortable with. Most of all, I was pretty easy to get along with, and though I didn't really smoke or drink, I more than made up for it with my ebullience in being ready to participate in anything fun. A midnight session of Doom 2, a game of squash at 2.00 am, or a practical session of crank-calling students. In short, I'd built a reputation as a fun guy.

In retrospect, then, I'd have got the roommates of my choice, and had obviously screwed my chances.

I slowly realised that most groups had been formed. People had waited for me to confirm and when I hadn't they'd just presumed that I had committed to someone else. Besides, I'd forgotten that the last date for confirming quad-mates was the previous day.

I came back to my room, got dressed more appropriately, and walked up to the Administrative Office and asked them if there were people yet to pick roommates. They gave me a list. Amazingly, the list did not include my name. I assured them there must have been a mistake and that I didn't have any roommates as yet. The list of quads was being prepared and they assured me they'd get back to me at the earliest.

I was alarmed. The last thing I wanted was to be stuck with people I didn't really know, or worse still, knew too well. There were far too many people chewing *paan* and chanting abuses in

The Fellowship of the Lost **51**

strange languages, for my liking. I wasn't exactly xenophobic, but when you are on the other side of twenty-five, you do really want to pick the people you live with. My ideal requirements were that my roommates should:

- Not smoke – I was allergic to the fumes of death.
- Be fun-loving – A humdrum life was no life.
- Be bolder when it came to women – I was hoping their bravado would in time rub off on me and help catalyse my own listless social life.

But I guess this was too much to ask for. I'd known a few groups which met these criteria, but I'd been too slow to cash in. Now I had to make my peace with what I believed to be roommates assigned to me on account of computer errors. I walked back to my room, switched on the air conditioner and opened the case book. Time was more precious than gold, and I didn't want to be cold-called in the first week of Term 2. Cold calling is like that dream you've had, when you walk into give your exams and realise you haven't studied anything, and even worse, that you've showed up without your pants. Abject humiliation. A professor will begin the day calling on random people in the class, asking them to state their observations about a case, and will take particular pleasure in kicking you in the balls if you as much as say that you aren't prepared, or will basically castrate you if he knows you are lying. I'm speaking figuratively of course, but I can tell you that 'castrated' B-school students will tell you it's pretty accurate.

Once a professor had you singled out, he always seemed to screw you again and again. Some sadistic gene seemed to be triggered in these otherwise benign creatures. I figured that all professors wanted to be Gandalf the Grey, but ended up changing sides to become Saruom the White the moment they saw ignorance in the eyes of the young.

❖

52 *Touching Distance: The Great Indian MBA Dream*

It was 6.00 pm now. I had dinner to eat and cases to read – long cases with lots of text and even more numbers. Then, I had a pre-class assignment to complete for the marketing class; and finally, needed to meet my study group to go over yet another marketing simulation game that we were going to begin working on the next day.

To top it all, I had just lost two hours to the stupid room-mate assignment nonsense, which could have been spent sleeping blissfully and gathering energy for what was to come later that night. Everyone slept between 2.00 am to 5.00 am, but how well you slept in the afternoon made the difference to how high your grades were going to be over a period of time.

I made slow progress and got all the way to page four in thirty minutes. Intermittent distractions included checking my messenger program to see if either of the two girls I had a crush on were online, and to check on cricket scores.

Finally, I decided to go to the cafeteria to get dinner. It was nearly eight and I was almost done reading the case. I walked out and strode rapidly to the cafeteria to save time. No student at ISB walked slowly unless he was accompanying someone of the fairer gender.

I grabbed a plastic tray, shared pleasantries with the staff (excellent people, they were) and helped myself to some paneer, dal and roti. I then grabbed some fruit and curd-rice, some mango pickle (old habits never die), and turned around.

I found Ranga sitting at a table. On another table were some rather hot Tamilian women arguing about something, and I loved that. Nothing like intellectual conversation from my neck of the woods over dinner. In the absence of rolling on the grass with hot Punjabi women, this would have to do. Not that the Tams shall not roll, but the sort that do are usually the Punjabi ones making their Sandalwood or Tollywood debuts in the so called 'South-films'. Dumbasses – don't they know the right term is 'South Indian films'? This is what the right amount of weight in the torso in the right

The Fellowship of the Lost **53**

gender does for you throughout your life. Gives you a head start, or two head-starts, no puns intended. I headed in their direction, but I heard Ranga calling out to me.

'I mean, like . . . dude, *baro illi* (come over here)', he said.

I walked up to his table and plonked my tray down.

'What's up? Read the case?' I inquired.

'I mean, like . . . I just kind of glanced at it. I was talking to the professor at dinner. Seems like a nice guy. May not cold-call me. Ha-ha', he replied while wolfing down spoonfulls.

Ranga was seriously in a different league. If you were a professor at ISB, you were sure to have Ranga eat with you, no matter when you arrived. I had the opportunity to sit with him at times, and he'd go on and on about strategy, models, banks and other such elements from *The Economist* or *Business Week* or *Filmfare*, for all one knew. Most of his talk was superficial, but it took a while for a polite Caucasian professor to figure that out, and in the meantime, Ranga was all over them. What drove him to such lengths I did not know, but he sure liked it. I gave him the benefit of doubt; maybe he was brilliant and therefore this was a forgivable quirk.

'Hey, by the way, I came by this afternoon to tell you about something', he said, as I chewed on cold roti and hot paneer.

'Yeah, I remember! Killed my sleep', I said.

'I mean, like . . . I've given our name as quad-mates. Us and Venkat', he concluded, apparently proud of himself.

Sputtering, I reached for a glass of water.

I looked at him, my thoughts were staggered, like when you get a fast bowler crack you in the nuts and your mind is suddenly clear before the pain comes. In that window of clarity, you can think of anything you want and suddenly the answers are there; its lucidity inspired by a few microseconds where the mind is not distracted by anything. It is simply sharp; sharp in the anticipation of the most overwhelming pain about to arrive.

Like me, Ranga was a vegetarian like me and did not smoke. He was from my city and had been neutral to me so far. I hadn't spent

54 *Touching Distance: The Great Indian MBA Dream*

a great deal of time with him yet. He always wore a white VIP vest and shorts, and looked like he didn't know what a comb was. His hair stood on end and through his glasses, he looked blankly at people. The south Indian version of Homer Simpson, as I'd observed earlier.

Not sure how to respond, I ate half a roti and finally looked up at him. He was chewing on some rice.

From what I'd seen so far, Ranga was idiosyncratic to say the least. He had no interest in sports and wasn't one to be a wing-man when it came to girl-hunting. Lastly, he was forever lost in a universe of talking about business strategy. Not exactly what I was looking for in a quad-mate.

'Dude, why didn't you ask me about this?' I said, trying to sound as composed as I could.

'I mean, like . . . I wanted to tell you today, but you were sleeping, OK?' he retorted.

'Is Venkat the guy with the Brad White beard?' I asked.

'Oh yeah. Don't worry, he's a cool guy. He's in my study group. I mean, like . . . he was in the army. Captain or something.'

Brad White was a Wharton Macroeconomics professor from Term 1. About sixty years of age, he was a genial giant of a man, standing at six feet and four inches. Put him in a red suit and you didn't need the reindeer or a sled. Lovable guy. He had a beard I'd never seen in India before, and that's saying something, isn't it? His sideburns dropped way down to his jaw and then curved in an arc to meet his handlebar moustache. While at first it looked comical, Brad, being so tall, heavily built and White, carried it off. Put some leather on him and get him to swing his trunk-like legs over a Harley Davidson, he would look like the quintessential weekend biker. Or a WWF wrestler. Either way, it fit.

I figured there was a very good reason no one in this five-thousand year old culture had sported a Brad White. It was bound to look really foolish on an Indian face. Venkat was about five-feet six-inches, Tamilian, and very slim. The first time I saw Venkat,

The Fellowship of the Lost **55**

he had a thick moustache, the kind without which you don't stand a chance in Telugu movies. Because Venkat was Tamilian, the moustache was understandable, given that he was in the army and needed to fit in with a bunch of bigger, burlier north Indians who probably threw their weight around, despising the smaller, and punier 'Madrasi'.

After the first week of Macroeconomics, Venkat had grown out his sideburns. After the second week the devastation was complete: he sported a Brad White and a huge smile to go with it. It was a conversation-starter no doubt, but I wondered if he really had a mirror in his room.

Venkat was among the oldest people in our batch, into his thirties. Before the beard, he was known to be mature and fun-loving, but what he was attempting with this beard was just beyond everyone. Needless to say, he invited the professors' attention, who let it pass, and Venkat didn't seem concerned. I'd concluded anyone who did something like that didn't really care about being serious, or simply didn't care at all. I was sure this guy was off his rocker. Maybe all those years in the sun-baked missile-pointing divisions had finally burnt or melted all the circuits in his brain. Or maybe the persecution complex developed from hanging around with so many testosterone-bursting north Indian men successfully attempting Hrithik Roshan moves at army parties while he tried a Rajni move lamely, had been too much to take. I didn't need to wonder if he was idiosyncratic. He had it printed on his face – with a Brad White.

I turned over all of this in my head and concluded that I had just been signed up for the zoo, and not even by my own self.

'*Yako? Bere yaaru sikliilva?*' I said in Kannada, translating to: Why? Couldn't you find anyone else?

'I mean, like . . . Venkat is pretty cool with quant skills. I mean, we can use him for our finance assignments!' he declared.

I was amazed. I didn't know exactly how to respond. Study groups and quad-mates either make or break your grades. I really

56 *Touching Distance: The Great Indian MBA Dream*

needed a decent set of grades to get a scholarship and cast off some of my loan. Results for the Term 1 exams were not out yet, but I believed I had failed a shot at finishing near the top of the class and wresting a scholarship. The right quad-mates would have gone a long way towards helping achieve that goal.

I looked around the cafeteria at people walking here and there furtively. Hmm . . . the universe had set me up to fail, it seemed. I thought back to all those inspirational talks from the bevy of businessmen and thought leaders, and decided to take on this adversity anyway. I was going to get that scholarship, no matter what. If I lived in a zoo, it wasn't going to matter. I was going to build myself a nice perimeter, then build a rocket that got me away to the stars in a blazing show of the timeless success of the human spirit against all odds.

❖

A few days later, at the end of the first week of Term 2, I was woken up by a knocking on the door. It was the movers. They came in and asked if I needed any help. I declined. I was only too happy to delay leaving my luxury and entering the zoo.

Every cloud has a silver lining, or so I told myself. All said and done, I did look forward to being in a quad. I'd missed all the fun I was hearing about from people in SV2. They were having a blast. Women were more accessible, and most of all, there was a lot of fun going on, like regular dunking in the pool. In contrast, at the Executive Housing, I felt like I was stuck in a luxurious cage, complete with a bathtub. My only interactions were at the cafeteria and they were limited as people really preferred to spend time with known faces.

I walked into the quad and was given a set of keys. I prided myself on some knowledge of Vaastu and numerology. I was a number three person. There were four rooms available in the block we'd been assigned. They were numbered J-8, J-9, J-10, J-11. I was

The Fellowship of the Lost **57**

given J-11 to begin with but I requested Capt to switch rooms. He didn't bother. I had J-9.

To my surprise, Capt reeled off a bunch of numerological calculations himself saying that the match was a good one. J-11 was better for him too, it seemed. That was a good start. I resisted the temptation to quiz him on the numerology that drove him to that beard.

The quad was pretty impressive. A large living area separated the twin rooms. Each two-room pair had a shared bathroom.

Massive windows opened out the rooms and the living room. My room window faced east (chosen carefully, keeping in mind vaastu compliance). The vista included Executive Housing on the left, the Atrium on the right, and a tree-dotted horizon straight up ahead. I breathed in the air and felt good about myself.

Ranga took the room next to mine. He was beaming with joy and so was Capt when they arrived. Capt and I somehow hit it off right at the start. Capt had this strange ability to laugh at the stupidest of things and it rubbed off on me. It wasn't so much what he was laughing at, but the fact that he chose to laugh at something so stupid that got me laughing as well.

Ranga was in high spirits. He unpacked in his room and we all stepped out to make tea for ourselves. Capt volunteered the tea leaves, milk and sugar. It was a great party. Just the three of us and the better part of a year to form bonds.

The good times seemed like they had just begun, but the next day was about to change all that.

◆

The following afternoon, once classes were done, the campus was abuzz with the news that the grades for Term 1 were going to be declared. I was excited. My experiences from school and college were excellent when it came to exam results. I had a bizarrely outstanding school record. I had stood first in every exam in school.

58 *Touching Distance: The Great Indian MBA Dream*

The same had continued through pre-university and engineering, where I was always near the top of the class.

Unlike school and college, there was no notice board where grades were posted. All grades were simply e-mailed to each student, and students could collect their exam answer-papers, if they so desired. Once grades were communicated, there was a second email that carried the distribution- or bell-curve. Based on where your aggregate grades were, you could estimate your position in class, i.e., you knew how many people were ahead of you and how many were behind.

I had prayed hard and I had given it everything in the last few days leading to the Term 1 exam. I opened my grades email; I looked at the bell-curve. Something was wrong, surely: I was in the second half of the class! Somewhere between suing ISB for erroneous valuations to resolving to deal with being a total failure in a huge bet I'd just placed, I found myself suspended in captivating silence.

I leaned back in my chair and let out a slow sigh. Beads of sweat formed on my forehead and face. My breath seemed to have stopped for a while as my brain stopped all functions except working out my situation. What the hell had just happened? Did this mean I was a failure? Would I ever get a job? Was I going to end up at the bottom in the coming terms? How was I going to pay back my loan? What would she think, the one I was so besotted with? Would she even respect me, leave alone fall in love with me? What was I going to tell to my friends? What about my family?

After the dust kicked up by thoughts had settled down and I'd stared for an eternity at the gently swaying trees from the silence of my room, I stood up, my mind an absolute blank. I wanted to know how this had turned out for the others. Misery truly loves company. I stood up and walked straight to Ranga's room. The door was open. He saw me at the doorway and looked away. He looked like he'd seen a ghost. No words needed to be exchanged.

The Fellowship of the Lost **59**

He walked up to the door and closed it. I didn't remember him carrying a strong rope in his luggage, so I backed off.

I walked up to Capt's room to share the bad news. I saw him meditating. I walked back to my room, sat in my chair, put my feet up on the table and stared into the blue sky. The trees swayed slowly, gently in the wind. In the distance, birds dotted the horizon as if nothing would ever shake their spirit. The blue tranquil sky mocked my performance. I gazed blankly through those enormous windows. To my left was the Executive Housing, where I'd spent the last month leading to this disaster, and to my right was the Atrium where I was going to be spending the next nine months or so. There was a heaviness in my spirit, and my heart pounded in my chest as if it was trying to smash the ribs with a sledgehammer.

❖

I must have sat in that position for a long time, for I felt my legs, and then my backside, go numb. I was shaken out of this reprieve by Capt's voice Capt who was just walking in.

'*Hari om*,' he said.

I turned around and looked at him, fully conscious of my embarrassment and shame.

He laughed. 'Didn't go well, huh?'

'Slaughtered. God, I've never taken a blow like this,' I said.

'Ha-ha . . . you've had a good academic life, hey champ?' asked Capt.

I was silent, embarrassed.

'I guess I had better give up on that scholarship dream,' I said.

'Hmm . . . you should've worked harder.'

'I know.'

Silence resumed as he sat on the bed and stared out the window at the blue sky.

'How did it go for you?' I finally enquired, my words heavy with feeling and barely audible.

60 *Touching Distance: The Great Indian MBA Dream*

'I was meditating and the quad went strangely quiet. I figured something was up. You monkeys have never been so quiet when I've been meditating before. I figured one of you must have died or something equally tragic might have happened,' he said.

'Well, I *wish* I'd died,' I replied.

Silence again.

'Tell me,' I finally said, 'did you even check your email?'

'I got screwed, *yaar*. But that's okay. I didn't expect to do anything great academically, anyway. I learnt a lot of concepts which have remained with me and that's enough for now. Who cares a shit about grades? I never expected to top this class or get into McKinsey anyway. I didn't come here for that,' he said.

'Okay . . . ' I replied, soaking in this new line of reasoning.

'There were other reasons. Anyway, I think as long as you feel like you're learning, that's all that matters. Trust me on this one,' he said.

'I know, I know. Grades aren't everything. They're all that is required to win a scholarship, though,' I said.

'Yes, that's true,' he agreed.

'I've put a lot of my savings into this, man. It is crazy. This is a beautiful place, and it's only human to enjoy it and be distracted, but at what cost? Now every time I step on that squash court or enter the pool I'm going to feel guilty.'

'Don't be, dude. Life is a lot bigger than this place. Like I said before, just learn. And make sure you enjoy yourself while you are here. Everyone knows what a scholarship is worth, but no one ever placed a value on happiness, right?'

'Doesn't make sense, Capt. I didn't come here to enjoy. If I wanted to enjoy myself, I'd have taken that ten lakhs and gone to some place outside India,' I said.

'I know what you mean. Trust me, life is too short. One day you'll look back at this year and say, I only wished I'd taken more chances and had more fun,' he declared.

The Fellowship of the Lost **61**

By now, I had just come to terms with it. I was upset as hell, but the blow had come and gone, and I was still alive.

Ranga walked in. He'd just woken up from a nap. From what I'd learnt in the last few days, this guy slept an awful lot. Sleeping was his way of dealing with everything.

Again, Capt and I stared at Ranga. Even before one of us could say something, it happened. That thing they call a catalyst which releases all that is latent in a brewing reaction.

He threw his head back and began to laugh uncontrollably. He held his stomach with one hand and took off his glasses with the other, laughing like he'd never laughed before.

'Screwed, OK. I mean, like . . . I'm completely screwed!' he screamed, laughing like a maniac. He rocked his head to and fro and laughed as if his lungs were going to burst. Capt and I exchanged glances, worried.

'I mean, like . . . I am so screwed, OK, that if my father found out, he would disown me immediately, OK. I mean, like he would shove an axe up my ass, then he would disown me!' he shouted, his belly shaking with laughter, like jelly.

'SCROOD! SCROOD! SCROOD!' he shouted.

'SCROOD! SCROOD! SCROOD!' I shouted. 'We are all so screwed!' I don't know why, but that uncontrollable urge overcame me as well.

Capt joined in and threw his head back. We laughed together for the first time since we'd written the GMAT. Strangely, we laughed in failure, not success.

The 'fellowship' had just been forged.

❖

From that one moment on, things changed for us. Gone were the masks. Every time Ranga said something from a Gartner report, Capt and I smiled, then laughed uncontrollably. Every time Capt said something metaphysical about meditation, we nodded gravely, then laughed.

62 *Touching Distance: The Great Indian MBA Dream*

Laughter was not a by-product. Strangely, it had become the air we breathed. It's priceless, this ability of people to laugh only for laughter's sake.

From an academic perspective, however, there were others who'd done well. Of the six of us in my study group, for example, two had done better than me, despite the injury that the Gillette assignment had inflicted on the marketing grades. Mohit had done extremely well, and his grades were the best in the entire batch. He had been the least social of my group members, and the one person who was somehow always angry and forbidding.

Nilima, the only girl in my study group, confessed that she had begun studying way before she arrived in Hyderabad. She had the best grades among the girls and looked certain to bag one of those scholarships.

I looked at my grades. There was almost no possibility of me finishing up in the top ten percent of the class the dean's list – by the end of Term 4.

This was a strange world, this ISB. Simultaneously cruel and delightful. Amazingly beautiful, yet so stressful. Forever filled with opportunity and a sword hanging over you. Above all, no one told me this group was going to be so competitive. No one told me I had to hit the ground running. No one told me the place would be so beautiful that it would enchant me into doing everything else but study for a while.

No one tells you these important things in life, I concluded. You simply learn from your mistakes.

Over time, I dealt with these issues. I became more regular and wasted less time. I was conscientious and did my best to understand things as best as I could. I also learnt to look beyond the cover of books and the appearances and faces of people.

I made more friends, among them Prosenjit Ray, also from Bangalore. He was deeply cerebral, deeply philosophical, and dead keen on a scholarship. I hadn't met him until then simply because he'd been hitting his books all through Term 1.

The Fellowship of the Lost **63**

The spirit of the apartment, however, was set by Capt. If there was one person out to make the most of this year, while working on his priorities assiduously, it was Capt. If it meant missing a class so he could attend an Art of Living, Sudarshan Kriya session, then so be it. If he had to miss a group meeting because one of his old friends from the army had called, then so be it. If he had to miss an assignment deadline because he was consumed with the need to meditate, so be it. He just didn't care, unless he did care about something deeply.

Prosenjit was the unofficial resident. There was a weird positive energy in the apartment, and it just bounced off us. I concluded I was the only one trying to improve my grades, and that was more out of habit than desire. At some level I too had wanted not to care. Ranga continued keeping in touch with relatives, friends and ex-bosses in the real world, and Capt, for his own part, kept in touch with his esoteric aspirations.

One of the fascinating things about moving to the quad was that there were people around 24x7. Half an hour didn't pass by without you talking to someone, hearing from them on the phone, or watching someone walk by.

In all the positivity, there always lurked the shadow of despair. Sometimes, she'd walk by and I'd be lost in thoughts so deep, I needed a mechanical crane to return to earth.

❖

Me: 'Do you feel like going for a walk?'
Her: 'Why don't you ask Trisha? You keep raving about her all the time, don't you?'
Me: 'Yeah, she's really something, huh? My God, she's so beautiful.'
Her: 'Why don't you marry her?'
Me: 'She's way out of my league.'
Her: 'Oh yeah? Too bad. Stupid idiot, how will you know if you don't ask her?'
Me: 'What about you? Are you seeing him?'

64 *Touching Distance: The Great Indian MBA Dream*

Her: 'Who?'

Me: 'Well, everyone's talking about it. Don't think I'm stupid.'

Her: 'Rahul? No way! He's a very old friend of mine, and that's it.'

Me: 'Come on, you guys are practically married.'

Her: 'No, that's not true. He's just an old friend.'

Me: 'No one spends that much time with an old friend.'

Her: 'I do.'

Me: 'How long have you known him?'

Her: 'A few years.'

Me: 'And nothing happened romantically? If I knew someone for four years, I'd be dating them and marrying them pronto.'

Her: 'You wouldn't. You're incapable of even communicating your feelings, leave alone anything else.'

Me: 'When have I not done that?'

Her: 'Who cares? You say you like this Trisha girl. How often do you call her?'

Me: 'Good point. I guess I'm too shy.'

Her: 'Yeah, that you are.'

Me: 'So, you're single?'

Her: 'Yes, I am.'

Me: 'Come on, that's really hard to believe. Someone as pretty as you?'

Her: 'I don't care what you believe.'

Me: 'Look, you spend every minute of your time hanging around him. That doesn't make sense! Either you are both seeing each other or at least he's got to be interested. He's a really nice guy, you should marry him.'

Her: 'So what if he's interested? I'm not.'

Me: 'Very hard to believe.'

Her: 'Good night.'

   Click.

Me: 'You there? . . . Damn!'

5

The Animal in J-Block

Let me have men about me that are fat;
  Julius Caesar, WILLIAM SHAKESPEARE

His eyes gazed vacantly at the Telugu TV channel playing raunchy film songs from the eighties. His right index finger was stuck in his navel, while his left arm supported his head as he reclined on the couch.

'But I tell you . . . talent is very important in life, OK?' declared Ranga, and smiled to himself. One of the many trains of thought in his serene mind had led him to this conclusion. You wondered if more was to follow that would make his assertion relevant to the present time. Silence. That train of thought had simply collided with another train or derailed by a stationary boulder. Such 'general truths' were delivered with sage-like distance, never mind the fact that they stood out in sharp contrast to their own redundant nature. That was Ranga. In love with simplicity, 'general truths' and strategy. He secretly lived in the belief that his ideas were always original and earth-shattering. In the stillness of his mind, he was the Van Gogh of the business world, except that he was more talented and wasn't about to cut anything off.

66 *Touching Distance: The Great Indian MBA Dream*

Half-listening to his declarations, I nodded gravely. I had problems of my own, and maybe some of them may pertain to talent, I reckoned.

I looked out the window, and soaked in the exquisite natural beauty. The sun was about to set in the horizon over the Deccan Plateau. The evening was in the process of painting an inescapably beautiful Hyderabad sky. The sun had burnt a few clouds to a beautiful cinder. The sheer beauty of the horizon quelled my thoughts for a few moments, much like the sight of an immense ocean that simply jumps out from behind a hill you just scaled, and for a few fleeting moments, takes away both, your breath and your pain.

As dusk approached, I considered the occurrences of the recent past and their effect on my current fate. My financial situation did not bother me as much as my performance in the first term exams.

As I contemplated my destiny and the forces that had placed me here, my thoughts veered back to the room. I had just made tea for my quad-mates but Capt, the resident Hare-Krishna on steroids, was yet to arrive.

Ranga's self-assured, navel-digging general truths did not come from his confidence in the future ISB months, but from his self-ejection from reality to a parallel universe, where I got the strange feeling that he might just be awake more often than he was in class.

Parallel universes were something of a necessity at ISB. All the students had watched helplessly as a new world began to rise around them. A world with walls of time, rivers of assignments, dams of ability and horizons of fate. Throw in options to swim, games to play, beautiful girls to court, and no time for anything but panic, and you have an ISB term.

A world bounded by steep walls one could not scale by hand, but could escape momentarily by spacing out to one's own parallel universe. Some escaped by design, while others were less fortunate.

The Animal in J-Block **67**

I feared Ranga's escape-hatch had shut behind him on one of those occasions when he had managed to climb out of his labyrinth. He never returned to reality, and I don't believe he tried either. It was too much work and he had chosen not to care. He'd decided he was stuck, or liberated, and he'd just pretend it didn't matter. His cocoon was now formed. In any case, his parallel universe was so much more beautiful than the stress-filled reality of B-school desperation.

I looked around the living room of my quad. My quad – J Block, Student Village 2. A set of four rooms, two pairs on each side, with a bathroom separating them, a large living area with an attached kitchenette at the centre of the layout.

'But I tell you, talent is, you know, like . . . kind of very important in life,' he repeated.

I nodded gravely. Talent was very important in life.

Ranga continued to surf channels on the TV, looking for another raunchy song. He wore his *chutney*-stained shorts and vest every day, till he washed these items of clothing some fine day when the time was right and the planets were in their respective favourable zodiac. In a strange new world, this chap from my city was an unchangeable oddity that was somehow calming and amusing at the same time. The predictability of his actions, demeanour and vacation of mind was ironically reassuring in a world where everything got more stressful by the day. He reminded me of a domestic farm animal which was contented and predictable in its daily habits. The fact that we could converse in Kannada, throwing ironic observations about our lives at one another, somehow made more sense than any professor I'd heard so far.

My gaze traversed to the TV. Ranga had lived true to his word. 'I watch only sex or *bhakti*, ha-ha-ha,' he laughed to himself. It was true. Always, if not a fat woman convulsing, he was watching a devotional movie made in the year that the Tollywood or Sandalwood producer had procured South India's first film camera. I was prone

68 *Touching Distance: The Great Indian MBA Dream*

to watching sports, and we took pride in the fact that we only watch 'sex, sports or *bhakti*' at our quad.

I left Ranga to his travails. From time to time, browsing those channels he'd shout something about some movie that had been a big hit in 1965 or something. His statements on movies were always prefixed by a very loud, 'Faaaaak! OOOOHHHH, Faak! This movie, OK? Was a great movie in 1970, OK?' The goddamned print was so bad you could barely discern the actor's face. I didn't know if Ranga was lying. After a while, I stopped bothering.

I walked over to indulge in my favourite pastime – looking out the large windows from our living room. The sun was about to set, and the day had just begun for the 150-odd students. Then my thoughts went back to her. I hadn't seen her all day, except in the class, and she didn't really make any eye-contact. Often I found her thinking hard, and I wondered . . . no, I hoped, that she was thinking about me.

❖

Me: 'We've moved to our new rooms.'
Her: 'OK, how do you like it? Roomies, ok?'
Me: 'Yeah, they're all right. Ranga needs to be potty-trained somewhat, but they're good people. Capt is a riot. How're your roomies?'
Her: 'Terrible. One of them is so dirty. One day I caught her brushing her teeth in the kitchen sink. I almost threw up.'
Me: 'You know what? I think I want to tell you something.'
Her: 'Go on.'
Me: 'It wasn't Trisha all along, it was you.'
Her: 'What do you mean?'
Me: 'What do you think I mean?'
Her: 'I don't understand.'
Me: 'Forget it.'
Her: 'You're telling me you like me?'
Me: '. . . '

The Animal in J-Block **69**

Her: 'Come on, I don't believe you. You've been raving about her all the time.'

Me: 'What didn't you get? I was too shy, I kept singing to you on the phone; I call you at every chance I get . . . '

Her: 'Are you serious? I just don't think you feel that way about me. You haven't even once said anything nice . . . '

Me: 'Well, I was shy. I thought I just explained that.'

Her: 'Are you serious?'

Me: 'Yeah.'

Her: 'OK . . . '

(after an awkwardly long pause)

Me: 'Did I scare you?'

Her: 'Yes, I'm not sure what to say to you.'

Me: 'Hey . . . just kidding. I was kidding. Don't be upset.'

Her: 'OK . . . Phew! You had me worried.'

Me: 'Why would you be worried?'

Her: 'Well, I just don't feel that way about you, and it would be hard to respond if you said anything like that.'

(longer pause)

Me: 'I know. And I also know that you're seeing him. I wouldn't suggest something as long as I knew that.'

Her: 'He and I are just friends.'

Me: 'So you're telling me you are still single?'

Her: 'OK, I've had enough of explaining this to you.'

Me: 'Why are you upset?'

Her: 'I'm not, it's just . . . never mind.'

Me: 'OK. All set for tomorrow's classes?'

Her: 'Kind of. I've been reading non-stop and it never ends.'

Me: 'I know. I don't think I worked this hard to even finish a terrible Electronics subject back in my engineering days.'

Her: 'OK, I have to go now. It's nice talking to you, as always. I'm just tired and I have to finish another thirty pages of this case before I can get any sleep.'

Me: 'Good night, sweetheart.'

70 *Touching Distance: The Great Indian MBA Dream*

Her: 'He-he . . . good night.'
Click.
Me: 'You there? . . . Damn.'
Click.

❖

6

Capt

But we are never gonna survive unless
We get a little crazy
No we're never gonna survive, unless
We get a little crazy

—Seal

Enter Capt. He had this big smile on his face, which obviously meant that he was coming back from some girl's apartment with whom he shared a strictly 'platonic' relationship. No kidding. As much as I'd like to tell you that Capt was having tantric sex with a bunch of women and was going to invite me to one of his orgies, I am sorry. These guys had turned out to be holier than me.

You had to know Capt to know that this was really the truth. Capt was older than both me and Ranga. We were twenty-six, while he was about thirty-three, but he didn't look it. If anything, he looked younger than both of us. He was fit as a Ukrainian gymnast, with a mind as quick as a mongoose's. Years of meditation and yoga had frozen time for Capt's body at some point in his teenage years. He was quite a unique creature. Coming from a fairly typical south Indian middle-class family, like Ranga and me, Capt differed

72 *Touching Distance: The Great Indian MBA Dream*

from us in that he was more evolved. Or at least he was convinced he was. It was perhaps the age gap. Or that all those years of meditation had finally paid off. Or that his distaste for Ranga's putrid existentialism and his knowledge that I hadn't thrown Ranga out the window but chosen to tolerate him, had encouraged him to classify both Ranga and myself in the same bracket of primitive individuals who were placed in his surroundings to challenge his spiritual fibre. After all, given that he was born into this world and ended up with us, gave him the opportunity to work through a few residual karmas before he achieved moksha and joined his gurus now living among the gods.

Capt's prior affiliations were more than consistent with his reputation. He had completed numerous courses offered by a number of self-appointed Indian spiritual gurus. In fact, a few of them knew him by name, which is saying something if you are familiar with the kind of following these gurus command. His guru-like inclinations may bias you to write him off as yet another spiritual hippie sitting in Rishikesh, looking for his next fix of hash. Only that you'd be mistaken. For one, Capt did not smoke anything other than his thoughts lit with the fire of his gods. Two, Capt was one of those who actually enjoyed existing in that spiritual and esoteric realm, meditating afloat the Ganges, even if it meant that the freezing waters may well leave his manhood frostbitten. He was well versed in several Indian spiritual texts and could quote, and still does quote, the *Bhagvadgita* at will. He had vowed to remain unmarried, in order to 'reduce the burden of new karma brought on by additional relationships that one is not born with, and which are of our own short-sighted choosing'. As you can imagine, testosterone-filled Ranga and I simply dismissed such claims as utter prevarications of the worst kind.

'What I say . . . you want Viagra, is it?' Ranga had once asked Capt.

In class discussions, Capt was an eager participant, leaning towards matters of the invisible universe at all times. He was

Capt **73**

prone to asking: 'What is justice?' if the subject was anywhere in the vicinity of philosophy. He would never ask: 'What is life?' he liked to believe that he already knew.

Sitting in my quad and looking at Ranga, who shared the bathroom between our rooms, I often wondered if Lady Fate had indeed conspired against me. My roommates were novel and interesting, but they didn't seem 'tuned into the requirements of success in the world'. Neither of them made any special effort to chase it, and didn't really care too much about networking, which is a huge part of what one needs to do in a B-school. Each MBA student hopes that he'd be enriched in material ways, that his quad mates would be business scions or brilliant people or Brazilian bikini-models looking for education in India. So far, Capt and Ranga were none of the above.

I'd learnt that you should get into the bathroom before Ranga did. If you didn't, you needed to hand him one of those room-freshner things, make him flush the toilet, and then put on an oxygen mask to go in. You also learnt that it was possible to have a million responsibilities and yet lie face-down on the ground and pass out for hours on end, only to wake up and beg someone to make you some tea. This guy was India's tribute to lethargy.

In contrast to Ranga, Capt was all that a disciplined soldier should be. He worked harder than Ranga, only when it was absolutely necessary, and he sure as hell took a bigger interest in the goings-on. He kept regular hours and always maintained a cheery disposition, which gave you the feeling that no matter what the debt, exams or interviews to come, it would all work out just fine, simply because Ramanna Maharshi said so and because the *Ashtavakra Gita* would liberate us all if we so desired. He was fond of saying, 'You are always only a thought away from enlightenment'. Given the number of thoughts I had, I wished I could believe him.

His smile widened with reassurance and his expression quickly changed to one of disgust when he saw Ranga in his trademark pose. Ranga lifted his eyebrow ever so slightly, to see Capt enter,

74 *Touching Distance: The Great Indian MBA Dream*

and went back to meditating on the oversized actress on TV. You see, by policy, Ranga did not move once he was in this position. His legs were firmly planted on the table in front of him. His potbelly had a Zen-like calm to it, having been bathed two days ago. Yes, Ranga was in his element, and nothing else mattered.

Capt shouted out his trademark *'Hari om'*, to thank the heavens that all was well with the Universe. Ranga has that quality to him, you know. His Zen-like state becomes a crutch at a high-pressure place like the ISB – a reference point, even, of better times ahead. If only we could all lie as languidly as he did in the heat of battle, we would indeed be blessed.

Capt dropped off his laptop in his doorway and walked back into the common living room and made himself comfortable on the chair opposite mine. I shouted a few light obscenities at Capt in greeting, more to underscore my state of irony than to be abusive, given as it was against my nature, and complained that I had so much to do in preparation for tomorrow's classes, but was busy keeping the beast alive, feeding it timely doses of tea. I asked Capt what the gods wished to achieve by putting me in this position. He laughed. I let out a scream.

Screams and complaints had become the unofficial handshake in our quad. Almost counter-intuitively, the screaming and shouting was in a way a tacit restatement of the fact that while things had become terrible for us, we still were in control and hadn't lost it yet. We were on the right side of madness, at least so far. That is not a fact to be trifled with. There have been instances of students who have not been so fortunate. Engulfed in the vortex of this extreme stress, some of these students had unfortunately succumbed to nervous breakdowns. For those who had been able to keep their sanity, a fellow student's breakdown was difficult to understand. In the environment of a typical hyper-competitive, grade-obsessed Indian campus, this was seen as a sign of weakness, no less. The ISB, I have to say, conformed to some stereotypes of an Indian campus: grades mattered.

Capt 75

There was a socialisation dynamic every time there was group-work involved. This dynamic was based on grade homogeneity, and configurations were simply based on who was understood to be grade-clever. For all the marketing material on diversity and learning from others, when it came to grades, the hyper-competitive ISB student kept it simple.

Book-smart? Hello.

Not book-smart? Not pretty to the point where you make team meetings worth it with your presence? Bye.

Anyway, like Ranga and me, Capt too was an engineer by education. He had worked a few engineering jobs and then chosen to work in the Indian armed forces, manning guided surface-to-air missiles on the border as part of the Short Services Commission. Strange, I thought, given his spiritual moorings. Maybe a mild case of schizophrenia, I often averred. It was just the case that someone so spiritual could also want to man some nifty warheads. It didn't make sense all the time, but I knew Capt to have a temper, and a very bad one at that. Maybe this whole army gig was his valve.

From time to time, we would elevate Capt in rank and shout out 'General!' or 'Major!' Capt smiled every time we promoted him. For a few minutes, Capt and I talked about the day and I ribbed him about possible breaches in the platonic foundation of his relationships. He let out his trademark deep laugh and assured me that his swimmers had not left their banks for good.

'Ha-ha, I fill voids of a spiritual nature,' was his frequent defence.

Ranga, immersed in the gyrations on TV, cast sidelong glances every now and then in our direction, wondering if we were talking about him.

In a little while, the inevitable happened. Ranga looked like he was about to pass out from the exhaustion of watching the oversized heroines dance. He was frequently passing out, either in his room, spread-eagled, on the floor, with nothing but his *chutney*-shorts on, face-down, with his legs making a perfect right angle; or in the living room, with the remote lodged between the several folds of

76 *Touching Distance: The Great Indian MBA Dream*

his skin, snoring to heaven's dismay. He would wake up in a few hours to take one of his innumerable dumps – he was perennially carrying some kind of a stomach problem, thanks to eating a lot of the rich food and not exercising at all.

Capt bravely dislodged the remote from Ranga's belly. Ranga offered a grunt by way of protest, but did not move. Instead, he went back to sleep. Capt and I then went back to our new-found hobby – watching Animal Planet. Steve Irwin—may his soul rest in peace—the Australian adventurer, was on, trying to get bitten by a snake or any other capable reptile that would care to. The thing was, both Capt and I were nature freaks, with Capt being the more experienced one with all his travails in the Indian landscape while on tour with the army. Capt just loved Steve and impersonated his Aussie accent the whole day, and for days on end when he was given to the mood. It was stupid, but numbingly acceptable.

After watching TV for a bit, I decided to carry out our ritual. Ranga was falling asleep and this was good timing. I say with pride that I invented this ritual. It involved screaming out as loudly as we could to let the stress out. It worked. We ended the ritual in fits of laughter, feeling a little better that we were not alone. I'm sure it was therapeutic at a very esoteric level because Capt was a willing participant. Capt never did anything that was bad for the body or soul or the universe. He was pretty well versed on that front, given his self-proclaimed evolution.

Ranga was startled, then realised what had happened, and shut his eyes slowly.

'Errr . . . Capt, *chai bana na yaar*,' said Ranga, trying not to sound imperious.

'Fuck you, Ranga. You never wash the vessels. The last time I made it, I found the same vessel lying there three days later with a crust of tea.'

Finally, it was decided that Ranga and I would wash the vessels. Capt sang to himself while Ranga browsed the channels to find the next treasure.

Capt 77

'Gaaawd, there's no sugar!' yelled Capt, and I added an expletive or two of my own out of sheer disgust.

'It's that son of a bitch Kajaria,' I averred, referring to this CA from across the landing in the quad opposite ours, who was always 'borrowing' our milk, sugar and tea to make his own beverage and conveniently assuming that three guys would walk up to his flat in any kind of weather and retrieve it, if they wanted to. I'm sure he secretly hoped that we would put the stuff back in his flat after we were done with it.

We tried to get Ranga to get the stuff, but he argued that he would be washing the vessels later so he couldn't logically be the one getting the stuff from Kajaria's flat. Goddamn it – if we didn't get the stuff, there would be no vessels to wash. That was the perennial beauty of Ranga's proactive energy and brilliant logic. But we loved him, anyway. You had to; he was Ranga, after all.

I got the stuff from Kajaria's flat and gave him many pieces of my mind, smoking hot. Then came the good part.

We sipped the wonderful tea that Capt made. The large windows were open, bringing in clean air from the outskirts of Hyderabad, and looked over some of the oldest rocks on the planet (I'm not kidding). That summed up the spirit of our quad. We were like the rocks of Gachibowli. No matter what, we got the tea made and drank it.

❖

Her: 'Hello . . . '

Me: 'Hello.'

Her: 'It's me, stupid.'

Me: 'Well, I'm just a bit surprised you called. You've never called me before, not without a reason.'

Her: 'Stop being a jerk.'

Me: 'Just stating facts. Anyway, what's up?'

Her: 'You tell me what's up. You've had me worried. You haven't called or spoken to me in three days. Was it something I said or did?'

78 *Touching Distance: The Great Indian MBA Dream*

Me: 'No, not at all. Been busy . . . so many things going on. How're things with you? How's studies?'

Her: Didn't you hear me? What's the matter? Everything okay at home?'

Me: 'Yeah, things are okay.'

Her: 'Why have you stopped calling me? What's the matter? You found yourself another girl to chat up?'

Me: 'Well, no. I told you, I've been busy.'

Her: 'OK. If you insist.'

Me: 'What does it matter if I call you or don't? You said it wouldn't matter, right?'

Her: 'Well, it's only civil for you to keep in touch. And yes, it doesn't matter. You've called me pretty much every day since we've been introduced, and that's a few days into ISB.'

Me: 'Not sure what I can tell you. Yeah, I guess I have called you everyday. I didn't know you cared whether I called or not. Anyway, I'm glad I was missed and I'm glad you called.'

Her: 'Me too.'

Me: 'Look. I've just been tied up. Besides, I have different groups to work with this term and as you know, that can take a lot of time.'

Her: 'OK, that's fine. I just called to check on you. Don't stress out too much.'

Me: 'How's the boyfriend?'

Her: 'I told you there's no one.'

Me: 'Come on, that's a lie . . . '

Her: 'Gosh, just let go now, will you?'

Me: 'OK . . . how have things been for you?'

Her: 'All's well. I just wanted to check on you. You said something last time we talked and I retorted to that. I figured you might be upset.'

Me: 'What, upset because you told me I wasn't your type? Come on.'

Her: 'OK, I'm glad you're fine. Do call. Don't disappear.'

Me: *'I will. Say hi to your boyfriend.'*
Her: *'Gosh, that does it.'*
Click.
Me: *'Hmm . . . '*
Click.

7

Satellite Attack

Slip inside the eye of your mind
Don't you know you might find
A better place to play

—Oasis

The library at the school was a structure worth beholding. It rested at the centre of the Atrium, which itself was built on pillars erected around the circumference of the well of the Atrium. The structure opened to the skies by way of a massive circular skylight about forty feet in diametre, which illuminated every corner of the circular facility. Completely lit by natural light, it had an enormous glass dome for a ceiling.

The library had two levels. The shelves were arranged in two large concentric circles at both levels, and were stocked with the most inspiring books – stuff that can really make you want to sit down and read. No matter what your subject of interest, there was something you could pick up. More than anything else, just being in the library would energise you. After a listless day, a trip to the library could remind you of all those dreams and aspirations which had brought you here in the first place. It had a silent calm, and

Satellite Attack **81**

a subtle, tangible energy which could only be experienced. Books must have an intelligence all their own.

Located as it was at a significant height, the large windows encircling it provided amazing vistas of the region, stretching endlessly over rocks, hills and the campus lake. The light inside the library changed from harsh during the day and took on a softer yellow and orange hue towards the evening when the sun's rays began to cool off. In 2002–03, given the smaller class size, the place also offered a location for reflection and quietude, far from the madding student populace and the tribulations, assignments and unfinished work items which never seemed to abate.

It was a place where people were usually in a sunny mood, and were always willing to have a laugh. It was also the perfect place to meet one of those pretty women and strike up an interesting conversation with very relevant opening lines, thanks to the books in their hands.

This evening, however, 'she' was with him again in the library. They were leaving through a different pathway towards their Student Village. I decided to take the long route back to mine. It was a lovely evening and I could use the walk. Besides, it gave me an opportunity to watch her leave in the distance and to see if my fears were unfounded or not.

I slowed down my steps, then sat on a rock that concealed my presence. I needed to know what was up. Halfway back to their SV, they paused, words were exchanged, laughter ensued. Nothing intimate there. I was a little relieved. How I wished I was him. He was always around her, and she didn't mind it. Maybe she sought it. Maybe there was more to it than met the eye. My eyes looked as keenly as they could and my mind stayed as calm as it possibly could. The forms disappeared in the distance. I turned around and walked back. Nothing had been resolved, and my angst was as acute as ever. Maybe I'd just have felt better if I saw them hold hands or kiss. Then I'd know I had no chance and could move on.

❖

82 *Touching Distance: The Great Indian MBA Dream*

Seen from above, the pathways leading from the Atrium to the Student Villages resembled the spokes of a wheel. These pathways were laid in stone, and cut across the beautifully manicured lawns. They were each lit by a few hundred CFL foot-level lamps on either side. The paths resembled runways, and given that the Atrium was at a height, it was almost as if you descended from the heights of learning in the classrooms and library to your abodes after a safe landing back on earth. The sun had set a few hours ago and the inky blue-black ISB sky, which was glittering as always, reminded me that the day had just begun.

The list of cases to be read that evening and the assignments I had to complete, tumbled through my mind, which began a balancing act of its own, attempting to optimise time and space. The breeze picked up and it was getting colder. I looked heavenwards at the glittering continuum. With so many thoughts cluttering one's head, it always helps to look at infinity, just to put things in perspective and to know that life is an illusion.

There were seldom any clouds over the city, leading to clear nights, which was great for star gazing. A moving spot of light caught my eye and I looked carefully. I was sure I had spotted a moving satellite. Hell, it might even be a spaceship. With everything that had changed around me, the horizons of my mind had expanded to embrace all that may be possible. Besides, there had to be something exciting out there in the infinity that could counter-balance the monotony of my books and the weight of the laptop on my shoulder.

Transfixed by the moving light, I nearly tripped over a couple of the foot-level CFL lights. Back in my quad, I decided it was up to me to make sure my fellow inmates vacated their work for the next few hours. I walked straight into Capt's room to tell him about the discovery. Stuff like that was sure to keep him charged up him for the next four hours. After all, the Martians may have arrived to announce that the most evolved being around was Capt, and he needed to be taken away to teach them about how they could be

Satellite Attack **83**

better space-beings. If, on the other hand, they were ill-disposed, the missile man in him reckoned there was none better than him to save the planet in its darkest hour.

The moving light in the sky was still visible from my window. Capt walked into my room. He had the stern look of a man who was sure that Martians were about to attack and he was the last man left on the planet, with a stick in his hand, and was destined to successfully defend it. Missile or not, he was God's chosen man in these situations.

'*Yaar*, yeah. It looks interesting. But it's not moving. It can't be a spaceship,' he concluded, an uncertain disappointment in his voice.

I didn't know that Capt had actually seen spaceships of any kind before, but I suggested that the Martians may have decided to park and take a pee. He let out a typical bellowing laugh, almost as if he was simultaneously happy and disappointed that he could be moved to laugh at something non-spiritual, and made an effort to hold back his opinions on the workings of Martian bladders. Anyway, I suggested that he look with more patience. He saw that it was moving rather slowly and was thinking of other ways to shoot the idea down. Capt always wanted to be right about things which were off the ground. If there was a flying saucer out there, it couldn't become one until he put his thumb on a stamp pad and pressed it against the Martians' green bottom, stamping his ass-port and authorising his entry over earthly skies.

Ranga, who was waiting for something to distract him, slowly strolled into the room with the look of utter disdain at Capt and me looking out the window. As far as he was concerned, there was no money, *bhakti*, titillation or food in that direction, and we were being completely stupid.

'Ha-ha-ha. I mean, like . . . if that's a UFO, fucking, I will get an A in Cost Accounting, OK. Ha-ha-ha. Balls, OK? . . . I mean, like . . . ha-ha-ha . . . Capt, ha-ha, you and this prick, OK? . . . you guys are pricks . . . ha-ha-ha,' he said. Once he had had his fill, he stopped picking his nose, gave his tummy a nice massage and

84 *Touching Distance: The Great Indian MBA Dream*

lay down on my bed, smiling at the ceiling, thinking of all those spaceships he could fill with his TechPlant stock options.

Capt, in the meantime, was looking out the window, paying as much attention to Ranga as he was to all the furniture in the room. If there was a spaceship outside, Capt did not want the Martians to see Ranga. He feared they'd attack instantly. Finally, he said, 'Let's go outside and take a look.'

In the background, Ranga babbled in Kannada that all of us had indeed lost it: coming to ISB on a ten-lakh-fee and all that, and how we had got conned, and how he would never have come if he had known how to calculate net present value (NPV) of his future cash flows because according to him, they never added up to ten lakhs anyway. He said that the only saving grace for him was that he had not gone mad like the two of us intent on chasing spaceships at midnight. He ranted that there were no employers on Mars and that Martian money was not good enough to repay our loans. 'Just look at yourselves: pathetic pricks ... ha-ha-ha,' he laughed. He walked slowly into the living room and turned on the TV. Much in the same way that the alcoholics turn to the bottle when they need a break.

We continued to look outside through the window and finally decided to go out, only to be stopped by Ranga in the living room.

'*Arrey*, Capt ... *chai bana na yaar*,' begged Ranga. He believed that implorations in Hindi may appeal to Capt's military past and sense of duty.

'Not now, you asshole. We're trying to look for a spaceship,' said Capt.

'Dude, don't worry. We'll catch up with it soon. They're here to meet us, I'm sure they won't mind a tea-break. If we were going to be beamed up for a bit, I'd rather have some tea first,' I said.

'I'll be out in a second,' I said to Capt as I closed the door. I had a call to make about weights hanging off my brain about creatures of a slightly different nature.

❖

Satellite Attack **85**

Me: 'Hello.'

Her: 'Hey, stud boy!'

Me: 'Missing me yet?'

Her: 'What? No. Why would I?'

Me: 'Look, you just told me the last time we talked that you missed me and all that.'

Her: 'Hey, mister. I didn't say I missed you. I just said that you seemed to have stopped calling and I was wondering what the hell had happened to you. I wanted to make sure things were good at your end.'

Me: 'He-he . . . okay. I still think you missed me, and if you insist that you don't, I have no option but to doubt you.'

Her: 'Whatever. Anyway, how are things? What's up? You called.'

Me: 'Hmm . . . Now that you miss me so much and all that, how about that walk I keep asking you for?'

Her: 'Where do you want to go? I'm not too keen on starting a scandal . .'

Me: 'Come on. There are so many people going on walks. What's another couple of students?'

Her: 'Mister, the ones walking around the Atrium are either couples or lovers, not friends.'

Me: 'Oh, come on!'

Her: 'Ok, let me think about that.'

Me: 'Think about what? Being a couple or being a pair of friend-walkers?'

Her: 'God! You're hopeless.'

Me: 'Ok, ok, sorry . . . I was kidding.'

Her: 'Were you? It's hard to say.'

Me: 'I was. I promise. You scare easy.'

Her: 'Hmm . . . okay. I almost believed you the last time.'

Me: 'When I told you that it wasn't Trisha I was in love with?'

Her: 'Yeah.'

Me: 'Well, I explained that I was kidding.'

86 *Touching Distance: The Great Indian MBA Dream*

Her: 'Yeah, you did. You want to explain why you look lost in our classes and why I end up catching you gazing at me?'

Me: 'I wasn't gazing at you.'

Her: 'OK.'

Me: 'So what if I was? You're extraordinarily beautiful, you should know that.'

Her: 'Oohhh ... turning on the charm, eh?'

Me: 'I'm just stating the facts. You have your own fan club and everything, right?'

Her: 'Yeah, right. They're just pulling my leg.'

Me: 'Trust me, sweetheart, they aren't. If you so much as threw your shoe into a pit full of alligators, those guys would kill each other to jump in there and retrieve it for you.'

Her: 'He-he ... very funny.'

Me: 'Don't worry, I'm not one of those in your fan club.'

Her: 'He-he ... good to hear that. I like having you as a friend.'

Me: 'Yes ma'am. Glad to help.'

Her: 'Anyway, I have to go now.'

Me: 'OK ... so how about that walk?'

Her: 'I need to think about it. Why all this walk josh?'

Me: 'I never get to catch up with you except over the phone. Your SV is so far away; and in the cafeteria, you're surrounded by wolves from the cow belt.'

Her: 'He-he ... stop it. Yeah, sure we will catch up. Bye for now.'
Click.

Me: 'Sigh.'
Click.

8

The Recruit on the Rooftop

I can feel it, coming in the air tonight, Oh Lord
—PHIL COLLINS

Ranga switched the channel to some Telugu *bhakti*-film from the last century. N.T. Rama Rao, the famed actor of yesteryears, was delivering a soliloquy about life and nothingness. Ranga offered to translate. I winced.

Tea was made and sipped, and with Ranga's commentary on NTR, we had abolished all thoughts of reading the case for tomorrow. Capt asked me if I had read it. I hadn't. I asked him the same question and Capt said, '*Shuru bhi nahin kiya, yaar.* Prof *zinda maar dega* cold-call *kiya toh*.' Capt was prone to speaking in Hindi from time to time when he was disgusted. The language-switch was highly correlated to his emotional state. After all, he spoke only Hindi while he had been in the army. He spoke it much better than us true-blue 'Southies' who infrequently ventured to contribute a newly learned profanity or two.

We both looked at Ranga. It was a strategy case of some sort, and given Ranga's fatal attraction to the subject and its simplicity, we reckoned he must have read it. After all, he must have read a

88 *Touching Distance: The Great Indian MBA Dream*

page or two on those several occasions when we saw him passed out on the floor, face-down on page three of any case. Ranga decided to emerge from a brief reverie. 'Ha-ha-ha-ha . . . the case . . . ha-ha-ha . . . Capt, asshole, in the interview, is the interviewer going to ask you what was in the case? I mean, like . . . what's important is not cases in B-Schools, it's learning from others' perspectives. I mean, it's exposure. And you know, it's mapping what is in the case to business models in the industry. I mean, in TechPlant . . . we were trying to do this . . . and . . . ,' he stopped short to swat a mosquito which had placed itself on Ranga's belly and was about to send in a sharp bite. He missed.

'Bastard mosquito!' he said angrily, disappointed.

Looking up, he said, 'I mean, like . . . ' then tapered off and went back to watching television as he caught sight of a pair of oversized protuberances carefully videographed to titillate.

By this time, Ranga's general truths had started irritating Capt. They were still amusing, but I think Capt had somehow accepted the first few and had given Ranga some credit for them, but when I began laughing about them later, he somehow blamed Ranga for having fooled him the first few times. At least, that's what I think. Capt, of course, will deny it. As far as I am concerned, give me a general truth once, I'd think you were a sage; repeat it, and I'd think you are Ranga.

Capt cursed a few of Ranga's close female-relatives, using the most common Hindi abuses and followed up with, 'Have you read the case, you asshole?' Capt was hoping someone could give him a quick summary before he went into deep meditation and waited for the gods to be on his side when he was cold-called in class the next day.

'Ha-ha-ha, I mean, I still don't believe you ask me these questions. But I'm really impressed that you have such high expectations of me . . . ha-ha-ha. I mean, anyone can answer questions in class and do class participation after reading the case. But you know, the real

The Recruit on the Rooftop **89**

talent is in doing that before reading the case,' said Ranga. I looked on mirthlessly. This guy was just unstoppable.

It was almost 1.00 am when we finished tea. Ranga screamed, '*Faak* . . . Oh *faaak*! OK guys, I'm going to sleep now. OK, I mean, like . . . you know, just crash onto the bed. I mean . . . George Day, OK, caught me sleeping in class and the bugger, OK . . . cold-called me, OK, God, I mean, . . . OK, just couldn't control it . . . just smashed . . . ' He rushed into his room and shut the door. It took him no more than thirty seconds to fall asleep.

'What is *this*?' asked Capt.

'What is what?'

'*This* . . . *this* excuse for a mammal that lives there,' he said, beckoning to the door that had just been closed, a smile appearing and then being replaced by a scowl.

I nodded gravely, pretending his question was serious.

'You know what, Capt, I have this sneaky feeling it really doesn't matter,' I said.

'What doesn't matter? His nonstop nonsense or his need for talking absolute bullshit coupled with his sloth?' asked Capt

'Oh, I was saying it doesn't matter if you don't read the case. It may not make a difference in the end,' I suggested.

'Of course, *yaar*. Nothing matters eventually, ashes to ashes, dust to dust, bullshit to cowdung,' declared Capt.

I allowed the silliness of the Capt's general truth to hang in the air as if I respected it. With a serious expression, Capt and I looked out the window at the lights which were now on in the gym.

Then, a brilliant idea struck me. 'Let's climb onto the terrace and check out the Martians.' Capt readily agreed.

We gathered our *chatais* and walked toward the terrace. The weather was just perfect. Capt had already started a story about how he slept somewhere even more dangerous when he was in the army, some place close to wild animals of the kind you could not hypnotise with your yogic powers. All of his stories were entertaining, and so no one ever complained, even when he repeated them. This one

90 *Touching Distance: The Great Indian MBA Dream*

was about the time he discovered a cobra in his toilet in the hills south of the Himalayas, just as he had unbuttoned his pants. I made a few obvious jokes about his anatomy and the rarefied mountain air, to the effect that illusions are fostered in these situations. He assured me that the cobra had indeed coiled itself on the toilet seat, waiting for him to arrive. He said that he stayed still and used the power of his mind to get it to leave through the window. I asked if he noticed the wet floor after Mr Cobra had left!

'You asshole-recruit Ranga! Come out and join us,' Capt roared.

'Recruit' is the designation given to guys who wear large *khaki* shorts and try to get into the army in the 'walk-in exercise programme+interview' deals. They are made to run around a big dusty ground till half of them drop, so that guys like Capt can deal with the 'shortlisted' fifty percent. This process is repeated till the manageable number of hundred or so remain, when they are given a pad and a pencil and asked to do some tests. I'm told that more than twenty or so faint at the sight of those tests. Capt said that Ranga would never get into the army and would be a recruit at best. Capt said I would have been a sergeant, which I'm presuming is something better, so I don't mind too much. Everything is about relative grading, at a B-School, after all.

Capt always regressed to addressing us in army lingo when he wanted to get us organised about something or the other. Like getting us to come to the living room to check him out in his new suit, or when one of his 'platonic' ladies was in our quad. He wasn't trying to show off the fact that he'd been an army guy when the lassies were around, but he didn't mind reminding them from time to time, using us sergeants and recruits as props. Ranga's theory was that Capt was trying to relive his youth before the ladies. Ranga was always going on about how he wanted to find a girl quickly before the end of the year. He said that everyone's member had an expiry date. Only that guys like Capt didn't know it. He had suggested that one of these days, Capt's member would break

The Recruit on the Rooftop **91**

off when he would be trying to launch his missiles and that Capt would not know what to do. He completed it with an animated demonstration.

I went downstairs and attempted to call Ranga to join us, but on my way down, my attention was caught by the sight of something that heightened my senses, set my pulse racing, and made me sick to my stomach.

I'd love to tell you I saw a cobra coiled with its hood spread, trying to deliver me from the vagaries of life, but what I'd seen was even worse. Not scary, just worse. Even at a distance of a hundred metres, she was unmistakable. Her gait, her hair, I even remembered her perfume from this morning when I walked past her while leaving class. And there he was, walking next to her, her hand in his. There are moments in life when you feel your spirit sink to the ground, leaving you motionless.

They walked alone under the halogen lights that lit the road and they were on their way back to their Student Village after the kilometre-long walk around the Atrium. At once, I was filled with jealousy, betrayal and shock. Strange. I'd been rejected before and had no chance here, but I suddenly felt a knife slice through my heart.

The main door opened and Ranga stood in the doorway.

'*Yako isthu kopa? Bartidde.* Just had to go to the pot first,' (Why do you look so angry? I was on my way out) he explained.

In his right hand he held a discoloured pillow and in his left, a similarly patterned blanket. We walked back up to the terrace and I was no longer interested in Martians or spaceships. I was filled with anger at myself, for allowing myself to fall so madly in love with someone who didn't care.

Ranga lay down. Capt and I listened as he began telling us stories about how he used to sleep under the stars when he was younger. I listened, without hearing a word. I stared at the belt of Orion in a fixed, insane manner.

We chatted for a while but the plan had already started to backfire. Mosquitoes had appeared out of nowhere and were attacking us

92 *Touching Distance: The Great Indian MBA Dream*

like there was no tomorrow. The Martians were the lesser danger now. We braved it for another ten minutes but Ranga's loud snoring didn't make it worth the while. We rushed back in at 4.00 am.

❖

Me: 'Hey.'

Her: 'Hey, what's up?'

Me: 'I tried calling you earlier. Didn't get through . . .'

Her: 'When? It's pretty late already.'

Me: 'Yeah. I just took a chance calling you. Saw you online.'

Her: 'I just got back. Was working on that case with Akshata.'

Me: 'Akshata?'

Her: 'Yeah.'

Me: 'What did you do in the evening? Did you step out at all?'

Her: 'No, I didn't. Been with Akshata all day.'

Me: 'Hmm . . . '

Her: 'What do you mean, "Hmm"?'

Me: 'No, I thought I saw you.'

Her: 'Me? When? Where?'

Me: 'I thought I saw you taking a walk.'

Her: 'Ah, ok. With Rahul? I stepped out for a walk earlier.'

Me: 'You just said you were with Akshata all day?'

Her: 'I forgot. What does it matter to you anyway?'

Me: 'Guess, I just believed you when you said that you were single.'

Her: 'I am single.'

Me: 'OK. If you say so.'

Her: 'What's that to you? You're not in love with me or anything, are you?'

Me: 'Hell no!'

Her: 'Anyway, I have to go.'

Click.

Me: 'Hey, you still there?'

Click.

9

Of Sofas and Shaktimaans

I used to rule the world, seas would rise when I gave the word
—Coldplay

One of the things the students at ISB were very conscious about was their past professional experience. Since everyone had some work experience or the other, it was understandable that they felt either positively, or negatively, about it.

At the risk of sounding biased, I aver that the coolest folks were the engineers. They outscored the CAs in every finance-related subject that had a few formulae, and were supremely confident about their ability to think through problems, given their very strong grounding in everything quantitative and their appetite for hard work.

The CAs were usually apologetic, given that they were frequently beaten at finance subjects. They stuck together somewhat safe in the knowledge that no matter what happened, the banks would always prefer them, simply because they'd fitted in before, and given that banks were banks, they liked to play it safe, unless they all decide to participate, rather unwittingly, in a synchronised meltdown.

94 *Touching Distance: The Great Indian MBA Dream*

There were a lot of people with different stories. The odd architect, the DJ, and a group of former army men who'd decided to trade the fervent patriotism for a more benign existence.

The ex-army men were full of discipline, but their brains were not necessarily in as great form as those of the engineers, and they did in some sense feel a little out of place when they saw the CAs sweating day and night over grades and books. The ex-army men, of course, were the most fun. If you could get used to their eccentricities and their constant need for acknowledgement, that is. Without too many sentries to salute them at every opportunity, they had perhaps started feeling their dignity shrinking a little. Once they got over the shrinkage, they did their best to blend in with us bloody civilians, who lived as it pleased them and did not have the table manners you were expected to display every time you saw a fork and didn't want it shoved up your ass.

All that you could say about ex-army men, was certainly true about Capt. In addition, Capt was mighty proud of having been in the army and never lost a chance to tell you about it. From where we sat, we learnt of the time Capt came face to face with a cobra, on a dark street, then walked right past it after doing a swami mind-job on the poor reptile, causing it to stand still while he walked away with all his senses intact. He had, at another time, come face to face with another snake coiled in the pot when he walked in, dropped his pants and lifted the lid. He didn't say whether he let the call of nature overcome the survival instinct, but I'd believe that to be the case.

Finally, there were innumerable stories of his bravery; like, sitting in trucks which were just about to roll off a hill as the merciless rain poured down hard but he kept the driver motivated to get the wheels and his ass safely back home.

Of course, from time to time we were happy there was no gun around. For all his spiritual attainments, Capt had a temper, and a bad one at that. He never really got violent, but he sure as

Of Sofas and Shaktimaans **95**

hell spat like one of those cobras that just had someone open a lid on it.

❖

In time, our apartment acquired a reputation for being a really fun place. We served tea, made mostly by Capt or me, and were always in good spirits. I was the only one who hit the books assiduously, while both Ranga and Capt were game for a break at any given point of time.

A frequent visitor to our apartment was a rather fun guy called Ajay. He was well built and looked like he could put his fist through a crocodile's belly if it ever disagreed with his hypothesis. He was that kind of guy – strong opinions, hypotheses and all. Splendid chap, mind you. Splendid enough for us to 'recruit' him in our Logistics and Supply Chain Management Group, which by itself turned out to be a total failure. As a group (Ranga, Capt, Ajay and I), we did miserably, and individually we did as much 'class participation' (read: holding our hands aloft while answering questions, or at least pretending to know the answer in return for full marks for participation) as we could in the final hours to give the professor's teaching assistant a huge headache. Imagine, one of the jobs of a teaching assistant was to note down who said what in a class! And you thought your job sucked!

Prof Mehta, who taught us Supply Chain, on the other hand, would smile from ear to ear, trying to hide his glee. He must have been convinced that he had done a splendid job gauging my responses in the final hours.

Anyway, to return to the scene of the crime, Ajay walked into our apartment to say Hello. Maybe he'd just come in for the tea . . . Anyway, Ajay trooped in one such day. I think we were approaching the time of placements. I stepped out for a while to chat him up. Ranga had passed out on the floor of his room, halfway between the bed and the desk. Anyone else would have called the ambulance, but I knew better.

96 *Touching Distance: The Great Indian MBA Dream*

This time it was just Ajay and me. I was on the couch, facing the TV. On either side of me were two single sofas. Capt trooped out from a deep sleep (he denied it, of course, preferring to convince people that he was in *dhyaan* or meditation so deep that Lord Vishnu himself was about to make an appearance to pat him on the head) and sat opposite Ajay. After a while, my stomach gurgled for tea, and I exchanged glances with Capt. He nodded. This kind of telepathy had been developed to a remarkable degree over the course of a few months.

I got up to make the tea, while Ajay droned on about work-ex or something, in the background. Capt, as was his wont, was trying to relate everything to the bigger picture and state a generalisation. I opened the large sliding windows and stirred my tea while enjoying the breeze, listening dispassionately to the listless conversation meandering on behind me. 'Those fuckers want work-ex, *yaar*! If they want ten years of work-ex, why the hell are they coming to our school? They should go to some old-age home,' said Ajay.

'Look *yaar*, work-ex is important. Bloody hell, in the army it's everything. Look what happens without work-ex; look at the dotcom bust with all these twenty-something CEOs. In the army you would never have a commanding officer who is twenty. Twenty-somethings get their asses kicked in the army, they don't get to kick ass. That's just the way it should be everywhere!' Capt announced with the finality of a judge throwing someone to the gallows for heinous war crimes.

Ajay wondered what the hell Capt was trying to say. I understood—Capt wasn't saying anything, he was just ruminating. Connecting random ideas from his experiences and boiling them in every situation was Capt's forte. If they helped vent his frustration against all things non-army and young, so be it.

They went back and forth like this for a while: Ajay, rather burly and brusque in speech when trod on, was looking at Capt with steely eyes, disagreeing. Capt had the wisdom in his eyes—the wisdom of a man who knows that he is right.

Of Sofas and Shaktimaans **97**

'Bloody bastards, *yaar*, those guys. My friend, Capt Vir from the engineers . . . those HR bastards didn't consider his army work-ex in the previous batch. Good chap, Capt Vir,' said Capt.

'Dude, why the fuck should the HR guys care about how long that guy sat in a Shaktimaan or some truck? Work-ex should be relevant,' said Ajay with all the conviction usually associated with stupidity.

I took a deep breath. If I had one of those time-machine things, I'd have told Ajay he was being the monkey who unfortunately shits where the crocodile sleeps. And it happened: Capt took a while to imbibe it, and then his brain lost control. He gripped the arm rests of the sofa and stopped breathing. His eyes glared wide open, and his face looked like the hood of the cobra that had its toilet lid opened in the middle of a siesta.

'You take your sofa and get out, you bastard!' thundered Capt, clenching his mug of tea so hard I was sure it would implode. 'Who the hell do you think you are and what the crap do you know!' He was fully awake now.

I turned to look at Arun. The rabbit was caught in the headlights and the sofa was equally frozen with fright. Arun had the look of a monkey crapping, who has realised that the series of white dots are pointed and sharp and the black unmoving blob is the eye of the crocodile.

It was one of those occasions when the *yogi* Capt blew his top. I'd never seen him like this too often. In one fell swoop, he had demoted Arun to a corporal, or a recruit, or whichever unfortunate layer of the army was at the bottom of the pyramid. I, for one, half-scared and half-dying with mirth, made a mental note to ask Capt whether he was going to buy us a new sofa if Arun was going to take that one with him.

Needless to say, Arun went very quiet for a while. The monotony was broken by Ranga, who'd heard some abuses.

He stepped out of his den, dressed in his vest and shorts, rubbing his stomach, eyes barely open.

98 *Touching Distance: The Great Indian MBA Dream*

'Who is shouting? You pay nine lakhs and can't even sleep. What kind of place is this?' he demanded.

Sensing the carnage in the room, he turned towards me and said, *'Lo, yenaito ee pishachige?'* (Dude, what happened to this demon?) dropping his voice and turning to Kannada, a language Capt did not understand.

I tried not to laugh.

Noticing that Capt was cooling off, I said, 'Relax guys, let's have some tea,' and filled their mugs.

'Guys, you going to the big party tonight?' I asked, attempting to change the topic. Parties were always happening at the ISB, at least one every other week, thrown by a group of people having their birthdays, and a few paid for by the students' fund that was set aside for buying the many bottles of liquor.

Ajay was a little shaken but chimed in with a, 'Capt, are you going?'

Capt had recovered somewhat and said, 'Yes, *yaar*. These civilians don't know how to party. All they do is drink. There is no conversation; just a bunch of blokes hounding a few girls who took the trouble to put on some lipstick and a push-up bra,' he observed.

'What's wrong with that?' I asked

'Nothing,' came the reply.

This time, Ajay didn't have any further comments about army parties.

We got up and rushed to our assignments, meetings and case books. Capt reopened his yoga mat and decided to meditate upon his loss of temper.

That evening at the party, Ajay and Ranga drank beer to the full. Capt arrived, dressed well, even if he wore a t-shirt tucked into his jeans and then walked around effecting military-like conversation and the regimented socialising that you see at *fauji* parties. His party t-shirts always had collars on them, in keeping with Indian army officers' mess requirements.

Of Sofas and Shaktimaans **99**

I ogled at the women who sent my heart fluttering and realised I just wasn't shameless enough to elbow a bunch of idiots out of the way. Besides, pretty women are the holy grail at all academic institutions and Lord Vishnu himself may not stand a chance in this crowd, I told myself.

'Guru, never say no to free booze and free food,' said Ranga

'Ranga, the booze comes out of your fee, you idiot,' I corrected. Ranga looked at me quizzically, sleep disappearing and a steely look in his eyes. He cursed himself for not drinking more at earlier parties.

◈

Me: *'Hey, thanks for the walk. I had a great time.'*
Her: *'Yeah, me too. Vivek saw me and the whole Student Village was abuzz with the news by the time I got back.'*
Me: *'Just because you and I went for a walk together?'*
Her: *'Yeah. That's enough, isn't it? It's a huge campus and I'm the one with the fan club.'*
Me: *'Yeah, I suppose so.'*
Her: *'He-he. Yeah, it's a joke, but they all sit around me at dinner and keep calling themselves president, secretary, treasurer, and what not.'*
Me: *'Gosh. I had better watch out and not get lynched.'*
Her: *'Yeah, you'd better. He-he. My roomies even said something like . . . hey, your skin is glowing.'*
Me: *'Gosh. One walk and all this!'*
Her: *'Yeah.'*
Me: *'Too bad I didn't hold your hand when they were around.'*
Her: *'Mister, I'd have kicked your ass if you had tried.'*
Me: *'So you agree with the deal I made with you on the walk?'*
Her: *'What deal?'*
Me: *'That if we are single four years after ISB, we'll get married?'*
Her: *'Yeah sure, why the hell not! Good luck to you.'*
Me: *'Well, I wouldn't mind it too much.'*

100 *Touching Distance: The Great Indian MBA Dream*

Her: 'I know you wouldn't. Bullshit. You talked about Trisha all the way.'

Me: 'She's the decoy.'

Her: 'Yeah, I almost believed you once before, but not again.'

Me: 'Why won't you believe me? Is it so inconceivable that I could be talking about Trisha to see how you react? There, I've said it!'

Her: 'Shut up. You like her and that's it.'

Me: 'Gosh. Why won't you believe me?'

Her: 'Stupid. Stop acting up and go study or something. You want to keep your grades up.'

Me: 'What does it matter? The scholarship is gone and I'm still single.'

Her: 'Yeah, that you are. Grades may still matter when it comes to McKinsey. So do your best.'

Me: 'Thanks. I know I have to.'

Her: 'OK, I have to go.'

Me: 'Come on, can't you chat for a bit?'

Her: 'No, I can't. I have this case to work on and I've already wasted a good forty-five minutes walking around the Atrium.'

Me: 'Come on. Don't say that. It was a beautiful evening and you had me all to yourself.'

Her: 'Yeah, all evenings are beautiful until it comes to placements and we're wondering what kind of jobs we are going to land with and what kind of money we are going to make.'

Me: 'Smell the roses.'

Her: 'I smell loans, and the pressure to get married.'

Me: 'Yeah, about that.'

Her: 'Yeah, yeah. I'll marry you if I can't find anyone else.'

Me: 'Huh?'

Her: 'I have to go now . . . bye.'

Click.

10

The Smile of the Mona Lisa

Look at the stars,
look how they shine for you
And everything you do
Yeah, they were all yellow.

—Coldplay

'Escape' by Enrique Iglesias, echoed off the sheer white walls of Student Village 3. The moon was in attendance, but not many bothered to give it the cursory look as they walked on, bottles of liquor in hand. The student DJ (well, he actually was a semi-professional DJ before he joined the ISB) stood at the turn-table (read: computer with mp3 files) and looked with disinterest at the screen, enjoying his cigarette.

The Tower of Isengard looked on with great dignity. Focused lighting ensured that no matter what, the Tower was the centrepiece of everything that would ensue in these parts.

The location was the 'Mirror Lake' at Student Village 3. The Mirror Lakes were conceived of by the ISB architects to hold a still plane of water, which they believed would lend a sense of aesthetics to the otherwise rubber-band-like over-stretched lives

102 *Touching Distance: The Great Indian MBA Dream*

of the students who lived around it. These two pools, measuring about fifteen-hundred square-feet each, and about a foot deep, were constructed side by side. They were splendid, no doubt. Little did the architects know that every now and then, the pool would be drained of water, and the students would convert it into a dance floor. On such nights, the only liquid that touched the floor of these pools was sweat and alcohol.

I was never much of a dancer. Never had been. I loved the music and the atmosphere and the congregation. I am a social animal, no doubt. Everyone at these parties was seen in a different, more relaxed light and such evenings held the potential for magic of all sorts, but never delivered. I guess that's what made them so nice. They lingered for that very reason, since they held within them the cocoon of possibility, where everyone is on the threshold of winning.

As the chorus rang into the night, bodies moved in half-delirium and undiluted fatigue. Everyone was having a good time. The few ISB girls who did show up were all either smoking, drinking, dancing or enjoying the attention of the large number of men who tried to get in on the conversation.

Sitting on the lawn, I leaned back against a rock that must have been around since eternity and rested my head on my palms. The air smelt sweet and the song was a personal favourite. It was another brilliant night in Hyderabad. Hyderabad will show you some of the clearest skies you will ever see, especially over the outskirts where we were located. I was never the first guy out of the blocks when it came to such parties. I liked to arrive, sit around, chat and watch; eventually, I would hit the dance floor and dance the night away but it was always a nice feeling to absorb the atmosphere on such occasions.

I gazed vacantly at the crowd, wanting to catch a sight of her, but no, she was nowhere to be seen. Trisha was around, surrounded by her folk, as was always the case. Why couldn't I be in love with Trisha, instead? Wouldn't it be easier? I could just

The Smile of the Mona Lisa **103**

tell myself it would never really materialise and that I had to let it go. But with her, I had all this hope. More than anything else, I wanted to believe her when she said that she was single. In some stupid way, it gave me hope that she may feel differently in time. One day, just one day if things turned around and she felt the way I did, nothing could ever be better. Everything would have been worth it: coming here, the pining, the pain, everything. Was the stress amplifying my emotions? I thought it might be the case. Maybe I could never feel so strongly if I wasn't here. If I was at my glass cage, maybe I couldn't care this much. It had to be the perfect storm—a girl I couldn't resist, immense academic pressure, and a tonne of inhibition that prevented me from even discussing this with anyone. I had to deal with this all by myself. One day, it would be the end of this year and this test would be over. My painful reverie was interrupted by a familiar voice.

'Hey buddy, what's up? Where's your drink?' Prashant walked up from behind, alcohol in hand.

'I still don't drink,' I said.

'Mind if I join you?' he said and sat down when he saw the look of approval on my face.

Prashant was someone who often found himself in a league of his own. An architect by profession, he was among those who lent true diversity to the ISB. The ISB had, and still has, a policy of admitting candidates who bring in diverse experiences. The repercussion of this practice had always been surprising.

In Prashant's case, they'd got it spot-on. A little over thirty, Prashant had more life experience than most people have in two lifetimes. He'd seen it all and done it all. From being an investigative journalist in Ladakh writing about the fragile health of monasteries, to being published regularly in the glossy architectural magazines of India, here was someone who had charted a course all his own. His friends were a who's who of the real creative club of geniuses in India—like Ken, the inspirational musician/songwriter of the

104 *Touching Distance: The Great Indian MBA Dream*

hugely successful band Silk Route, etc., etc. Everyone held Prashant in the highest esteem.

Soon, we were joined by a string of guys who decided that there was just too much competition around the abysmally few girls—another inescapable observation at these parties. The girls arrive at these parties, looking much better than they did during class: lipstick, make-up, perfume all in place; and the men gather around to get a closer look at these artefacts. Some wanted to develop the art of conversation with members of the opposite gender, for success in social life in the years to come (and these were the ones most likely to go home with no positive experiences) while others merely wanted to smell perfume. There were yet others who just wanted to get closer. The latter were never disappointed. I'll let you do the math on that.

Sooner than later, one of these blokes would watch his inhibition dissolve in the steadily increasing alcohol in his bloodstream, and ask the girl to dance. The rest of the watchers in the crowd would curse the slow pace and fear inside their own blood cells and seek to join another group where the artefact wasn't yet moving to the music. If you ever wondered why the prettiest girls always danced first, you should know that inhibition dissolves faster in such cases (alcohol is the catalyst, of course).

Eventually, as more girls would get on the dance floor, these guys would either begin dancing with each other or retreat to the supply of alcohol. I never can understand guys dancing with other guys in our country! I see it everywhere: at parties in the office, at educational institutions, everywhere. I get that most people are shy, but why not dance alone? Why do you need someone from the same gender, for heaven's sake!

Back to our conversation, Prashant was on something of a roll.

'Why aren't you on the dance floor yet?'

I told him that I didn't like the fact that I needed to shove drunken men out of the way to dance with one of the girls there.

The Smile of the Mona Lisa **105**

And besides, I knew that when the time came for me to shove-push and seek someone out, I needed it to be for someone important. I am quite an old fashioned guy who prefers intent, in such matters, to immediacy. And I hadn't found 'the one' at the ISB. Love had to strike, and strike hard. Unlike some others, I wasn't keen on dancing with, or on being seen to be dancing with X, Y or Z.

Prashant understood. He continued, caught in by the fact that what I had said probably struck a chord somewhere. 'Yup. Never let instances like this push you around.'

I nodded.

We continued making observations about the untruth and fragility of the human condition, especially in situations where inhibitions and fear were located. The conversation veered to truth and honesty that we all lose sight of at one point or another.

Prashant then began to recount an anecdote that he had encountered earlier.

'I'm going to tell you a story. There was this young man who was in the midst of a revolution in Paris. Like others around him, he felt compelled to engage in the destruction and chaos that was being heaped on the world. One day, the mob he was part of attacked a museum. After the destruction was complete, the boy emerged from the museum, protecting something within a clenched fist. He never opened his palm until he was alone. What he held became a personal treasure, never shared. It gave him solace and hope.'

I had the questioning look in my eye and he responded, 'In his palm he held the smile of the Mona Lisa.'

It was a long time ago, but this anecdote stayed with me. I guess all of life comes down to a set of memories and experiences which we carry in our palms. We look at them from time to time for direction, hope and energy, and lastly for our true-north of inner truth – our own smile of enigma and possibility, which keeps us going.

❖

106 *Touching Distance: The Great Indian MBA Dream*

Me: 'Hello.'

Her: 'Hey, stud.'

Me: 'Didn't see you at the party this evening?'

Her: 'Oh, I decided to go out.'

Me: 'OK, cool. With your friends?'

Her: 'Oh, no. It was just Rahul and me.'

Me: 'OK. Dinner plans?'

Her: 'Hmm . . . yeah.'

Me: 'Nice. Romantic dinner, eh?'

Her: 'Look. I told you we're just friends.'

Me: 'OK, OK, I believe you. He asked you out?'

Her: 'Well, not really. I did.'

Me: 'OK . . .' (Sigh)

Her: 'How was the party?'

Me: 'Well, you know how I feel about these parties.'

Her: 'Yeah, Mr teetotaller, you need to loosen up a bit. All this south Indian Tam-Brahm puritanical goodness isn't going to get you anywhere.'

Me: 'Well, I guess so. I am what I am, what can I say?'

Her: 'Yeah, I appreciate that. I like people with principles.'

Me: 'Well, you don't like them enough.'

Her: 'Why do you say that?'

Me: 'Well, you've never asked me out for dinner.'

Her: 'Oh, come on. We've spent time together walking.'

Me: 'That's fine. I'm a little tired. Just wanted to say Hi. Hadn't seen you and you weren't around so I thought I'd check on you.'

Her: 'OK. All well with you? You don't sound so great.'

Me: 'I'm fine. What did you guys talk about?'

Her: 'About ISB, the people here . . . I guess with the kind of people here you can talk forever, right? I mean, there are so many talented people and so many pseudos.'

Me: 'Did you talk about me?'

Her: 'Yeah, a little. Rahul wanted to know what I was doing strolling with you. He-he.'

The Smile of the Mona Lisa **107**

Me: 'Is he upset that I'm spending time with you?'

Her: 'Why should he be?'

Me: 'Come on, you might as well admit it. You guys are together, right?'

Her: 'Hmm . . . Gosh. I can't believe I'm telling you this. But yes, we are.'

Me: 'WHAT?'

Her: 'We are . . . together . . . have been.'

Me: 'Why did you deny it all these days?'

Her: 'I just didn't want to talk about it.'

Me: 'I mean, I kept asking you if you were seeing him.'

Her: 'Well, I just wasn't comfortable talking about it.'

Me: 'Anyway, he's a great guy. I'm sure he will make you really happy.'

Her: 'Yeah, I've known him for years now and he's been wonderful.'

Me: 'Yeah, he's a great guy.'

Her: 'I'm so glad we reconnected here. We had split up.'

Me: 'When I asked you if you were single in Term 1, why did you say you were?'

Her: 'Because I wasn't sure I wanted to get back together with him back then.'

Me: 'OK. I thought you were single.'

Her: 'I was, and I wasn't. You'll still go for walks with me, won't you?'

Me: 'I don't know . . . what does Rahul think of it?'

Her: 'Well, he actually thinks you're quite safe and a gentleman. He can't go out with me that often, else the whole world will know and we're not prepared for that, and he'd rather see me walking with a gentleman like you than anyone else.'

Me: 'So, I'm the red herring?'

Her: 'Well . . . he-he, if you put it that way. You don't mind, do you? You're anyway drooling all over Trisha.'

Me: 'Is he really okay with my spending time with you?'

108 *Touching Distance: The Great Indian MBA Dream*

Her: 'I told you he is. He thinks you're a nice guy.'
Me: 'Hmm . . . I don't know if I want to give him any ideas.'
Her: 'You don't. Anyway, what's your problem?'
Me: 'Nothing, I guess I just have to go now.'
Her: 'Ok, take care.'
Me: 'Good night.'
Click.
Me: 'Sigh.'

11

The Laws of Conservation

Once divided,
there's nothing left to subtract
Some words when spoken,
can't be taken back

—Pearl Jam

She ran around the tree as fast as her dripping saree would allow. Her girth was only exceeded by his tumbling, perverse, rotund layers of adipose. The *nada* of his *lungi* looked ready to retire from its painful and disgusting occupation. They ran towards the sea and he lay on top of her as the song gained tempo.

Ranga smiled. This was the kind of stuff to die for. Wow, forget C.K. Prahlad and all those phoney professors who came to the class to give him a hard time; none of that mattered as long as he got to see these money shots on a Saturday morning.

I stirred, woken by the strains, the literal 'strains' of the Telugu song. I trooped out, groggy-eyed and said, '*Lo, nan magane Devar haad kelud time idu. Belage belage shattadtara porn nodtaiddiyalla.*' (Loosely translated: bugger, this is the time to be listening to devotional songs. What the hell are you doing this early in the morning watching this filthy porn?)

110 *Touching Distance: The Great Indian MBA Dream*

'*Nan magane, hannondu aitu,*' said Ranga (Bloody son, it's 11 o'clock).

He had a point. I had woken remarkably late. I hadn't been able to get much sleep. I returned to my room. My thoughts veered back to the previous night.

I remember sitting still looking out my window for what seemed like an hour. I remembered thinking for an eternity about how I felt about myself and what I could do to move forward, away from it all. Away from the darkness of an unrequited emotion that had consumed me for so long. It held me in a vice-like grip, and it was up to me to deconstruct all that. Slim hopes, even slimmer chances holding the proverbial castle in the night air—it had all come crashing down. Everything I had denied, even to myself, was finally blurted out in short sentences. Why had I failed to admit it to myself? And having somehow known the truth all the while, why had I allowed myself to go down this rabbit hole.

It was a harsh morning. The grass around the Atrium was dazzling white as the burning sun reflected off it. The boulders were so hot they created a mini-oasis atop them. Illusions of hope; how bloody poignant. Once the veil was lifted, all that was left was a hellish heat and searing reality.

I went back and snuggled into my bed, turning on the AC and the fan to full throttle. I had closed the door behind me but it failed to shut. From the depths of my solace and pain, and I could still hear the Telugu drums climaxing in the background. I could only imagine the visuals. Too tired, too depressed, but awake, I pulled the blanket over my head and tried to sleep. The song ended and I heard Ranga switch channels. He hit some colourless news reader. I heard him chuck the remote on the table, get up and go to his room. The TV was on and I was too frustrated to ask him to turn it off.

Then, the main door to the living room opened and in walked Capt. '*Hari om,*' he announced. I heard him switch off the TV. This was going to be fun. Capt absolutely hated wasting electricity.

The AC and the TV were on when he walked in and no one was around. This was pretty regular when you lived with a human animal who believed in consumption as a means to growth and all-round prosperity.

He looked at me lying in bed and walked into Ranga's room. Ranga was lying on his back and smiling at the ceiling, ruminating on the darkest secrets of that Telugu song.

'You asshole Ranga . . . Last night when I came back, you fucking left the TV on and were fast asleep. Bastard! This is the third time this week!'

Ranga turned his gaze to Capt thundering in the doorway. Capt really was one for losing his cool at these things. Imagine, this was after regular rounds of Sudarshan Kriya and his oh-so-frequent meditation or *dhyaan* sessions. Ranga went back to staring at the ceiling and attempted to gather his thoughts leading to the climax of the song. He was hoping Capt would leave now. Capt didn't. Capt had simply had had enough.

'You bastard! What the fuck? . . . Are you listening to what I am saying?' he continued, smouldering like one of the fuses of his anti-ballistic missile.

Ranga said, 'I mean, like . . . I mean, I think I fell asleep. I mean, like . . . maybe someone else switched it on . . . ask Steve, OK? I mean, why the fuck are you suspecting me? Anyway, even if I switched it on and left it . . . I mean, like . . . so what? Why can't you switch it off?'

Stress can get you to do several things which are illogical. Like get you to want to save electricity when you don't pay the bills, or make you want to come up with alternate names. The short anglicised naming phenomenon was again something I take credit for. Over tea, I once remarked that given the state of the economy, we'd all end up working for a call centre and would be forced to come up with short English names. These names are a reality in the industry; for example, a Rachna may become a Rita, and so

112 *Touching Distance: The Great Indian MBA Dream*

on. You get my drift. I christened Capt 'Vincent' and Ranga 'Rob'. I thought I'd be called 'Steve'.

Capt said in a soft threatening voice, 'You asshole, let this be the last time, OK? Next time you do this I'm going to fuck you real bad.' He went back to his room, fuming.

Ranga went back to the living room and turned on the TV. The Telugu song was forgotten and he needed new ammo for the day. He sat in his Zen position, and smiled.

Another day, a really typical one at the ISB: roomies, Telugu songs, blazing sun, fighting, screaming, yelling, in the midst of assignments, deadlines, midterms squash, gals, parties and class participation—it was a bloody circus out there, and, we the clowns, who had to get in. After brushing my teeth I walked into the living room and headed for the newspaper. Ranga asked me to make tea. He was always in the best spirits, no matter what. A little act by Capt wasn't going to ruin his day.

'Capt . . . do you want tea?' I yelled. He mumbled a reply in the affirmative. He still sounded pretty upset that someone couldn't follow a few domestic rules in the interest of discipline. Ranga had his tea and continued to watch TV. I took Capt's tea to his room and we chatted about his resemblance to Sri Sri Ravishankar of the Art of Living fame. Capt loves that; over the course of the year, I'd learnt a few things about the people there. He was returning to his good humour and my purpose was served. I took my tea back to my room and turned on my laptop to play some music. The dreaded emails had arrived: my groupies wanted some meeting or the other to discuss some case . . . dammit! It was bad enough I had to pay for all this without having a peer group torturing me as well.

As I replied to a few emails, listening to 'Boondein' by Silk Route, Ranga walked in. 'I mean, like . . . you know, ha-ha-ha, I mean that actor . . . OK? I mean, like . . . NTR, man, he is a real stud, OK? That movie was like a big hit, OK?' I smiled. I loved it when Ranga went on and on about something I didn't understand or care about. His enthusiasm for the forgotten and the irrelevant amused me.

The Laws of Conservation **113**

'Let's go for lunch,' he said. I reminded Ranga that I had woken just a little over an hour ago. He laughed and talked about how he always woke early and had a timely breakfast and how I was always the late riser. He said I did not demonstrate enough *sattvic* tendencies. Yeah, right.

I didn't tell him that he woke up at seven, was the first guy at breakfast, came back to watch TV, and then slept till lunch. He stayed awake for a few hours between lunch and tea, waking up from his nap just as I would start making tea. Then, he spent a few more hours after an early dinner chatting with us and then hit the sack somewhere between 1.00 and 2.00 am, when our day was getting started. Sometime during the day, he left to attend a group meeting which he wasn't really keen on attending, and his group did not complain when he did not show up. At other times he tried to read a case or two and attempted to study from time to time since he perceived that he should be doing something in the hope of recovering all that money he'd put down.

He trooped out whistling some Kannada song, while walking briskly towards the food. The animal was hungry.

I went back to looking at the spreadsheet open on my laptop. Some surreal Pink Floyd music kept me company.

A few minutes later, I heard Capt walk out of his room and scream out again. 'RANGAAAA! Where the FUCK are you? Son of a bitch!'

By now, I was singing along with Dave Gilmour.

Do you see your days blighted by darkness
Is it true you beat your fists on the floor
Stuck in a world of isolation
While the ivy grows over the door

He heard me through the half-open door. He walked in and muttered, 'He did it again. Both the TV and the AC are on. This time I'm going to teach him a lesson. How can he be so irresponsible, *yaar*?'

114 *Touching Distance: The Great Indian MBA Dream*

I nodded sympathetically. 'What do they do to someone like this in the army?' I said.

'They fuck him till he can't tell his face from his ass,' he thundered. I stopped singing and laughed spontaneously. He was hopping mad now; yelling some more, he switched off the TV and went back to his room. The years and years of army discipline had had their effect. I switched to a song by Metallica to reflect my new energy levels.

After some time, I heard the door open and Ranga whistled his way into my room. '*Lo,* ice cream *matra sakkataagide,*' (If nothing else, the ice cream rocks today) he said.

We chatted for a while and he told me about the intellectual masturbation he had accomplished about corporate governance with some professor.

He stepped out to the living room, looking for the remote. '*Lo, yello remotu?*' (Where's the remote) he shouted. I said he had used it last. He repeated the question, louder and with more panic. Sensing what had happened, I walked out just in time to see Capt stepping out of his room.

'Where's the remote?' Ranga asked, looking at Capt with some anger, hoping to pre-empt an attack. But while Ranga had been loading up on strawberries in his belly, Capt had been planning a full frontal attack, missiles loaded and all grenades with pins off.

'You bastard! What the fuck did I say in the morning?' He meant business and looked it.

Ranga, as always, was looking for the path of least resistance. In a slightly angry voice, he said, 'I mean, like . . . what are you talking about? I mean, are you like talking about the TV?'

'Yeah, asshole. Why the fuck didn't you switch it off when you went out to go fuck some professor's head over lunch?'

Ranga attempted to ignore Capt and began thinking about possible places where the remote could be. He dug his hands into the crevices between the cushions, opened the refrigerator, and

The Laws of Conservation **115**

then proceeded to check the kitchen cabinets. Flabbergasted, we looked on as he lay bellydown on the floor, scanning the undersides of the cabinets. Never had we seen Ranga blow so many calories in such a short time. All of this lasted five minutes. Frustrated, he looked back at Capt and said, 'I mean, like . . . Capt, where's the remote, OK?'

Capt shouted his question again, 'Why the fuck didn't you turn it off, asshole?'

'I mean, like . . . because I was going to come back and watch TV, right?' he replied.

Standing in my doorway watching all of this, I couldn't take it anymore.

'Because I was going to come back and watch TV!' I screamed, bursting out in laughter.

Capt's face turned red. He failed to find a response. They stood facing each other like Neo and Agent Smith, while I fell to the floor clutching my stomach, convulsing with laughter and pain.

Over my laughter, I heard Capt blazing now, reaching his crescendo. 'You fucking recruit, here's your punishment: no more TV for you today. I'm not giving you the remote.' Capt walked back to his room.

Ranga searched in all the places where he didn't have to make the effort to bend his body and burn some calories. He didn't find it. He yelled, '*Saale* Capt, *zyada baap mat ban* . . . I mean, like . . . this is too much. OK?' Why Ranga needed to speak in Hindi, a language he knew very little of, I had no idea.

Ranga looked around but a patient and thorough search was too much for him. Moreover, the ice cream was getting burnt up faster than he had planned and dinner was a full four hours away.

Muttering obscenities, he walked back to his room and turned on his laptop to watch some movie he had saved. Half an hour later, with the standard fifteen minutes before lunch was due to close, Capt and I walked briskly to lunch.

116 *Touching Distance: The Great Indian MBA Dream*

Back in the flat, I walked into Ranga's room and asked him to come outside, luring him with tea. Capt was back to his normal smiling self and said, 'So Ranga, ha-ha-ha ha,' and stabbed the remote into Ranga's belly.

Ranga quickly tuned in to Delta TV and sipped his tea, smiling at the screen. Capt took his tea and walked back to his room. I opened the sliding windows and watched the cirrus clouds washed to a bright orange in the setting sun. The good times rolled on for a few more minutes before I had to leave for a group meeting.

◈

Me: 'Hey, how are you?'

Her: 'I don't want to talk to you anymore.'

Me: 'What? Why?'

Her: 'Well, you haven't called me in ten days.'

Me: 'I was busy.'

Her: 'Don't give me that shit. After I told you about . . . anyway, it's all about you, isn't it?'

Me: 'What do you mean?'

Her: 'It's all about what you want.'

Me: 'I didn't know it mattered if I called you or not.'

Her: 'Well, it doesn't.'

Me: 'OK, so what's the problem then?'

Her: 'You can't just disappear like that. You're the one who used to call me everyday, right?'

Me: 'Yeah, that's true. You never called me, so why does it matter? You probably have more time for whatever it is you want to do.'

Her: 'Yeah I do. Thanks a lot for calling today. Now if you don't mind, I have to go.'

Me: 'Hey wait. Don't be angry.'

Her: 'I wouldn't waste my anger on you.'

Me: 'I'm sorry I didn't call. I was dealing with stuff and I've been busy. Why couldn't you call me?'

Her: 'You're the one who always called. It's that simple.'
Me: 'I don't get it.'
Her: 'That's fine. I'm hanging up.'
Click.
Me: 'Hello!'

12

Hoo Haa Hoo

We didn't start the fire,
It was always burning since the world's been turning
We didn't start the fire,
No we didn't light it but we tried to fight it
—BILLY JOEL

I now proceed to recount the incidents that painted one of the most colourful days at the ISB. A day when I had no idea whether Capt would jump through a window or throw me through another. A day when Ranga was conspicuous by his absence and several people nearly wet their pants when Capt's antics assumed their violent form.

It was the day of Holi, the festival of colours. I had no idea what to expect. We'd been told that the party was going to be at SV2, the more populous Student Village.

Parties were well attended. From random parties to birthday pool dunkings, which were always well attended when we were celebrating the day a girl was born. The attendance was directly proportional to the physical beauty of the subject in case, more specifically with respect to the natural genetic endowments that

Hoo Haa Hoo **119**

draw so much attention when they are covered with drenched fabric. On such days, all the men stood by the pool, their tongues hanging out, waiting to catch a sight of the forbidden fruit. The less shy men attempted to participate in the dunking, hands on. The rest of the males took the ogling route – 'low risk, high return'.

Back to the festival of colours; I don't know what the deeper designs behind serving *bhaang* were. Agreed, most ISB parties were well stacked with booze. Give most people half a chance for a free drink, and they will take it. At ISB, you didn't have to bring your own booze – those who didn't drink, subsidised it for you at the beginning of the year. Under the umbrella of student community activities, each student shelled out a tidy sum, which helped inject the necessary doses of alcohol in the bloodstreams of those who did the drinking. However, there were returns for the teetotallers as well. If you have hung around people that get drunk, you know what I mean. If you have had the chance to hang around interesting, funny, intelligent, stressed-out people who get drunk big time and sporadically, you definitely know what I mean. The beast of freedom, lurking within each of those poor students, was beaten into submission by repeated assignments and cold-calls at the time of class participation. Free alcohol was the key that unlocked the beast, nourished it and finally gave it a kick in the butt to goad it to romp all over the clean rooms that the mind had helped build in endless hours of academics.

The beast living within Capt was a special kind. This one had been trashed several years ago. Not by ISB, but by Capt's spiritual pursuits. All but dead, the beast hung on to dear life by manifesting itself during the odd occasions like at the Shaktimaan events, or when Capt yelled at Ranga or when one of two girls obviously attracted to Capt, like fireflies to fluorescent lights, called on him. On these occasions, the beast made a return of sorts, briefly albeit, before being trashed into submission by the constant chants of '*Hari om*' or the occasional hour of meditation. I still think he was taking naps sitting up.

120 *Touching Distance: The Great Indian MBA Dream*

Like all others, I went to the celebration to have a good time. Almost all of ISB had turned out. The spirits were high, understandably. It was like one giant dunking party. No, jokes apart, there was a lot of clean fun to be had, and in fact it was much more than I had bargained for.

After hours of dunking, I was approached by a student we knew well. He said, 'Capt *ko chad gayi hai. Ladkiyon ke saath baitha hai, yaar. Pata nahin kya bolega ya karega.*'

Like a flashback from a bad Hindi move, Ranga's comments from the morning struck me. Ranga had warned: '*Lo, hushaaragiru . . . bhaang hodbittu sumne mutkoltaiddare mutkoltane irtya.*' (Listen, be careful. If you drink *bhaang*, you will begin touching yourself and keep doing it.)

Ranga didn't have to say where he got that data from. It was inevitable. As expected, he denied ever having been embarrassed by it. Somehow, his absence from the celebrations was an uneasy coincidence after his statements.

Moving back to the present, my thoughts were not on Capt, but on the beast within him. I could literally see the beast salivating and baring its teeth at the prospect of 'flesh' and blood, having been deprived of it for thirty-two years of life on earth.

I walked in the direction of the scene of a probable crime. Capt was down on all fours, like a dog. He then picked up a plate of *jalebis* in his left hand. He was laughing uncontrollably. In front of him sat two girls wondering what he would do next. I walked up and crouched near him. His eyes were shut by the force of laughter and he could not recount the joke despite repeated requests.

Finally, he said, 'There are so many *jalebis* on this plate, *yaar* Steve. Ha-ha-ha.'

Confirmation about his inebriated state received, all those around me gathered closer to see what he would do next. It was like watching the beginning of the great Indian rope-trick in fifteenth-century India.

Hoo Haa Hoo 121

Then he rolled onto his back and laughed with uncontrollable delight at the sun. He rolled from side to side like an uncertain drum, and squealed, trying to scratch his back against the grass like a dog. The girls took a step backwards and kept a close watch on his hands and other ominous parts of his anatomy. The men laughed and patted each other on the back, secure in the knowledge that for now, this was all fun at someone else's expense. Some of them laughed in fear that the time to knockout was closing in as the *bhaang* in their blood began opening channels in the brain that had hitherto remained untouched.

Capt, in the meantime, was going berserk, and I suggested he go into the shade, much like you want to put an elephant in *masti* in chains and get the hell away from its organ. Besides, the blazing Hyderabad sun could do no good to his state. I fought off several internal demons and other ISB students who implored me to allow them to watch a little longer.

I led him to the general-purpose room housing the tennis table. He saw some pottery articles made by the students' spouses and began to stare at the clay. In a few moments, seduced by the growing interest in his current state, he decided to cut loose. I had always nursed the suspicion that Capt was really fond of public attention. As much as he tried to distance himself from all things material, he was deeply drawn to public adoration. He sat cross-legged in the lotus posture, and began to chant, 'Hoo haa hoo . . . Hoo haa hoo . . . Repeat after me!' in a frenzy. For some of the members of this *yogi's* cult, the *bhaang* was beginning to strike. For the others, this was the best and safest contribution they could make to ensure that the show went on. Any which way, the chanting moved to a crescendo, as the gods became insecure with a true feeling of befuddlement at the object of his invocation.

'Hoo haa hoo . . . If you're singing a song . . . Hoo haa hoo.'

'Hoo haa hoo . . . If you're working on a morn . . . Hoo haa hoo.'

122 *Touching Distance: The Great Indian MBA Dream*

'Hoo haa hoo . . . If you're standing on a corn . . . Hoo haa hoo.'

'Hoo haa hoo . . . If you're munching on a corn . . . Hoo haa hoo.'

In subsequent stanzas, he replaced the middle phrase with other sentences which made no sense to anyone around, least of all to Capt. Also, by this time, Capt had become slightly more creative and had added some hand movements to his swaying back and forth. The crowd was erupting, and it had now swelled to a group of fifty. Students, spouses, professors, security-folks, all of them gathered around to watch the great Indian *bhaang* trick. Soon there was a suggestion that Capt be moved to the portico outside the room for the benefit of the rest of the populace. Faced with certain bodily harm, I complied. Capt was jumping up and down like a primate as I tried to move him towards the door.

In between psychedelic colours and images which bounced in his brain, creating a million impulses, leaving him no time to act on any of them, Capt also sensed the effect he was having on his ardent devotees. Pleased, he complied.

Soon, he had taken his place at the helm of a semi-circle. The crowd was growing in number and interest. Capt said, 'I'm lost in my mind, *yaar* . . . what was I saying?'

'Hoo haa hoo,' I suggested politely.

Capt nodded. 'Thank you, Sarge,' he said.

'Zindagi se bharosa uth gaya hai mera
Zindagi saanp, to jeenae wala sapera.'

The crowd went delirious. Someone in the crowd shouted something, trying to grab attention. 'Silence in the ranks!' Capt bellowed.

He repeated the second line of the song, this time making a snake's hood with the palms of his hand while moving his torso from side to side like in the B-grade, old Hindi movies. Thrilled,

Hoo Haa Hoo **123**

the crowd egged him on. From somewhere, a camcorder emerged and now there was evidence.

> *'Jo jeena jaane, woh saanp nachaata*
> *Jo na jaane, usko saanp das jaata.'*

This proceeded for a while. From the corner of my eye, I saw Anant sitting in the lawn, staring intently at the grass. I walked over to him and saw another group of people watching him closely. He looked at me and tried to say something, but was unable to. Later, he told me that he was trying to stand up but couldn't.

I told Capt that it was time for us to go back. He agreed. He said, 'Steve, pick me up, *yaar*.' I helped him up and he leaned onto me for support. A professor looked at the two of us and smiled. Through the mess of glazed colours in his eyes, Capt recognised him. Capt was trying to do a standing march, hopping on his toes, one foot at a time. 'Steve, I hope this professor doesn't think bad of me, *yaar*,' he said. I looked at the professor. He smiled back in sympathy – for me.

I dragged Capt all the way to our apartment and told him, 'Capt, you need to bathe! Now!'

'Hoo Haa Hoo . . . Hoo Haa Hoo . . . Hoo Haa Hoo . . . Hoo Haa Hoo,' he replied.

I walked to the windows and attempted to secure them. The last thing I wanted was Capt trying to fly through on the strength of his mind.

I dragged him to his loo and said, 'You really need to have a bath now.'

'What is a bath, *yaar* . . . Ha ha ha, it doesn't matter if the body is clean or dirty, *yaar*. Anyway, the bath only cleans the body.' I nodded in agreement.

I went into my own bathroom and proceeded to use at least two cakes of soap to get rid of all the colour. I stepped out and looked across at a sight that truly blew me away. Capt was standing

124 *Touching Distance: The Great Indian MBA Dream*

exactly where I had left him. Only now, he had his arms extended upwards. I recognised the snake pose. His body was violently moving, assuming the curved shape of a whiplash. He would bend his knees, arch backwards and do a whiplash break-dance move, resulting in his snake hood lashing out at the mirror. Dazed, I continued to look at this elastic-body behaviour for a few more minutes.

After I gained some nerve, I walked up to him and said, 'Capt, have you bathed already?'

'No, *yaar* . . . I'm trying to move the energy from the base of the spine to my head and have it go through it. I think my *kundalini* may be rising and enlightenment may be close.'

'Look, Capt. Will you please just bathe? You don't want to meet Lord Venkateshwara looking like this, do you?' I asked.

'He-he-he . . . yes, you are right, *yaar*. Perumal knows I am clean from the inside, but out of respect for him I think I should clean up on the outside as well, don't you think so?' he retorted.

'Excellent idea, sir,' I said.

'OK. Then go now. I shall bathe.'

I stepped back into my room and looked out the window. I was tired and somewhat amused. In the middle of all the academic stress, this was an explosion of madness. I looked at the trees, now taller than they were when I first looked through these windows. The sun was bright and the day was getting hotter. Some people seemed to be getting back to their senses and were walking back to their apartment blocks.

In the foreground, I saw him.

With all that colour covering him from head to toe, it was unmistakably him. Capt had escaped like a lifer who had found the key and killed the sentries. He walked bravely back to the other block, the scene of the party. His cargo shorts were unbuttoned and unzipped. I put the pieces together. He'd begun to undress for his bath and had decided that what he needed was *bhaang*, and not ablutions. I watched him walk in a straight line, occasionally hopping up and down. The hopping didn't do his shorts any good.

Hoo Haa Hoo **125**

They hit the floor and he tripped, falling flat on his face. I stormed out the room and ran down the stairs, trying to save him from humiliation no one would let pass. He was fifty metres away from me when I shouted out his name. He turned around, stood up and shouted back

'I'm not going to bathe now!'

Then he ran, leaving his shorts behind. Damn it, he was fast, and even faster with all those poppy seeds going crazy in his brain. He ran like the wind and ran straight to the party. A stunned group of students watched this spectacle. Capt, coloured from head to toe in a riot of a rainbow gone berserk, with only a loincloth-like brief protecting his modesty. He ran straight past the students and to the cauldron of *bhaang*. He picked up a glass, filled it up, and panting, gushed it down. Then he did it again.

I slowed down my pursuit and started walking. The damage was already done. Cameras went buzzing and even in their inebriation, the students knew a Kodak moment from a hallucination.

As he filled himself with more *bhaang*, I walked up to him, panting, and said, 'Look, enough. Let's go back. You're almost nude, man. Look at yourself.'

'Get away from me, I want to be dirty!' he shouted, then looked down, and all around. A crowd had begun to gather and he seemed to like it. He smiled at all of them and shouted, 'Get away from me!' laughing wildly, and reaching for that loincloth covering, threatening to pull it off.

The women covered their eyes and the men looked disgusted. I'd given up all hope of saving the day and stood with arms crossed, watching in amazement.

He then proceeded to recite his verse of the snake and life, with plenty of errors thrown in. Perhaps he was tiring, after all. All that steroid-assisted running from our Student Village to this one had clearly taken its toll. With exhaustion, some sense seemed to be returning. He looked around, then down at himself and

126 *Touching Distance: The Great Indian MBA Dream*

said, 'Sorry, everyone. You've seen more than you should have,' and giggled.

'But then, I have never felt so liberated as I do today. I am God and you are my subjects.' He dipped his glass into the cauldron one last time, gulped his *bhaang* and ran towards the ring-road. He took a wrong turn and instead of running to our Student Village, ran towards the main gate.

Someone called the security folks and told them we might have a deserter amidst us. He was to be arrested and returned safely to Student Village 2 despite all claims of divinity.

I walked slowly back to my room, smiling from ear to ear. What the hell had just happened? I walked into the apartment and stood shell-shocked. Would wonders ever cease? There he was, standing in front of the mirror, looking at himself, hands joined together in the serpent pose. He seemed to stop short of resuming his dance move as he watched me enter.

'Gosh, man, where the hell did you run off to?'

'Ha-ha-ha . . . sorry. I realised I wasn't wearing my pants.'

'But you ran off to the gate.'

'Yeah, I ran through the Atrium and headed back. I couldn't go further without my pants.'

'OK . . . so . . . what do you plan to do now?'

'OK, OK . . . leave me alone. I promise to bathe,' he said and laughed.

He finally did bathe, but by then I'd had enough. I'd returned to my room. I figured I couldn't help this situation. I could lock him up until the *bhaang* wore off, but this could be too much fun anyway.

When I stepped out half an hour later, I found him sitting on the couch, muttering to himself. He greeted me enthusiastically. The effects hadn't worn off completely yet.

He had done a shoddy job of washing the colour off his body. All the colour on his ears was intact. Dry even. It was almost as if

Hoo Haa Hoo 127

he had forgotten that he had ears! When he continued to mutter for another fifteen minutes, unintelligible rants about life, I pushed him into his room and begged him to go to sleep. As entertaining as it was, I simply didn't have the energy to watch him for another couple of hours. Moreover, there really was a chance that he would exit through the first floor window in the living room.

I pushed him into his room and he complied. He covered himself with a blanket, and continued to mumble something. I said as loudly as I could, 'Capt, you have to sleep now! Do you want the AC?'

Eyes shut, mumbling to himself, he said, 'Sergeant, don't raise your voice.' Tired, demoted to sergeant, I trooped to my room.

When we woke up four hours later, he seemed okay until I heard him mumble, 'Repeat after me, I will never drink *bhaang* in my life.'

Ranga walked in just as tea was being brewed. He looked at Capt and said, 'Ha-ha. I mean, like . . . I knew it, OK . . . Ha-ha-ha, you guys have no capacity . . . I mean, like . . . ha-ha-ha, did Capt shag in public?'

'Intellectually, yes', I said, exhausted.

'Hoo haa hoo,' I added. I was just glad all of us were alive.

❖

Me: *'Hi. Are you okay?'*
Her: *'Fine. How are you?'*
Me: *'I'm good. Are we good?'*
Her: *'Yeah, why not?'*
Me: *'Would you like to go out sometime? Grab a cup of coffee or something?'*
Her: *'I don't know. Let me see.'*
Me: *'That's great. First time I ask someone out and they shoot me down—'*
Her: *'First time? You're so boring. Anyway, let's see. If I so much as step out, my absence is going to be noticed.'*

128 *Touching Distance: The Great Indian MBA Dream*

Me: 'OK, in that case, let me know. I really haven't been out ever. It's all these assignments with no room to breathe. I'd like to just get away from ISB for a bit.'

Her: 'Yeah. We'll see.'

Me: 'This week is pretty okay. Not too many assignments, at least for me. How about sometime this week?'

Her: 'Let's see.'

Me: 'You can tell Rahul; we'll go as friends.'

Her: 'Yeah, we'll see.'

Me: 'Thanks.'

Her: 'OK.'

Click.

13

The Curse of the Minority Investor

Mephistopheles is not your name
I know what you're up to just the same
I will listen hard to your tuition
You will see it come to its fruition

—Sting

Prof Samuel Old was a brilliant man. He had to be – he was consulted at every MNC that could afford him, and taught at every premier management institution, from Harvard in the West to Hong Kong in the East. If that wasn't enough, on more than one occasion, I heard from different sources that he was in the running for a Nobel. He carried a titanium Apple iBook and spoke with an accent which had alighted somewhere between Guangdong and San Francisco. His rasping voice communicated a well cultivated boredom over the wireless microphone he strapped onto his manicured Ralph Lauren Polo t-shirt before he began his class. He was rich, smart and successful, and like all other rich, smart, successful people, he knew it.

Mind you, he wasn't one of the management consulting partner types who needed to perform for a living. These people are rich and

130 *Touching Distance: The Great Indian MBA Dream*

successful, but need to watch what they do. They are on camera, candid camera; they have to think, sweat, act, speak, appease, suck-up, smile, etc., according to the occasion. They have no power, and their security lies in your willingness to buy their show. They live in the hope that someday, the present value of past earnings will exceed the present value of future earnings. Then, on that fateful day, they quit.

Old, on the other hand, didn't care. I loved that about him. What's the word . . . ? – self-assured! He was the kind who, if he bent over at the dining table and farted accidentally, would not bother to explain because he didn't need any more money or favours or anything else. Self-assured.

Expectedly, Prof Old made a huge impression on Ranga. In the twilight of his Neanderthal existence, whose longevity was constantly being narrowed given that he needed to share a bathroom with me, Ranga had found another who could possibly fart and not care about it. Ranga was the archetypal existentialist. He existed: he ate, he farted, he left. 'I mean, like . . . deal with it, OK?'

This summer afternoon, I sat in the living room, reading a case and watching a cricket match while Capt was attempting some yoga postures he claimed had been revealed to him at a meditation camp in Rishikesh.

'*Abbe* Ranga, *kahan se aa raha hai*?' inquired Capt. Ranga stood in the doorway, his thick coarse hair standing on end, raising the alarm of daytime lightning strikes in Hyderabad to the uninitiated. Ranga didn't care; it was his regular hairdo or the lack of it. I imagined his hair looking exactly like that on his wedding day – his in-laws, fingers crossed, sending a silent prayer to the heavens as they imagine his genetic contribution to the progeny. Some years later, I was to see an ad for a chewing gum: *Center-fresh: hila ke rakh de.* The ad was set in a barber's saloon where the patron wanted a 'hair-on-end' styling and the old barber pops a unit of gum into his mouth. *Hila ke rakh de.* . . it all made perfect sense now.

The Curse of the Minority Investor **131**

'I mean, I'm coming from the corporate governance class. Capt, tea . . . *pleeeaseee*,' Ranga pleaded.

'You moron! Why are you sitting in that class when you are not taking the course, asshole?' Capt secretly nurtured the hope that one day, he would find the energy to sit in the classes for which he had no time or strength to take on as credit courses. It angered him that there were crazy, energetic, non-spiritual guys who did stuff he wished he'd do.

Prof Old taught corporate governance, a subject right up Ranga's alley. 'I mean, I like . . . that professor, OK? I mean, like . . . he is an amazing guy. I mean like, look at Enron, I mean, like . . . even MCI Worldcomm, OK? I mean, like . . . Minority investors . . . poor guys. I mean, they get screwed, OK? Capt. I mean, you don't get it, do you? You may make your bucks, asshole. But what about minority investors?' Just the kind of thing that defined Ranga. He always believed that he needed to worry about the highest of problems, so long as he had others in his study groups to crunch the numbers for him and complete his work.

Capt gave Ranga the once-over and bent into another yogic posture. Like me, Capt knew that Ranga had found the latest set of buzzwords to fill his daytime management vocabulary. Ranga rambled on in his room while I continued to watch Sachin step out to Glenn McGrath, raising my hopes. The earth went around the sun, and long shadows of the ISB Student Village towers were cast on the rocks of the Deccan Plateau. Elsewhere in the Student Villages, a large number of men fantasised about a small number of girls, some of whom fantasised about a professor or a rich guy or a high-paying job. It was that kind of listless day. On the other side of the globe, another dirty, rich Wall Street investment hand executed a trade based on insider-information at Parmalat, while another Wall Street Wharton grad did the math and sucked on the same trade, to be fired in due course. Somewhere, some minority investor actually suffered, as he saw his blue-chip stock tank, taking with it his life-savings. He cursed the system, oblivious

132 *Touching Distance: The Great Indian MBA Dream*

to the wisdom that a part of his karma just got balanced. All was just as it should be.

Yes, we lived in the time of Enron and MCI-Worldcomm, not to mention Arthur Andersen, from where came half the chartered accountants in our class – full of integrity. Integrity, that I used to joke about being probably left unused, given the fate of the company. Integrity, methinks, is a living thing. Like a plant. Use it like a packaged vegetable and you might as well put an expiry date on it. Of course the idea is to erase the expiry date on it so that someone might actually buy the package.

Evidently, the global issues in the recent past had a huge impact on Ranga. That a minority shareholder—never mind the fact that he may be a rich white American stockbroker with seven Latino girlfriends or a Cuban drug lord having his enemy's arteries for schezwan noodles at lunchtime—would suffer when a big company's stock tanked, was outrageous to Ranga.

Ranga was the self-proclaimed defender of the minority investor. He didn't stop to think who these people might be: they were minority investors who needed to be protected by his brain. So what if it was a drug lord in Columbia? It could also be the beggar in Lucknow. Of course beggars in Lucknow don't hold stocks, but that didn't matter when Ranga spoke with the zeal of a part-time Christian missionary promoted overnight to replace the dead pope.

Corp governance was the highest of the high issues Ranga had encountered.

Make no mistake about it: Ranga was once regular like the rest of us. He went to one of the best technical universities in the country and also represented the state at table tennis. Having played him several times, I can attest to his skills with a paddle. It's just that he'd lost his moorings in a new world full of possibilities where you could abdicate reality and live in a dreamworld of simple and powerful ideas. He liked to believe that once he had his MBA, the rest of his life would be spent sitting around a table talking about

The Curse of the Minority Investor **133**

what is right and what is wrong while the commoners outside did the grunt work to bring in the business.

Prof Old, for his own part, didn't worry about the ISB one way or another: the same eager faces who had plonked a good amount of money in hope of succour, the same neat and perfect classrooms and nice air-conditioning no matter where he went. Globalisation and its discontents may well be, but everything worked to his advantage.

Anyway, he made me laugh on at least two occasions. Once, when I attended his first lecture, sitting next to my good friend Navin—the quintessential chocolate-boy of our batch whom every girl wanted to either adopt, marry or molest—and at another time, when I heard an interesting incident second-hand.

Navin was another chartered accountant who came from Arthur Andersen and wore his nature on his sleeve. You liked the guy instantly; he was unassuming, kind and participative. He took class-participation seriously on occasion, with inconsistent results. Although he'd spent a few years at AA, he claimed he never used a paper-shredder. I believed him. He was that kind of guy: clever, and without conceit.

Prof Old was making a point about how the partnership structure becomes meaningless from a Corp Gov viewpoint when the number of partners grows beyond a certain number, as in the obvious case of AA. At this precise moment, Navin woke from his slumber, and his neurons, in a blaze of brilliant synapses, put together the perfect counter-argument that the world was never to hear.

As the class sat listening in rapt attention to the erudite Prof Old carry on, Navin raised his hand. Prof Old majestically paused and looked kindly at him.

'Yes?' he said.

'Err . . . sir, I'm from Arthur Andersen,' said Navin, introducing himself.

'Oh, congratulations! . . . Do they still exist?'

134 *Touching Distance: The Great Indian MBA Dream*

The first couple of words of the sentence were spoken with an icy edge – laced with a disinterested, callous aplomb, like biting into vanilla ice cream on a searing hot Hyderabad summer afternoon only to find that it was full of razor blades; or, sitting down on a slab of ice to douse the flames of your burning arse only to discover that the slab was made of frozen oxygen.

Navin's pale Sindhi complexion rapidly went from white to red while I was torn between being polite and laughing my guts out. The others in class had no such compunctions and let go.

Another time, Prof Old arrived after lunch and was projecting his slides, as the students trooped in with cups of water, coffee and a tired but surviving need to get a return on the investment that this class and program had cost them.

Prof Old noticed that there were a full four minutes to go before the class began. The extra glass of orange juice and cold water, coupled with the rather cold air-conditioning he had been suffering in class-room AC4 (Academic Centre 4) for the last ten minutes, combined to pump large quantities of urine from his kidneys into his bladder. Ordinarily he would have waited for the first break to relieve himself but what the hell, he had four minutes to troop around the corner to the restroom and come back well in time. Besides, he was an existentialist and a successful one at that. If he wanted to pee, he went.

Prof Old passed a couple of students on their way in, who greeted him with exemplary AA consulting manners. He nodded in marinated kindness and walked calmly to the restroom. He admired the wonderfully clean and well-maintained facilities at the ISB. Indeed, a good leak that relieved a full bladder often gave him as much pleasure as a note that his latest paper was being published by some hallowed institution or the other.

He walked up to the first available urinal, unzipped, and let go. 'Aaaaahhhh!' he remarked. The sound of the stream striking the flawlessly clean white porcelain urinal was unnaturally loud. Must be echoes, he ruminated, remembering his high-school physics

The Curse of the Minority Investor **135**

instruction. He wondered if the echoes could be amplified to a frequency of perfect interference if he increased the fluid velocity. His was a brilliant mind given to random experimentation. He pressed on the accelerator, raising the sound to a loud but well modulated hum. It worked – the sound was clearly louder than the incremental input delta!

He was almost approaching ten seconds. Man, this was a good one. Pleased, he flushed, washed his hands and dried them. Relieved, he walked back to the class with two minutes still to go. He was pleased; this gave him enough time to return, clap on his wireless microphone and get to the first of his slides.

AC4 was ablaze with laughter when he returned. Nearly every student had his head on the table, face down, avoiding Old's eye, while shaking violently in uncontrollable mirth. He even caught sight of someone who fell off his chair and rolled on the floor at the back. Moe Harper was the only one who was polite enough to speak up.

'Professor, seems like you had your mike on,' said Moe, pointing to the small black appendage clipped onto Old's expensive blue Ralph Lauren Polo t-shirt.

◈

Me: 'Hey, thanks for taking the time to come out.'
Her: 'Why did you go to all this trouble? Who's car is this?'
Me: 'It's Prosenjit's. He's happy that someone is driving it. It's been rusting over the whole year at the ISB. You look really pretty, by the way.'
Her: 'Gosh, I just told them I'd be going to the library, and stepped out before they could ask me any questions.'
Me: 'Does Rahul know?'
Her: 'No. It's not a problem. You're the only guy he trusts around here. I didn't want to tell him anything. Besides, we are only going out for half an hour or less, right?'

136 *Touching Distance: The Great Indian MBA Dream*

Me: 'Yeah, I have to get back and study too. OK... anyway, we're halfway through. What a year it's been, huh?'

Her: 'Yeah. I'm so glad I met Rahul again. I'm just hoping everything works out and he and I get a job in the same city.'

Me: 'Yeah.'

Her: 'Look, you don't have to pay for the coffee.'

Me: 'I insist.'

Her: 'So why did you ask me out today?'

Me: 'Nothing much. I guess I just needed some fresh air.'

Her: 'It's a nice evening. I don't have much time.'

Me: 'How long do you have? I thought we could do dinner?'

Her: 'No, we can't. I'm meeting Rahul for a study assignment. I need to be back in about twenty minutes.'

Me: 'Are you sure?'

Her: 'Yes.'

Me: 'OK, let's go back, then.'

Her: 'So, when are you going to make your move on Trisha?'

Me: 'I don't know. She's way out of my league.'

Her: 'Come on.'

Me: 'Besides, I need to feel sufficiently strongly about someone before I do something like that. It's too scary otherwise...'

Her: 'So, who have you felt strongly about?'

Me: 'Hmm... honest?'

Her: 'Yeah, honest.'

Me: 'Never mind, I don't want to talk about it.'

Her: 'It's me, isn't it?'

Me: 'Phew!'

Her: 'That's OK. I always knew.'

Me: 'What do you mean you always knew?'

Her: 'Even Rahul doesn't call me every single day and sometimes twice on the same day. He doesn't sing to me on the phone randomly and he never sent me poetry I inspired.'

Me: 'Gosh, I don't know what to say.'

Her: 'You don't have to say anything. You're a sweet guy.'

Me: 'I don't get it.'

Her: 'What do you mean?'

Me: 'Why did you entertain my calls if you weren't interested in me, knowing how I felt about you?'

Her: 'I don't know. You're a nice guy and I liked the attention you gave me.'

Me: 'OK, I think I need to turn this car around. I don't think I can deal with this now.'

Her: 'Hey, relax. It's no big deal.'

Me: 'I know it's no big deal. I just lost my appetite, that's all.'

14

Poolside Stimulations

Jai Guru Deva Om,
Nothing's gonna change my world

—THE BEATLES

Two distant planets aligned with four other stars in a distant universe, forming a hexagon of scintillating perfection. Cause led to effect. Dean Sujay Manmohan felt a bolt of lightning in his medulla oblongata. Later that afternoon, he was to take steps toward ensuring that the ISB had at least one session where students would be initiated in the activities of the Image of Giving foundation. Elsewhere, a bearded man clad in white robes smiled. In Capt, the Dean would find a spiritual ally so willing that his zeal would only be matched by the aggression and acridity of the Image of Giving (IOG) instructor who would arrive.

The Universe had acted as it always did – on its own.

The IOG idea was received with muted caution by most of the populace. Of course Capt, who had pretty much done all the courses they had to offer, and had invented a few more in his own mind, was excited and was entrusted with the task of negotiating the rates with the Foundation and making sure we

Poolside Stimulations **139**

got a hell of an instructor who would cleanse the souls of these fortune-seeking lads and lassies, most of whom were on the verge of selling their souls to the Devil, or any company willing to come within smelling distance of the asking price. Capt did spend a lot of time figuring out the logistics and suchlike. Of course, Ranga and I had to attend. Capt was a friend and quad-mate – the unwritten rule applied.

It wasn't much of a struggle to get us on board. I was always up for something new, especially if it was spiritual, and Ranga, contrary to his every outward appearance and behaviour, feared and respected God more than he did any Strategy professor anywhere. He had a sneaky suspicion that God, and not Michael Porter, invented strategy.

The course was to be held over the weekend. We began in right earnest on the Saturday morning. Capt got us up at maybe 5.30 am, which wasn't too bad, except that I distinctly remember that I had gone to sleep only about a couple of hours before that. I rushed out and was happy to see that Ranga was safely tucked in bed. That gave me the opportunity of first use of the bathroom and I certainly didn't want to begin a spiritual day after inhaling the animosity of Ranga's refuse before the sun had a chance to cast at least a few cleansing rays into the bathroom.

Ranga had hit the sack a lot earlier than me. He specifically mentioned that he wanted to get a good night's sleep in anticipation of the spiritual day ahead. Today, he had passed out with his neck at an obtuse angle to the rest of his body, positioned like da Vinci's Vitruvian Man except that he lay facedown.

Bathed and ready, we trooped out into the morning and walked to the swimming pool, by which the course was to be held. The setting was tranquil and beautiful. Sarovar Park, the guys who ran the services at the ISB, had done a great job as usual. White mattresses were laid out and a number of girls had turned out as well; for a moment, I wished this was the Osho ashram.

140 *Touching Distance: The Great Indian MBA Dream*

I remember the usual suspects – Nishant Golli, Dhamit Pathak, Anu, Rangarajan, Sudhir and wife, Preetam Singh and (then) girlfriend Simran in tow, and a few more who play no greater part than the set already mentioned. Save for one: Rangarajan. Rangarajan was a powerhouse. Literally. He was a huge guy, standing at over six-feet and two-inches tall and weighing at least a hundred kilos. He could have easily flattened most of those who said anything unsavoury to him if only he had ever considered aggression. Rangarajan was what you call the archetypal gentle giant.

Rangarajan was also several other things: a poet with skills to make you cry each time, no matter what the theme of the poetry. To this day, Capt is troubled by the fact that Rangarajan stood up at every given opportunity to unleash the dogs of poetry upon him. Poor guy, his curse was not just his poetry, but the blind self-confidence that knew no fear.

There are many ways to incense Capt, but one of them is to suggest to him that Rangarajan's poetic skills were better than those meted out to Capt by Mother Nature. Every time Rangarajan stood up to unleash poetry, the populace applauded, unwinding at the utter simplicity of honest cause leading to completely random results. Rangarajan, to them, represented human nature in all its innocent glory, trying everything it can and falling flat on its face. In this case, it was consumed by a search for rhyme while chained to a huge iron ball of lyrical incompetence. One of the first things he said to me was: 'I'm not a faffer.' Well, he was right in his assessment, and he was wrong in everyone else's. Faith has its illusions.

And so, to borrow from Mario Puzo, we literally went 'to the mattresses' to squat on them and receive spiritual initiation.

Preetam, for his own part, was smitten. He beamed like an eager child when his love interest Simran walked up to sit behind him. Preetam was the prototypical MBA aspirant. He was smart, had a few skills and loads of ambition. He had framed his idea of the ideal year: impress as many people as possible, marry the

Poolside Stimulations **141**

prettiest lass in your class after making her fall in love with you, and join McKinsey.

However, ISB was a very misleading place in such contexts; I distinctly remember that I had perceived Simran's affections to be directed elsewhere. When I saw them together, her eyes did betray the yearning that you otherwise notice in honest lovers.

My suspicions were, unfortunately, right as usual. In a few months, Simran was to move on and catch up with the boy she had left behind in her city, secure in the knowledge that he indeed was her true love. In fact, I learnt that she had chosen to experiment with Preetam to establish the strength of her affections for the earlier beau. In her cold heart, this was simple experimentation. As for Preetam, this rejection probably hurt less than that of prospective employers of choice. When I heard about Simran's experiment, I remember nodding gravely, as was my wont, knowing that this was as abstruse as was footnote 21 on page 387 on any 900-page finance textbook.

And now, for the instructor. He turned out to be a real piece of work. This guy had flown in from Delhi and had a name that sounded like he came from one of those business families. Not the ones who made it big, but the others who are happy to take their loot home to stay under the tax radar. I can't quite remember it. Anyway, he first expressed concern that we were a few minutes late and worked on his baritone to sound important. Then he went through a few exercises which increased everyone's pulse a little. He then made everyone say, 'You belong to me,' in turn. All well-intended, of course, but try as hard as he could, every shred of emotional muscle had been hardened by the tribulations of failure and frustration, not to mention sleep deprivation, that the unsuspecting students began to wonder if they were actually doing it right. For my own part, every time I looked deep into the other person's eyes to say 'You belong to me', all I saw was the same thought in my own head: 'What the fuck are you doing here? Let's skip this touchy-feely crap and get to the part where

142 *Touching Distance: The Great Indian MBA Dream*

we all gain supernatural powers to hypnotise recruiters, women, bosses and professors.'

When he began to teach us a breathing technique in which you take deep breaths while constricting the nasal passage, he requested that everyone go to him to ascertain the quality of their efforts.

Capt's spirit, already soaring over the stars, now caught fire. Here was an opportunity for Capt to firmly establish what he suspected the others had not deciphered so far: the unquestionable truth that he was more evolved than everyone else in class. Having done these breathing exercises on many occasions, Capt went up to those struggling with the breathing, like me, to tell them how to get it right. He said vague things like, 'Try to hear a gushing sound as you breathe in,' or 'Your thoracic passageways are flexible . . . try and constrict your larynx,' etc., etc.

This really got to our middle-of-the-road-businessman from Delhi. How dare this silly guy with a moustache, who is part of his ashram as a student, dare seek a part of his stage? How dare someone set up shop right next to his own in Delhi!

The guy bellowed, 'You there! You go to the back and sit-down! If you don't have complete knowledge how can you teach?'

Capt stood his ground. 'I have done the course,' he replied.

'So what? A little knowledge is dangerous,' said the middle-of-the-road businessman turned fraud instructor.

Ranga stowed away the statement in the vast empty expanse of his mind for future class participation.

I was angry as hell. Firstly, let me tell you that I don't like aggressive, I'm-the-guru sorts who are playing games of king-of-the-hill. Secondly, I'm always upset when such well-meaning enthusiasm is shot down like a dog in the street. For his own part, I had no idea why Capt complied. He just slunk away to the back, philosophising this rebuke as a small part of God's greater plan that helped balance a part of his outstanding karma somewhere.

Poolside Stimulations **143**

To this day, I give Capt credit for taking the high road. Not too many others would have acquiesced the way he did. I even saw him accompany the fraud to dinner that evening.

Anyway, time passed and we had a session of the breathing technique, the best part of which was you got to roll back on the mattress after you were done. I fell asleep. The sound of the water being circulated in the pool, and gentle breeze waltzing over the Deccan Plateau, and the ample cloud-cover created the perfect stillness for my soul to call 'timeout'. Anu woke me up a short while later to tell me I was snoring.

For my own part, I really did have a bad cold and my unblocked nostril was trying hard to suck in as much oxygen as it could. If that is snoring, so be it. After I woke, I sat like everyone else, looking around not quite sure what we were all doing. I'd so much rather be asleep, but I had to look around, try and be sociable and look interested. The fraud instructor went about, asking for feedback on what experiences people had. He asked if anyone heard a bell in the distance, or if anyone heard music playing, or if anyone felt like crying, or laughing. I was hoping he'd ask a more real question, like, if anyone felt like snoring!

Anyway, most people I knew to be honest replied in the negative to all these questions. Some others, who I had suspected to be rather pretentious, were just not going to miss out on the opportunity to establish their superiority.

Sambhra wasted no time in saying that one moment she was laughing while the other she was crying.

Closer to home, Rangarajan said he felt like dancing. I saw Capt grimace. In his mind he had imagined Rangarajan dancing to his own poetry set to the music of Metallica.

Ranga scratched his head for the most strategic description of the nothingness he had experienced. I nodded gravely.

Preetam said he had done this course abroad, and many times at that, but he'd never experienced anything there either; I felt my heart

144 *Touching Distance: The Great Indian MBA Dream*

swell up in sympathy for the geographic diversity of his devotion and also rolled my eyes at his need to state his travelogue even in a context that was designed to enable us look inward. Simran looked impressed, and satisfied silently at her ability in picking a winner, at least for the time being.

We then watched a video on the bearded guru himself, and some of those on the mattresses fell asleep in front of the TV. One of them was rather ingénue in estimating the risk involved. He was wearing blue cotton track pants and stretched out in front of everybody. He stretched his legs out and closed his eyes, and began to fall asleep. He put his hands under his head to pillow his empty thoughts. Gifted with more than a little prescience, I knew this was a bad idea. When you are asleep, you don't have too much control over your thoughts. Thoughts which are suppressed well during our waking hours don't surface easily. If they are not well suppressed, they can raise their heads. In some cases meditation can help alleviate our inhibitions. In cases where one's mind is usually filled with non-spiritual thoughts, meditation can actually alleviate anatomy as well. It can create a safe environment where these thoughts believe they have a right to exist in all circumstances since God loves them as much as all other thoughts.

If you still haven't got my drift, you are better off being blissfully unaware. Being the good Samaritan that I am, I looked around quickly for a blanket, but here none was in sight. Before I could think of Plan B, one of the women sniggered. Fifty-six seconds later, everyone had caught on. Someone said something about a sweet dream. There lay Ranga, in all his beatitude, with a huge, embarrassing, unmistakable and nauseating part of his anatomy, blissfully unaware of the angels fleeing away in utter scandal.

Elsewhere in the universe, the bearded man in white robes chose to smile, seeking refuge in the knowledge that God loves fun. I nodded gravely.

❖

Poolside Stimulations **145**

Me: 'Hey.'

Her: 'On your way back, Mister?'

Me: 'Yeah. You have a good term-break, too.'

Her: 'I'm so looking forward to meeting my mom and brother.'

Me: 'Marriage plans in full swing, huh?'

Her: 'No . . . As usual, Rahul doesn't want to commit.'

Me: 'What's the problem?'

Her: 'Well, he has a bunch of things on his mind. Also, his sister needs to get married before him.'

Me: 'OK, that's understandable.'

Her: 'Well, I don't know.'

Me: 'This is the problem with people like you who live in some la-la Bollywood world. What do you really know about family responsibilities?'

Her: 'Agreed. Are you going to lecture me now? I don't need that right now.'

Me: 'OK. Anyway, I have an idea . . . why don't you give me your horoscope? I'll show it to someone in Bangalore while I'm there.'

Her: 'Buddy, I don't have a horoscope.'

Me: 'Not a problem. Just email your date, time and place of birth, and I'll generate it.'

Her: 'Hmm . . . I'll have to check the time with mom.'

Me: 'I know . . . that's why I asked you to email it. You girls are really slow on the uptake. Give me some credit. I now know you well enough to know what to expect from you, don't I?'

Her: 'Hmm . . . if you say so. Anyway, is this diviner accurate? I've never really talked to an astrologer before and have never had anyone tell me what's going to happen.'

Me: 'Well, I was like you, but then I became curious. Every time I think about going there I ask myself if I really believe this or not. In any case, think of it as entertainment. I can tell you, skilled or not, this person is a really nice Tamil gentleman. He's not a charlatan on the sidewalk looking to make a quick buck.

146 *Touching Distance: The Great Indian MBA Dream*

> *He used to be a corporate law expert for forty years, and this is his retirement hobby. He's a third-generation astrologer.'*

Her: 'OK, whatever. I'll send it to you. Hopefully he'll say I'd be married soon.'

Me: 'I don't want to sound like Morpheus from the Matrix, but he shall say what he shall say. I'm getting late. Ranga's waiting and we need to get on that train.'

Her: 'OK. Safe trip!'

Me: 'You too.'

Click.

Her: 'Will you call me from Bangalore?'

15

The Great Mysore Sandal Soap Robbery

Oh, life is bigger.
It's bigger than you.
And you are not me.

—REM

It was another hot day in Hyderabad as I trooped back to J-9, laptop bag hanging from my shoulder. We had returned from our term-break a few days ago. As I walked back, my mind wandered to the three-day-long term-break I'd enjoyed in Bangalore.

Among other things, I had made a trip across town to meet the astrologer, Srinivasan Ramachandran. We exchanged Tamil pleasantries as always and chatted about his recent trip to Selam and my desire to begin reading the *Sri Bhasyam* by Ramanujacharya. I then slipped him the horoscope I'd printed. He looked puzzled. There was no name on the page.

'Sir, this is a classmate's horoscope. She wishes to know if she'll get married this year.'

He looked at me, wondering if I had any investment in the matter. He held his glance just as long as a stream of incense

148 *Touching Distance: The Great Indian MBA Dream*

smoke wafted across my determined eye, and decided that he would not worry about it. He'd known me long enough to know that I was full of questions about the future and he gave me the benefit of doubt.

After what seemed like an eternity, he said, 'I don't know if you would know the answer to this question, but does she want to marry someone at this present time?'

With my eyes betraying some steel, I replied in the affirmative. He slowly looked back at the horoscope. I looked vacantly out the window, at the tree outside, as the smell of wet earth wafted in. It was going to rain in just a little while.

Then, he began to look back at the page and muttered to himself, counting planets and constellations on his fingers, as always. I watched dispassionately, bracing for the news that would leave me stranded on my relationship island, teaching me to swim all the way back to life again.

After a while, he said, '*Saar*, it is difficult for me to comment on this, but two things are certain: I can say that her chart suggests that she is inclined to marry someone. She may even know the person already, given that her Venus is strong at the present time. The year has potential for marriage and it might well happen. In fact, I should say that marriage is almost certain for her in this year.'

'So, she is going to marry someone she knows at the present time?' My question was formed even as he was speaking, my mind polishing the crystal-clear image with great disgust.

'I cannot predict that, *saar*. Please be careful; I only said the possibility of marriage is high and that she may be attracted to someone at the present time. Both conclusions may safely be made.'

'Sir, thank you. I shall communicate the same to her. Is she going to be happy in her marriage?'

'*Saar, adu yeppadi sollradu* (how can that be said)? How can I answer that question without matching the groom's horoscope?'

The Great Mysore Sandal Soap Robbery **149**

he said, trying to sound as neutral as possible, looking at me as if to say that I should have known better than to ask such a stupid question after all these years.

In the distance, thunder struck, and the Bangalore wind picked up. Bangalore never has the howling kind of wind, but is silent and strong, bringing with it dramatic rain that makes you wonder if the sheet of sprinkling water could ever look as beautiful elsewhere in the world. For a full minute I considered calling her to ask for Rahul's details so that Mr Ramachandran could pronounce his prediction on compatibility. As he looked at me, trying to read my thoughts, another thunderclap filled the sky and the inevitable Bangalore domino fell. The lights in the room went out, thanks to that oh-so-predictable power cut, leaving the burning incense carrying the unspoken questions into the air, as he shifted to reach for the emergency lamp. I knew that he continued to look at me questioningly by the light reflecting off his spectacles in the dimly lit room. It was nearly 5.00 pm, and was getting dark outside. I realised from the certainty of his movements, which had a certain conclusive quality to them, that he intended for me to leave and let him go downstairs to his family for some filter coffee.

I prostrated, like that tree in the forest no-one heard, as he muttered *shlokas* in blessing. I walked to my car and looked up as the first tiny raindrops fell on my eye-lids, almost in tender sympathy. The die had been cast and I just had to come to terms with what was going to happen. As I turned on the ignition, the thunderclaps boomed loudly and the rain came crashing down. With wipers turned to full speed I looked at the water running down the windshield and resolved to let time pass me by.

◆

Some of these thoughts stood out in sharp contrast as I walked back to my room under the hot Hyderabad sun. As the beads of sweat began to gather on my brow, I thought of the empty apartment. Ranga was returning later today after meeting his pre-ISB employer,

150 *Touching Distance: The Great Indian MBA Dream*

and Capt was indulging in some intellectual frolicking with the lassies in the cafeteria. The TV would be lying in wait for me to turn on and so would the AC. My island of peace beckoned. Some quiet TV time, a nice shower, followed by a quick nap before my meetings with study groups later in the afternoon. It was all good. Extrovert I can be, but I need my downtime with no humans around to recharge the inspiration. With these serene and happy thoughts I reflected upon the next few moments before the frenetic meetings were to begin.

I reached there to find the door already open; I distinctly remembered locking it before I left. I walked in to hear Ranga talking to someone on the phone. '*Ranga, nan magane yaavaglo bande?*' (My idiot son, when did you come back?)

'Like . . . ten minutes ago. I mean, like . . . the company paid for my flight.'

Ranga's company had been kind. He always found a way to screw them over. There went my afternoon TV and AC peace time. Ranga would want to buzz around my ears for a bit. He'd want to tell me that the folks he spoke to only worried about execution, without caring about how they could dramatically increase profitability through the application of strategy. Even if he wasn't in a buzzy mood, he'd want to come and shoot the breeze so long as he was awake.

'*Capt yello?*' (Where's Capt) he bellowed, inquiring about the co-ordinates of the third animal of our territory.

I unlocked my room and turned on the AC and fan. I was going to lock it and simply pass out, waiting to yell 'Fuck off!' if he was going to knock. Suddenly, I heard noises emanating from the bathroom between our rooms. I was surprised. Then I was immediately angry. Ranga had asked me where Capt was, and Capt had his own bathroom which he shared with the guy across his room. Then who the hell was in here?

'*Lo . . . Yaaridare bathroomalli?*' (Who's in the bathroom?)

Ranga walked into my room, standard black shorts and white vest. He had changed quickly out of his travel clothes into his

The Great Mysore Sandal Soap Robbery **151**

apartment fatigues. If you didn't know better, you'd have thought that he was contracted by Rupa (of '*Rupa underwear aur baniyan*' fame) to wear their sleeveless vest the whole year.

'I mean, like . . . this guy I met, OK? He's like applying here . . . like, for next year. I mean, like . . . on the flight, OK? He was coming here for an interview. Like . . . I told him to share the cab. I mean, you know Avinash Agarwal, OK? I mean, he is his cousin *ante,*' ('ante' in Kannada translates loosely to 'it seems').

Ranga looked at me and his voice had taken on a rather apologetic and tenuous tone as he came to the end of his explanation. He knew what was coming.

'What! What on earth man? Why the hell is he defecating here? Why the fuck did you bring him here? *Lo nin maado kelsavella intadde* (All the things you do are just like this). *Nan karma nin jatege sikkakondiddu* (My karma is to be blamed that I'm stuck here with you).'

I was upset. I had enough trouble sharing the loo with Ranga and could do without having to share it with a complete stranger with his own signature bacteria and odour. When it comes to loo matters, I prefer independence. If you said I was bordering on obsessive compulsion when it came to bathroom cleanliness and hygiene, you're right. That's one criticism I would happily take. I'm a cleanliness freak, and I don't care for a moment if you throw the book at me for being one.

As Ranga began to wonder why he had invited this stranger in, my mind began ticking over. He had probably popped into the bathroom without his own soap. He was probably using my soap, which was a little more colourful than Ranga's 'Mysore Sandal Gold.' Did he flush? How much of a mess could he have made? God, no . . . I began to conjure images of his supposed relative on campus and tried to imagine his bathroom manners and attempted to juxtapose them on a relative within the accuracy of two standard deviations. The results weren't good.

152 *Touching Distance: The Great Indian MBA Dream*

Ranga, in the meantime, had walked out of my room and returned to his own. He put his feet up and turned on his laptop. As far as he was concerned, there was no issue. Whatever he had set in motion would be cleaned up by the earnest guy across from him. As I heard his thoughts echo in my mind I wanted to kill him.

I walked into Ranga's room, searching for answers and means to deal with this situation. The questions formed in my mind with rapid precision – did he have a place to stay? Had Ranga informed his cousin? When was he going to leave? Did he have diarrhoea? Did he know how to work a flush? As I saw him staring at the laptop trying hard to avert my gaze, I just gave up. I aborted the attempt and shut the door. I needed a few minutes to myself before I lost it.

'*Naraayana*,' came the war cry a few minutes later. Capt had entered the building and had walked into his room. I did not have the energy to explain the occurrences to Capt. Ranga did not have the courage. Staus quo was the emperor of the lacuna. We stayed in our rooms and I was just angry. It was just the kind of thing that Ranga did. Among his many traits was an unbearable stingy attitude, which had caused him to drag this loser into a cab or autorickshaw just so he could save a few bucks. There was nothing I could do. I wanted to get Ranga to clean the damn bathroom with his toothbrush, as a punishment.

A while later I heard him conversing with the stranger. I walked out to take a look at the new specimen. I braced myself. He was true to form, a native of the cow belt. He had just showered and hadn't dried himself completely and had worn his clothes on top of his bathed self. He looked like something Ranga would drag in on a perfectly dry day. He extended a wet hand toward me. Disgusted, I smiled as genuinely as I could, telling myself this was an opportunity for spiritual growth, and shook it bravely.

I introduced myself. This intruder guy was yet another chartered accountant (who else would jump into a cab with a guy whose hair looked like he was a futuristic conductor, to save a few bucks?). He

The Great Mysore Sandal Soap Robbery 153

had applied to the school and was here for an admissions interview. He had, in his wisdom to optimise events, decided to have the interview in Hyderabad so he could see the campus as well. Talk about balancing your bleedin' books and cutting costs.

'Where will you be staying? With Avinash?' I ventured leadingly, knowing that niceties had no place in this context and the sooner he realised he should go, the better. I was hoping that he'd apologise for using our shower, state that he'd been unable to get to his cousin on the phone and that he was simply sorry for any inconvenience caused. I have to say that I knew I was going to be wrong.

'I haven't met him yet. Actually, I wouldn't mind staying here,' pat came the reply. I shuddered; Ranga looked bemused.

In his infinite hospitality, Ranga looked at me and said, 'I mean, like . . . dude, why don't you put the extra mattress from your room out in the living room. He can sleep there.'

'OK, OK,' the intruder replied happily.

Now I was really mad! Why the hell wouldn't this guy go live with his cousin, if he indeed was his cousin? Was he one of those hyper-*desi* dudes who believe that the whole world is a joint-family and it's perfectly okay to pile on? Was Avinash really a relative? Or was he a relative of a friend of a friend's third cousin's first ass, which theoretically made this guy's bloodline interminably connected to his. And who did Ranga think he was, ordering me around to serve people he had met two hours ago!

I glanced into the bathroom and found my soap completely soaked with disgusting froth. I squirmed. Ranga's Mysore Sandal, or what was left of it, was soaked too! That was strange. This guy obviously believed we were putting up a buffet.

'Actually, Ranga, I'm using both mattresses to rest my back. Don't think I can spare mine,' I averred.

I know I hadn't been super-Biblical or anything, but there were some really serious things at play here. Here was some stranger in our flat, shitting in our pot and bathing with my soap. Ranga had no history with him except for the fact that this guy had split

154 *Touching Distance: The Great Indian MBA Dream*

a taxi fare. He had brought him into the school simply based on the information that he wanted to appear for the interview. All the identification the intruder possessed was a cousin he was loath to visit and a suitcase which was large enough to carry at least four WMDs. Lastly, he looked nothing like someone I'd have liked to introduce as an alumnus of the school. Call me judgmental if you will, but someone with absolutely no consideration for others and with no sensitivity to pick up vibes does not belong in my good books.

As I walked away, I heard Ranga calling housekeeping for an extra mattress.

I walked into Capt's room. He was sitting at his table, pants and fly undone, allowing his lower abdomen the airing it needed. He had indeed been talking with a few girls for a couple of hours and his vows of celibacy to gurus and invisible gods had prevented the erection of any human or physical aspirations. I reckoned the extreme dichotomies at play had caused overheating.

'*Haan*, tell me,' he mumbled, trying to smile.

'Do you even know what the fuck is going on here?' I began.

Capt gave me a blissful blank stare, which began to develop traces of concern as I recounted the incidents of the previous hour.

I had to step out for some assignment meetings later that evening. I told Capt that he needed to drive some sense into Ranga's head and have this intruder thrown out and then make Ranga use his toothbrush to clean every square inch of the toilet before I came home. I returned later at night to find the intruder asleep in the living room. I hosed every human touchpoint in the bathroom with water, and took a shower with a new cake of soap, chucking the old one away. I returned the soap to my room. If the intruder wanted to clean himself, he needed to do it with Ranga's Mysore Sandal Gold soap henceforth.

Too tired to speak to anyone else, I entered my room and crashed. The intruder was snoring blissfully.

I was awakened by a knock on the door.

The Great Mysore Sandal Soap Robbery **155**

'*Yaar* Steve, it's me,' said Capt.

Trying to organise my thoughts in the Sunday morning light, I opened the door. Capt walked in with a grave look on his face and shut the door behind him. In a strange way, he seemed concerned. I'd never seen him like this.

'*Yaar*, this guy—what's he doing here? He shows no signs of leaving. Today he opened his second suitcase and laid out his clothes. This morning, he was washing his dirty clothes in our apartment. What's he up to? I also saw him making some tea for himself and settling down with the morning newspaper today.'

'When's his fucking interview?' I said, bleary eyed, but mind prepared to launch a frontal attack.

'I don't know, *yaar*. He said sometime this afternoon when I asked him yesterday. Today he says it's been postponed,' Capt replied. 'Should we tell the security guys? What should we do?' he added.

I was really surprised at Capt's train of thought. Was this the moment that Capt was waiting for? Was this that event in time when all of Capt's army training came to our rescue. Would the well-cultivated nose that smelt the incorrect angle of tilt of SAM missiles be remembered in history for smelling out this potential terrorist?

'Look, Capt. There's no point raising a hue and cry. Let's just tell him to go stay with Avinash. It's his goddammed cousin and I don't know why he wants to live here. Tell him I'm going to shove Ranga's toothbrush and laptop up his ass if he isn't out of here!'

'No, dude. Earlier I had heard him tell Ranga that he had told his cousin that he was going to stay with us since he was quite comfortable here.' Capt was sweating.

I walked up to my phone and dialled Ranga. He was taking his post-breakfast pre-lunch nap in his room. I told him to come by immediately.

156 *Touching Distance: The Great Indian MBA Dream*

Capt carefully opened the door to let Ranga in. He closed and bolted the door behind him, convinced that this was an operation requiring adherence to the highest security protocols. In sharp contrast, Ranga was digging his navel with one finger and had another in his ear, looking like he had just come out of coma, and wanted to make sure all his anatomical cavities were exactly where he'd left them.

After we were all on the same page, Ranga began to recount his grievances.

'I mean, like . . . I was shocked, OK? This guy, like, has used my soap, OK? I mean, like . . . so what if it's one-week-old, OK? I mean, now I want a new one. So I asked him to pay like, fifty bucks, OK? That's what the Mysore Sandal Gold soap costs. Then, on the first day I had allowed him to use my phone to call his home, OK? So I like, told him to pay me fifty bucks per call on average.'

Capt's jaw dropped. While he was conjuring images in his mind about what he could do to avert this terrorist threat, and I was wondering how I could get this guy to join other members of his cow-belt moorings, Ranga had been busy inventing profit opportunities. I wondered if Ranga had collected any rent for the night.

I finally realised I had to take charge.

'Ranga, does Avinash know this dickhead?' I asked.

'Yeah, I mean like . . . cousin or something,' replied Ranga, looking sheepish as hell.

'Fine, it's settled, then. Ranga, throw this guy out. Tell him to pack his bags and go stay with Avinash. Dunno what the fuck he wants here. You're the dickhead who bought him in. You're going to make him leave.'

'Steve, should we interrogate this guy? I mean, who knows?' said Capt.

Stunned as I was at Capt's insistence on being celebrated a hero, I said, 'Why the hell not?'

The Great Mysore Sandal Soap Robbery **157**

We never got to interrogate him. Ranga saw the fire in my eyes and I repeated my toothbrush and laptop threats to him directly this time. He knew I meant it.

Now fully awake, he was determined to fix it. As Ranga left the room, he walked straight up to the idiot sitting in the living room and in his own inimitable way said, 'I mean, like . . . you need to go stay with Avinash. I mean, like . . . the other guys are getting uncomfortable.'

The intruder knew something was up, so he was all set to scram.

As Ranga watched him pack, he said, 'I mean, like . . . did you eat the bread? Damn, the tea is finished as well. Dude, like, we just bought all this stuff . . . I mean, like . . . just give me two-hundred bucks so I can replace it.'

The intruder looked puzzled as he paid Ranga. Flabbergasted, Capt left my room. We'd been watching through the ajar door.

I went back to sleep. When I woke, the intruder was gone.

As we sat down in the living room that evening, discussing Ranga's stupidity and berating him, releasing our academic and non-academic stresses in the process, Ranga was pretty unmoved.

Ranga remarked that the intruder was an *atyachaari* (oppressor). Capt had been a *krantikaari* (rebel-star). Ranga himself had been a *vyapari* (trader). He then threw his head back and laughed. Strangely enough, he was accurate.

I mentally pictured putting my fist through his teeth. Capt made a face at Ranga, looking like Mt Etna about to explode again. He proceeded to carpet-bomb Ranga's very being with expletives. Ranga continued to laugh his guts out.

'I mean, like . . . he had offered to pay for half the cab fare, OK?' said Ranga. Capt walked out, shaking his head. '*Hari om*,' he said, just as he left, imploring the gods for liberation.

'*Hari om*,' I repeated.

❖

158 *Touching Distance: The Great Indian MBA Dream*

Me: 'Hey, welcome back.'

Her: 'Hey.'

Me: 'Missed me?'

Her: 'He-he, you wish. How was your time away from this cauldron?'

Me: 'Pretty good. By the way, I did ask about you when I met my astrologer.'

Her: 'Cool. Is it good news?'

Me: 'Well, yes ... he said it seemed like you liked someone at the present time and that marriage was in the air this year for you.'

Her: 'Oh, good. Did he say if it would work out?'

Me: 'Well, he couldn't obviously. He didn't have the prospective groom's horoscope.'

Her: 'Stupid ... why didn't you take it along?'

Me: 'What do you mean? I didn't have the details to generate it. Besides, shouldn't you be thanking me? It is pretty good news, right?'

Her: 'Hmm ... I guess. It's just that I have so many doubts.'

Me: 'Huh? Now what?'

Her: 'Well, nothing, my mother is hounding me to get married.'

Me: 'OK, that's good.'

Her: 'And Rahul has all these problems ... he always has a great reason to put this off.'

Me: 'Hmm ... Well, it's going to work out, don't worry too much about it.'

Her: 'I don't know. He did this before a few years ago and I forgave him once.'

Me: 'You don't know how difficult things may be for him. He has an elder sister. I know what that's like.'

Her: 'Yeah, yeah. All you nice boys with your elder sisters.'

Me: 'Hey, come on. You don't know what it's like to be us. Rahul is not some teenager with some 100cc bike that he can rush

The Great Mysore Sandal Soap Robbery **159**

you away on whenever you want. Besides, it does seem like the wedding will happen, at least based on what the astrologer is saying.'

Her: 'I don't know. My heart says no such thing. Anyway, I'm done talking . . . I have to go now. Bye.'

Me: 'Anyway, what else is new?'

Her: 'Nothing else. I'm just worried that this is déjà vu. I should never have trusted him.'

Me: 'Come on. Give the guy a break. You are not in his shoes.'

Her: 'I'm done listening, I have to go now.'

Click.

16

The Sermon on the Rock

I've been sitting on top of these rocks,
Watching the waters run,
Everyone that I have loved, has gone floating by,
I've been waiting for the King of the World,
To come and rescue me,
From land that's lost in dreams

—JAMES

At yet another late hour (which has no definition at the ISB), I walked alongside Capt back to the apartment. We were returning from the library after another wasted attempt at conquering thirty-odd pages of some obscure textbook, in the hope of decimating whatever assignment existed on our desks for the morrow.

Trisha sat in the library, surrounded by her bevy of kinsmen, and as usual a casual wave and a cheery 'Hi' was all I could get out as I walked past her on my way back to my apartment. This love story was not going to happen, I'd concluded. There was too much else going on and as pretty as she was, there was an impenetrable forcefield of alert guys guarding the gates to conversations with her. My other venture, which had swept away my very being continued

The Sermon on the Rock **161**

to be a secret that I shared with me, and myself alone. The deepest truths are the ones you cannot share.

'Capt, this place is full of goalkeepers,' I said.

'Ha-ha, I know what you wish for, my friend. But let me tell you that it's an illusion. All of life is. Just look up and tell me that it's not,' he declared pointing at the inky-black infinity overhead.

'Capt, let's not discuss Vishistadvaita and Advaita now,' I said.

His tone had that all too familiar ring to it, suggesting that he was feeling other-worldly today.

You couldn't blame him. In 2003, ISB existed in a faraway part of the city, far removed from everything else. There was no light pollution at night and the climes were starry and inky-black. When the moon was out, the Atrium seemed to float against the sky, and you couldn't help but feel that anything this beautiful had to be an illusion. We walked back slowly, both of us looking up at the perfect night sky. Capt reeled off names of constellations and I simply marvelled at the amount of natural light there was at 1.00 am.

The path out of the Atrium and back to the Student Villages was paved with granite slabs and lit up with foot-level CFLs. In many ways, it was a beaten trail out of academic perfection into the riot of human chaotic vibrations emanating from student life. The Student Villages in themselves had become the bedrock for a study of accelerated emotional output, a study in which new thoughts and emotions were discovered and experienced, only to be obliterated with newer emotions that sometimes scarred deeper, and at other times grew even more fragrant as time rolled on. On some days, it was a fear of an unfulfilled aspiration – maybe personal, maybe professional. Within moments, this was strewn aside by moments of inspired flirting or a memorable conversation with a beautiful girl. The gamut of emotions continued to roll at their pace, with the certainty of a setting sun followed by a determined, laden monsoon.

162 *Touching Distance: The Great Indian MBA Dream*

The half-kilometre trail across the perfectly manicured lawn to Student Village 2, where we were staying, was rather pleasantly marked by a large rock of the Deccan Plateau. This rock stood out, exhibiting a character that spoke to all the eons that had passed and held stories for all those eons that were to come.

Halfway across the lawn, I stepped off the trail, walked across the dew-soaked lawn, up to the rock, and sat down, the cool surface calming my senses and evoking memories of simpler times when to sit on a rock was perhaps all one wanted to do to muse over all that one needed to do.

Capt followed, parking his own beaten behind on the other side of the large rock. I stretched out on the rock and looked up at a cloudless sky that revealed a zillion stars that lit up the corner of the universe where I existed.

My mind began to wonder as it often did on questions of faith, and I said, 'Capt, can you resolve the duality of free-will and destiny?'

'Is your question coming from experience or intellect?' asked Capt.

'Intellect mostly, but also intuition. I know the world is an illusion. I just don't know if it's worth anybody's time,' I replied.

'Good point,' said Capt. 'When the intellect matures, the mind begins to spiritually question reality. The next step is always experiential.'

'Can experiences tell you whether the notion of human life itself is really worth anybody's time?' I wondered.

'That depends on the experience and your ability to see its supernatural facet,' he declared.

'Have you ever had a supernatural experience?' I asked.

'Yes, once.'

Capt did come across as someone with a great deal of maturity and understanding in human situations, while at other times, he could just be as simple as any of us in the shallow negative emotions that swim in the waters of our soul, waters whose depths necessarily

The Sermon on the Rock **163**

remained shallow to absorb the constant agitation of the stresses we dealt with. Any deeper, and the turbulence would be far too unhealthy. Over time, each one us had learnt to expose a small quantity of our soul to the world, to keep our essential natures as unchanged and original as possible. There were yet others who lost themselves in the storms of human cravings, and felt a little depleted at the end of it all.

To waft back into the mists of this spiritual inquiry, I sought to push Capt further. Capt was necessarily someone who was pretty open and honest about his truths and lies. When asked about his spiritual experience, he spoke about a revelation.

'It was a long time ago. During an advanced meditation course in Rishikesh, I had undertaken silence for a few days and sat on this large rock by the banks of the Ganges. After a few hours of meditation, I opened my eyes to see life in everything. The rocks, the water, the plants. I did not want to step on the rocks for fear of hurting them. I saw that they all had a consciousness that I recognised as my very own. There were no boundaries. It brought tears to my eyes. I guess I realised at that point what it meant to be One with the Universe.'

I listened intently, gazing at the stars. You don't make up something like that for kicks.

'Hmm . . . interesting. Then why come back? Why the MBA?' I asked.

'Time, and readiness, I guess. I came to understand that I was unable to commit to a spiritual path. I realised that I needed to cling to the material world for longer. One of the ways to do that irrevocably, was to commit to a material burden like debt and higher education,' he replied.

I understood the gravity of this argument. It revealed a completely different dimension of life's experience and choices – choices of a nature that I was yet to experience.

'It's funny how much of this school, and indeed everything else with respect to institutions, is in line with the Indian culture. This

164 *Touching Distance: The Great Indian MBA Dream*

school is like a temple, isn't it? It's adorned with affiliations to the best three schools in the world. The professors are great, but the knowledge can so easily be attained by renting these books from a public library for less than what it costs to spend a day here,' I commented.

'Yes, you are right,' he said, nodding with gravity.

'So, you are here for some more idol worship, I guess. So am I. No judgments whatsoever,' I said.

'Yes, *yaar*. It's quite true,' he said.

'On a lighter note, this must be a sign of the times, Capt. Maybe this is the way things work in the *kaliyuga*. The distortion becomes the norm. The very notion of idol worship was a substitute to vedic *homa* worship,' I continued.

He nodded 'Right, again.'

'Hmm . . . still doesn't answer my question, Capt. Let me tell you why I came here. It was so because I wanted to receive the blessings of a great degree, the hope that I'd be all that I could be if I had a great stamp on me so that I could be recognised. That's the reason 99.9 percent of the folks are here. A better salary is part of the reason, but mostly people actually want great material lives and recognition, isn't it? Everyone wants to be interviewed on TV as a powerful guy,' I said.

'Hilarious, but true. Everyone also comes here expecting to top the class, get a scholarship and fall in love,' he said, mocking me. I let it pass.

'What's up with you, Capt? You should be out there getting married and raising children at your age. What makes you plonk down so much money and sit and listen to me asking you these pesky questions? Did you just want to make a clean start after the army?' I said.

'No, *yaar*. Growing up, I had a deep desire to study at a challenging and great institution, and be taught by great minds. It was a strange wish, in the sense that it was almost like a residual dream from a past life, a deep desire. At certain points, I thought

The Sermon on the Rock **165**

that this wish would never be fulfilled. And yet today, I think I am experiencing that.'

Consistent with his behaviour, I observed. Strangely, Capt was among the few of those I worked with who chose not to seek the holy grail in the crusade for grades. He was among the few who cared more about the knowledge available rather than the badge of competitive superiority. We talked for a little longer about manifestations of the supernatural on earth. Capt recounted stories about a close friend of his who had exhibited significant control over nature at varying points and had paid a heavy price for it. He could make it rain, he could move clouds, etc., but died a very strange death.

The stars continued to shine on these deliberations, the vibrations of which rang silently into a Universe and echoed in the annals of a greater intelligence that continued to watch over these illusions.

I got up to walk back to the apartment, and Capt followed suit.

'Capt, how the hell am I going to find a girl here with all these men crawling over them like bees in a hive?' I asked.

'Ha-ha, don't chase after mere illusions. That will only bring you pain,' he said, smiling to himself.

'Whatever, dude. No matter what you say, we all suffer in the real world. Even if you know everything is an illusion and there is reincarnation and karma and all those things. It is a fact that I have this enormous crush on Trisha and that this is neither the time nor the place to do anything about it,' I lied.

'True, this place sucks big time. Not exactly the kind of place you want to come to, if you have love on your mind. What the hell are you going to do? Forget studies and placements and learn some Hindi or Punjabi so you can fit into the right circles?' he said mockingly, reading my thoughts.

'Yeah, hell. It's a pain in the ass, this crush thing,' I said.

'You're doing your best. I've never seen you turn up so regularly to play football with those people,' he remarked, smiling.

He was right.

166 *Touching Distance: The Great Indian MBA Dream*

For an institute starved of time, the students at the ISB were a remarkable lot. While there was a large percentage of people like me who swore they were here to top the class, a lot of them also swore they would make this a year to remember – for themselves and for everyone else. This really was philanthropy of a unique nature. Students working overtime to organise activities to keep spirits up and to ensure this wasn't a year that people would forget in a hurry. God bless their sort.

Inter-class cricket and football matches were organised and saw tremendous participation.

The first four terms had the entire batch divided into three classes of about fifty-sixty each. I was in Section A. This was the time for getting your feet wet in the ISB scheme of things. Study groups, checking out the girls in your batch to realise that there were indeed no Miss Worlds.

But well, here's the thing. I was the ultimate romantic, never one to hold back from having a crush. I had a crush every other month when I was in high school. In the boat of my mind, there was this beautiful girl, her hair glistening as the rays of a setting sun bounced off them, a mystical smile playing on her lips as she drowned in my eyes to find my soul already encased in her own. There have been times when I met a girl either at the workplace or during my engineering days, and created a beautiful pedestal in my mind and placed her with great care on it. She sat on that pedestal and never cared to contemplate on how she ever got there. I turned out to be a faceless, fearful, un-rejected romantic in those cases. I never tried. You see, nothing ventured, nothing lost.

Anyway, coming back to the football. I was a footballer of some repute in my undergrad days – a pretty acrobatic goalkeeper. However, for my class I showed up and told them I wanted to play as a striker. Given that I could kick pretty decently, they bought it.

The good thing about these tournaments was that the women of the class turned up. In some cases, one or two women actually played with us as part of the team.

The Sermon on the Rock **167**

Prior to the matches, practice sessions were held, which gave everyone an opportunity to exercise a secret desire. The desire to frolic on the picture postcard-perfect rolling lawns of the ISB. While no one I knew of actually got away with the real thing, the closest most people came to it was rolling on these lawns after a rather embarrassing fall.

Early in Term 1, a motley bunch of us turned up on one such cloudy evening. I was surprised to see some representatives of the softer gender. How was this to work? I had no idea. Anyway, the important thing was that Trisha appeared, wearing dark track-pants and a white t-shirt. Who is Trisha, you may ask. Well, Trisha is one of the youngest people in the class. Very talented, and with a host of accomplishments in competitive horse-riding and shooting; she is also extremely beautiful. In body and in mind. Guys who had the good fortune to cross her paths under the Godsent guise of assignments, were absolutely smitten. 'She's so gorgeous! And she is such a nice person!' was what you consistently heard. For a north Indian Punjabi, she was slim – more like a naughty version of a rather svelte Aishwarya Rai than someone like a super-athletic Maria Sharapova.

On that first day of football, there she was, looking all flushed and excited at the prospect of having a good time with the folks. That was what you loved about her – an innocence only to be found in young children when they spot a nice park and a football, and can only rush off to kick the ball and chase it. She was refreshingly human, and represented all that is pure and native to the newborn soul.

As fate would have it, she was in the opposite team. As such, I couldn't even yell out her name, even under the guise of requesting a pass. A few minutes into the game, someone passed the ball to me and I ran towards the goal. She was playing defence, and paying no heed to my size or velocity, ran at me, trying to tackle me. Ah, the innocence of innocence. I made the cardinal mistake of looking up at her. The setting sun highlighted her soft features, irradiating

168 *Touching Distance: The Great Indian MBA Dream*

magic in the evening light, like a soft melody playing in the distance while you walk along a twilight beach in your most sensitive and sensuous dream. I dared not run at her for felling her, even by accident. Moreover, when someone so beautiful wanted something, they should have it, I reckoned. Before I knew it, she had kicked the ball away and no sooner than I had realised what I had done than a million comments began to ring out, exhorting me to stay focused, to concentrate on the game and not on the players. For her part, she received a loud cheer, not just from her team-mates, but also from mine, a testimony to her Hellenic beauty.

Capt had been there playing, and had seen all of it, no doubt. Later, he set down to counsel me.

'Look, dude. Don't worry about the girl thing. I promise you one thing: the whole desire thing is an illusion,' he said.

'It's not the girl. It's the chase,' I said.

He nodded. 'Yes, I know . . . that's what all desires are. Our need to chase, with the object mostly just incidental.'

'Anyway, changing tracks. Do you worry that the whole economy may tank as we head into placements?' I asked.

'I do. But I seriously don't care beyond a point. All it means is that it will take longer to pay off this loan. No matter what, I am going to get a job and deal with it in the coming years,' he replied.

'What about marriage? Isn't there any pressure on you?' I asked.

'Oh yes, there is. But then again, I'd rather not marry,' he replied.

'Why . . . *karma*?' I asked.

'Yes. I think I'd prefer to lead a simple life and do society some good. I don't want to get married, have a bunch of kids and spend my days trying to hoard wealth,' he replied.

'I agree. But it doesn't always crumble the way we'd like it to, right?'

'Yeah, you're right. When you look up at the sky, you have to submit to Ramana's statement,' he replied.

The Sermon on the Rock **169**

'You mean the one on *prarabda karma*? That you are not in control of what happens?' I added.

'Absolutely. You know it too, right? Look at how hard you've tried. You can't control outcomes in a dead-heat,' he said.

'What do you mean?' I wondered.

'I've seen you on your walks,' he said.

'What walks?'

'Never mind.'

I let it pass. I was too embarrassed to do otherwise.

◈

Her: *'Hello.'*

Me: *'Hey.'*

Her: *'So, champ. Had a hot date at dinner, huh?'*

Me: *'Why?'*

Her: *'You were sitting with Malini.'*

Me: *'So what?'*

Her: *'Total south Indian scene, huh? I even heard you speaking in Tamil.'*

Me: *'So what?'*

Her: *'Nothing. Just happy for you. I hope you'll stop calling me now.'*

Me: *'Hello, if I remember correctly, you called me, didn't you?'*

Her: *'Yes, I did.'*

Me: *'Anyway, why are you all excited?'*

Her: *'Nothing, just happy for you, that's all. So are you guys going out on a date?'*

Me: *'Look, she saw me sitting alone and joined me. Capt joined us later. What's the hullabaloo about?'*

Her: *'Well, I told you before . . . I've heard she likes you.'*

Me: *'So what?'*

Her: *'You don't like her?'*

Me: *'What if I did? It's not like you're marrying me tomorrow or even considering me for anything other than a phone call, right?'*

170 *Touching Distance: The Great Indian MBA Dream*

Her: 'Yeah. I have Rahul and it's going to work with him.'

Me: 'Yeah, you've said that so many times, I'm now hoping it comes true. Malini's a sweet gal. Maybe I will fall in love with her and marry her.'

Her: 'Good for you.'

Me: 'Anything else?'

Her: 'Will you tell me if you guys go out?'

Me: 'Why does it matter to you?'

Her: 'Well, just curious.'

Me: 'What the hell? He-he . . . is this some Plan B thing? You want me to wait on the sidelines and watch you canoodle someone else? You need to sort your head out.'

Her: 'Oh, please. Flatter yourself.'

Me: 'Forget it. I have to go now.'

Her: 'Ok, bye. Sweet dreams, Malini included. Give her a big kiss tonight.'

Me: 'Thanks. I will. I wish you a sleepless night.'

Click.

Her: 'Hello?'

17

Blink

Today was gonna be the day that they're gonna throw it back to you
By now, you should've somehow realised what you've got to do

—OASIS

As I recollect the events of a rather remarkable day described later on, I believe Malcolm Gladwell had some truth in his claims that we make our best decisions using intuition, in the blink of an eye, even before we use our left brain-hemisphere to rummage through data and apply that thing called 'logic'. I'm as intuitive as they come, so Malcolm, I hope you are right as rain. May your tribe increase.

Time rolled on and one fine day, I looked out the large windows of my flat to see a large group of people trudging along from the other Student Village, across my own, to the football pitch at the far end of the campus. They looked pretty fired-up. Someone saw me standing in the window and yelled out, 'Let's kick their arses!'

Inspired by divinations of unlimited slapstick comedy in the offing, I grabbed my soccer shoes and could scarcely contain my mirth, not to mention the blood thumping through my funny bone.

172 *Touching Distance: The Great Indian MBA Dream*

I rushed to the football field filled with adrenaline and testosterone. The marching army had already begun executing formations of a rather comical leaning, and most people were trying to stay on their feet as they attempted long distance shots at goal, all in the guise of warm-ups.

We were playing Section C, probably the weakest section when it came to football. When the game began, I picked up a stray pass almost immediately and put Kailashnath Ganti through on the left. Ganti was a local lad, and all his years studying engineering at IIT Delhi had not eroded his flair for a good game of soccer. He had established himself as the self-proclaimed captain of our team.

The first configurations would have made any football coach or strategy professor throw up with absolute nausea. Wherever the ball went, everyone, save the goalkeepers, chased it. It was ridiculous. Even hungry monkeys chasing after a single banana being tossed around would have demonstrated more strategy. As my pass reached Ganti, he was confused and terrified as the mob ran towards him. The more creative ones invented a battle cry. Ganti closed his eyes and covered his genitals in a primitive show of self-preservation. A cloud of dust erupted and almost magically the ball rolled towards the goal in front of me. I bolted toward it, unleashing a war cry of my own. I then looked up to see little Manik Mathu running towards the ball. We were headed for a collision. The prospect of this scared me a little since Manik was a stocky 5' 3" and when crouched and running straight ahead, his head was right in line with my tender possessions. This guy was no Trisha, but resembled one of the short, stocky guys from those American-Italian Mafia shows on TV.

I knew I would not reach the ball but I stuck out my foot in order to stop the pass. As expected, I was well short of the mark. Manik seemed mesmerised at the sight of my foot missing the ball and stared down. I was confused as hell. Did this guy not get the idea that he needed to go after the ball?

Blink **173**

I was the first to react. The ball was rolling behind Manik, and remarkably, towards the goal. I rushed towards it, Manik in hot pursuit. By now I was convinced that all Manik wanted to do was crash into me and somehow live to tell the tale. Ball at my feet, I raced towards the goal, my pulse racing at the prospect of greatness. Everything became quiet as my being retracted into my soul and gathered its divine energy to harmonise body, mind and intent. I looked up. What the hell? Rupa Josephine was guarding the goal. Gosh, was this my lucky day! Section C had not found a guy to stand in goal. I'm no chauvinist, but the way Rupa positioned herself between the uprights, it was pretty apparent that it was her first time on a football pitch. I took aim and unleashed a right footer. Manik threw himself in the path of the ball in an act of heroism, but was too late and finished up yelling in pain as his rear end created sparks against the gravel. The ball continued on its way, curved a little towards the left post, past Rupa, who wondered what was happening. It went straight into the back of the net. I had scored, and done so from the edge of the penalty box! I took off like an airplane in celebration.

We won that game pretty comprehensively: 4-0. I still remember Ganti's email titled 'Four fucking zip', sent to both classes after the match. Email sent, he resembled a chest-thumping guerrilla rather than a pitiful Desmond Morris subject.

❖

Our second match was against Section B, the class which contained the beauty Trisha and the lucky guys. Preetam was there as well, and I was to remember this one for the fight that almost broke out between the teams. Preetam, all of forty-five kilos, was messing about, and Rohan lost his cool. He held back at first, but when Preetam did not learn his lesson and messed around a little more, Rohan reacted like he had never done before and was never to do again. He yelled out a few things of which I caught 'Preetam . . . You want to play rough? I will just lift you up, throw you down and

174 *Touching Distance: The Great Indian MBA Dream*

break your bloody neck!' As he said these words, he raised his leg and imitated breaking a dry twig against his thigh. Rohan weighed twice as much as Preetam and was at least a foot taller. Had you met him, you would know he could do it. That was enough for Preetam. He had to make one great effort to not pee in his pants. He was just glad the folks from McKinsey were not around. They might have dinged him on courage and conviction.

It was a really scrappy game with one moment of great luck. Rohan, probably one of the best footballers, made one big clearance from the centre, which bounced once in front of the goalkeeper, over his head and into the goal. Trisha came to play, but did not have much of an effect as we just found it too easy to keep scoring goal after goal.

And so, suddenly, we were in the finals.

❖

We turned up on a sultry evening as the clouds gathered in the distance, carrying with them the gods of the universe who wanted to catch a glimpse of the low-quality, high-entertainment football. We were playing Section C once again. This time, they had rounded up a slightly better team. However, given the strength of our team, we were expected to win easily. Some women from each class turned up to cheer. From the midfield, I caught sight of Trisha in the distance. The game began. I played behind Aranjit Banerjee, a strong striker. I fed him a couple of times and we were up 2-0. Section C pulled one back.

In the second half, I was doing all I could to run into areas and create some intelligent moves. I was the playmaker that day. Certainly Aranjit was more than a handful for their defence. I could hear Trisha egg her team on.

With the game headed our way and with me not receiving any passes at all, I began to do what I did best. I began to space out, drawing conclusions from football as they applied to life and the

Blink **175**

campus, understanding people through their actions on a football field. I then thought about the rest of the year.

My sight wandered toward Trisha in the distance, cheering her team on with complete conviction that her encouragement would beget the will of the gods. What a beauty! Within these ruminations, my thoughts steered to life and love. Why was I so risk-averse? There was Trisha, pretty close to a human angel, and as much as I appreciated her, and I never did venture closer. I was not someone who would walk up to her and start an idle conversation which started with wit and ended with love. Why wasn't I capable of doing something great? Did I not believe in myself enough? Yeah, that was maybe it; she was way out of my league. I wondered if she ever thought of me. Of course not, I told myself. She, like every beautiful girl in India, found herself surrounded by a bevy of guys wherever she went. She never had the time to consider anyone who wasn't in eyesight. You couldn't blame her.

I continued to ruminate, watching eager young men push, shove and jostle in vain. How much like life! – I thought. We never know what we are fighting for. And we never stop to think. Maybe if we did, there would be nothing left to fight over. But life would require less energy, or at least, lesser energy of the obvious sort. Between thoughts I sneaked a look at Trisha. I wondered what she made of all this testosterone on display.

My thoughts and jogging up and down the field were interrupted by a pass. Arindam kicked the ball to me from thirty feet away and I stopped it with my right foot. I looked up. I was bang in the centre of the field, almost at the kick-off circle. The goal looked strangely clearer. In the goal stood Nataraj Venkateshan, not usually known for his athletic skills. Any doubts were dispelled by his fluorescent yellow shorts. The ball bounced. There was no one nearby and everyone was just waiting for me to either pass the ball or run at them. After all, I was in the middle of the damn park! What else was I going to do?

176 *Touching Distance: The Great Indian MBA Dream*

Something snapped. My thoughts began to calm down and slowly disappear. I pushed the ball further, allowing it to roll just a few inches this time. By now, everything in my mind went deadly quiet. I knew I was on the verge of something. Everything seemed to move in slow motion. Thoughts evaporated, time slowed down. Strangely, my body seemed light. I stepped up to it and without any thought, ferret, notion, or idea, just kicked it as hard as I could. I remember it being a hard and well-timed kick.

Airborne, the ball did not rotate, just held still, travelling in a perfectly straight line. I had kicked it fairly high so I, for a moment, thought it was going over the goal-post. At that opportune moment, the wind picked up and assisted the ball in its flight toward the goal. The ball began to now rotate slowly and kept moving. I began to hear sounds again. Strangely, no one was talking anymore. I just heard the sound of anticipation, like the first rays seen through the foliage of an Amazonian rain forest.

The ball had now travelled half the length of the field and I was convinced it was headed towards the goal, straight for Venky's face. Twenty feet from Venky, the ball began to shape away, toward the right post. Venky looked up, mouth open; the ball sped toward him, dipping and curving. As he watched, hands raised, the ball entered the back of the net, billowing it with its force.

I did not know what to think. I realised that I had not thought, but had simply acted. I had scored the goal of my life.

I had the strange feeling that anything I did that day would work. Rohan later said to me that Trisha had her hands cupping her cheeks as she watched the goal being scored. I had given her a memory, in return for several that she had gifted me.

I had blinked. I really should do it more often, I thought. One of my closest friends, Prosenjit, was to write in my Yearbook: 'You should take more chances'. He was right. Sometimes, you never know if you can seize the moment if you don't stretch out your hand.

❖

Her: 'Congrats, superstar. I heard you scored like some super goal?'

Me: 'Well, yeah. It was a bizarre day. Where were you? I score the goal of my life and you weren't around to see it.'

Her: 'OK. So you dedicated it to me, huh?'

Me: 'Well . . . '

Her: 'You'd better say you did.'

Me: 'OK, I guess I did.'

Her: 'Was Trisha there?'

Me: 'Yeah, she was . . .'

Her: 'Oh, cool. And Malini?'

Me: 'She wasn't. She had gone to the city.'

Her: 'Oh, that's too bad. I'm sure she'd have given you a big kiss, huh?'

Me: 'What does it matter to you? Sounds like you're jealous.'

Her: 'So, what if I am?'

Me: 'Doesn't make sense. You said you don't want me.'

Her: 'Anyway, is Malini going out with you on Valentine's Day?'

Me: 'Well, we might. We haven't discussed anything yet.'

Her: 'If I said I'd go out with you, would you pick me?'

Me: 'Gosh, stop kidding again.'

Her: 'No. Just for argument's sake.'

Me: 'Argument . . . I don't like arguments, you know that.'

Her: 'I'm telling you there's a good chance you can go out with me on Valentine's Day.'

Me: 'Why?'

Her: 'Rahul may be away . . . he has something else to attend to.'

Me: 'Sorry sweetheart, I'm not going to be your Plan B, in case the wheels come off this Rahul ride. Besides, he's a nice guy.'

Her: 'OK, but don't regret this later. What's between you and Malini, anyway? Do you like her as much as she likes you?'

Me: 'I don't know if she likes me. I don't know how I feel, anyway.'

Her: 'Do you like me?'

178 *Touching Distance: The Great Indian MBA Dream*

Me: 'Look, I can't be just an option for you. I can't help feeling the way I do, but I will live through this nonsense that I'm going through.'

Her: 'OK. I'm just glad I know where we stand.'

Me: 'You've told him you're going to ask me out?'

Her: 'Don't be silly. In any case, I'd have wanted to go as a friend only. I am with Rahul and I'm pretty sure of that.'

Me: 'Oh yeah, I'm the nice, harmless south Indian guy who can chaperone you, right? You know what, I never did think you could be so farsighted.'

Her: 'Well, relax. I don't think of you any other way.'

Me: 'What, I'm no longer Plan B boyfriend material?'

Her: 'He-he-he . . . you definitely are Plan B boyfriend and Plan B marriage material. You're pretty cool!'

Me: 'You and your problems. Since when have you become a sadistic? I have to go now. In any case, stop playing yo-yo with me. It's not funny . . . not anymore.'

Her: 'OK, OK . . . relax. I do like you, you know that, right?'

Me: 'Yeah, in some Plan B chaperone kind of way.'

Her: 'Well, yes, but . . . '

Me: 'But what? You don't like me enough?'

Her: 'I guess so . . . I don't know . . . I'm a woman . . . sometimes I can like more than one person, can't I?'

Me: 'Sure you can, just as long as it doesn't include me in your consideration set. Now, good night.'

Click.

18

Valentine's Day

Please forgive me, if I act a little strange
For I know now what I do
Feels like lightning running through my veins
Every time I look at you

—David Gray

It was Valentine's Day. As far as I was concerned, it was going to be pretty uneventful, considering that the other twenty-six before this one were dull as sand. I mean, you have all these cards and roses on sale. Just no one you would want to buy them for. Hallmark would be so much more profitable if they bundled women with the cards and roses.

As for me, I wondered which sentiment to choose this year: 'It will happen someday,' which also sells cards, or 'Screw it,' which leaves Hallmark in the lurch. Not too many cards or money in those dispassionate emotions. I chose the latter. I was pretty convinced I was the dispassionate kind of guy. Especially when there was no passion anywhere in sight. Anyway, that's not the point here.

There I was, sitting in the cafeteria with some friends and having a great laugh discussing the effort of one young lad who

180 *Touching Distance: The Great Indian MBA Dream*

had sent roses to all the ladies on campus. He didn't even spare the married ones. I know for a fact that some pretty girls got a bouquet. He put a nice forty-five degree line between beauty and number of roses. Good lad. Success or failure, he sure left his name etched on the flower market in Hyderabad. There's a role model for all the struggling men of this world. Anyway, before you get carried away, I should hasten to add that it may have set him back by a few thousands, but it sure as hell did not get him whatever it was he was trying to get.

That much was apparent from his face as he sat having lunch with us, and dreading the truth in the general banter that the husbands' association was calling an urgent meeting and hiring some local goons to take care of 'rose boy'.

I remember sitting with Capt and a few others at lunch, having a laugh at the lad's expense. Sitting a little further on was Priyanka, who needed little or no introduction to anyone who had anything to do with ISB. Suffice it to say that she was either ahead of her time or behind it, but she certainly didn't belong to 2003. I suspect that realisation was in the process of attempting to dawn over her. However, that realisation probably ran to the hills when she lit her next cigarette and blew in its face.

Diversity, diversity – the mantra of all new age B-Schools. We will have wild animals in class a few years from now, for sure I pity those animals. Anyway, to amuse myself (I had finished eating and found nothing better to do), I began singing to her. I'd got to know her a little and while this would surprise her, it certainly would not be met with anger. I'd become a little bolder at the ISB – the place does change you. As for the singing and putting people in a spot of surprise, it's the kind of thing I did sometimes. Just for kicks, you know. Not that I did it out of dislike. I was curious and loved pushing their buttons. Some reacted just the way I wanted them to. Others didn't. I learnt, I tried – it was a nice game. A little dangerous at times, but fun anyway.

Valentine's Day **181**

The singing was just the kind of thing that gave her the much-needed reassurance that was her oxygen for all practical purposes. She ran the standard sequence: I'm pretty, boys know it, they sing to me, oh God, why did you make me so pretty!

She responded with the rather predictable 'Why is he singing to me,' spoken as loudly as her fake accent would allow. Anywhere else, heads would have turned, but not in this case. Nobody was listening to her. People learn from experience.

All those around the table had a good laugh and Capt and I headed back to the quad. He made some esoteric observations about human nature and humanity's insatiable search for appreciation.

We walked through the door and saw Ranga sitting in his usual position on the couch staring listlessly at the TV. He looked at us sideways and seemed to disapprove of our presence. A few of my devious neurons fired and something struck me.

'Ranga, Priyanka was looking for you. You son of a bitch, you gave her a rose, didn't you? She said so herself. She wants to thank you, bugger . . . congratulations!'

Capt joined in without batting an eyelid. '*Abbe, kya kar raha hai aajkal?* Huh, Ranga? Didn't know you had a soft corner for her, man. You never told us. She was down in the cafeteria asking us about you. We were shocked, *yaar*. We told her we didn't know where you were. How long have you been in love with her?'

Encouraged, I carried on, 'Where did you get the rose from? From the same guy who supplied Jai? Great going! Dude, are you going out for dinner tonight?'

The spontaneity of our attack woke the sleeping animal and shook him into action. Ranga had that sinking look. His eyes actually opened and his face was quickly losing his postdump zen calm. 'Fuck off. You pricks, you're just lying. I didn't send anyone any rose.' His tone, though, had more fear than conviction. I think the fact that we caught him just after a nap may have calmed his grey cells into believing us.

182 *Touching Distance: The Great Indian MBA Dream*

I climbed right on top immediately. I hadn't expected him to be this easy.

'Look, *yaar*, she seemed a little angry. I think she may have gone to the Dean with this. You'd better call her up or send her an email and sort this out as fast as you can. You'd better hurry, dude.' Ranga did fear authority and the Dean was someone Ranga was trying to impress for some reason. Now the urgency in my voice and my suggestions were too much information – he had to get working. It's like a freak accident. You have no time to wonder *why* it's happening; all you can do is roll, roll, roll.

Ranga rushed into his room, muttering to himself. He began raining Kannada curses on Priyanka and the two of us. He still wasn't sure, but he was shaken for certain. It doesn't take much to shake Ranga out of his boots. And when he panics, he really can't put a sequence of cogent thoughts together. Note that the phrase 'cogent thought' in Ranga's context does not amount to redundancy.

He rushed into his room and did not emerge. Capt and I were beside ourselves with success. I sensed that this may be a little more fun if it lasted a little longer. I rushed to my room and shot off emails to Priyanka and her quad-mates, asking them to play along. It worked like a charm.

After more leg pulling, Ranga had simply lost it. He had sent Priyanka a stinker of an email. The email read: 'Priyanka, I want to make it perfectly clear that I have no interest in you. I did not send you a rose today. Whoever sent you that rose, it sure wasn't me.'

That evening Priyanka called Ranga and thanked him for the rose. When he said that it wasn't him, she said that it was OK for him to be shy and she knew how he felt. I couldn't have done it better myself. Ranga pleaded, 'Ma'am, I swear I didn't send you a rose. It's a prank.' I couldn't believe he was calling her 'Ma'am'! I had no idea he was that scared.

Later that night, Surabhi, Priyanka's friend, went a step ahead and shouted to Ranga from across the lawns, 'Ranga, you gave Priyanka a rose! What about me? Where's my rose?'

Valentine's Day **183**

I was a genius, and if Sir Isaac Newton were around, he would have applauded.

Well, Ranga didn't know what hit him. The snipers were all over the place. He finally pinned the blame on Capt and me, saying, 'I don't know who did this! But you know . . . I think it's you pricks, OK? I mean, like . . . I don't know why you do these things, OK? Like, if you wanted to give her a rose why were you giving it on my behalf! Yes, yes . . . you guys have given a rose saying it's from me. Pricks, I didn't give any rose. Fuck off, OK?'

It was hilarious. Finally, Surabhi broke the truth to Ranga the next day. Capt and I had the laugh of our lives and Ranga was OK in a couple of days. I don't know if he spoke to Priyanka after that. I'm guessing he didn't. Ranga wondered what was next.

Years later, after we graduated, I called Ranga at work, pretending to be a Citibank employee. I politely informed him that there existed an outstanding amount of rupees five lakhs on his credit card. He hadn't made a payment for the last three months. I asked him if he'd like to convert it to a short term loan at twenty-two percent failing which, I would be required to have him meet with collection agents at his office. When he protested and said there was a mix-up, I told him I knew his office address and his official phone number, so I had the right person and there was no mistake. I called him ten minutes later, and he said he couldn't talk then because he was desperately busy trying to call Citibank to clean up a misunderstanding. He sounded like his bowels were about to burst.

'I mean, like . . . you know. *Faak*, these bastards are trying to fleece me. I mean, I don't even have a Citibank card. I mean, I have to like, call you . . . like later or something.'

I couldn't take it anymore. I let the cat out of the bag. Ranga was upset for a day but forgave me again.

❖

184 *Touching Distance: The Great Indian MBA Dream*

Me: 'Hello.'

Her: 'Hey, I'm sorry.'

Me: 'What's up with your phone? I've been trying your number since eight and there was no answer. I thought we were supposed to meet at 8.30!'

Her: 'I know, I know.'

Me: 'What the hell happened?'

Her: 'Well, Rahul surprised me.'

Me: 'Huh?'

Her: 'Well, he showed up at my door just as I was getting ready and he took me out for dinner.'

Me: 'OK . . . and you couldn't call me?'

Her: 'I . . . forgot, I'm sorry.'

Me: 'Gosh, you're unbelievable, you know that?'

Click.

Her: 'Hello.'

19

Strategically Yours

Remember when you were young
You shone like the Sun
Shine on you crazy diamond

—Pink Floyd

'What are your aspirations?' asked Sumant Singh, the manicured partner, looking secure in the security that only an Armani suit could provide. Security from the penetrating client looks of suspicion and disdain.

'I mean, like . . . I want to change things strategically. I mean, I don't think you guys think straight? I mean, like . . . imagine starting a call centre for retail . . . like B2C in India. I mean, like . . . people should be able to call McKinsey and ask for strategic advice, OK?' said Ranga during the interview.

'Oh, how interesting. What would they require advice on?' cooed Sumant, in a voice calibrated to turn on Jeff Immelt's soul and open GE's wallet, should the opportunity arise.

'Yeah . . . I was getting to that when you interrupted me. OK, so here's the use-case. I mean, like . . . please don't interrupt my flow of thought. You already did that once. I mean, like . . . my

186 *Touching Distance: The Great Indian MBA Dream*

time is short, so listen. Whether or not I take this job is irrelevant. What matters is that your business benefits and I am able to add some value with my values. OK? So, I mean, like . . . any individual should be able to call like . . . a milkman who wants to make better milk, or say a housewife who wants to understand how to make better kids. Or like a guy who wants to buy a better tyre for his bicycle. Or say, a fruit vendor who wants to sell sweeter mangoes, or oranges that provide the best RoI on a one-day horizon. I mean, can you imagine the opportunities? I mean, you guys don't think big. I mean, in India, we have like one million . . . Oh, sorry, we have like . . . ten billion . . . or is it one billion? Yeah, it's like a big number and you guys don't see the market. I mean, if each piece of advice can be sold for one rupee each, you have a trillion dollar business. I mean, do you see the model?'

Sumant, and the other partner in the interview, Ranjeev Chopra, felt their souls rise to the roofs of their small hearts. The promised consultant had arrived. They had stumbled on a rare genius. While they wanted badly to pour out their hearts' problems and those difficult spreadsheets to Ranga, they held back. As manicured consultants they had a job to do – they had to act stiff and disinterested.

Ranjeev interjected, 'Mr Ranga, you have posed some interesting ideas. Where would you locate this call centre and how many seats would you have?' Ranjeev had the answers nailed having sold some packaged analysis to some old white guy a month ago. He was not prepared for what was to strike him.

'Ha-ha-ha ha! Are you sure this is a good way to spend my time? I mean, like . . . why don't you refer to my blog on the strategic importance of call centres? I am running it as a service to my US CEO friends. I have some spreadsheet-based RoI calculators that you can rip off there. I mean, usually that's something you are used to, aren't you? Some of them are so simple even you can use them. I mean, you just input the location and RoI you need and it will

Strategically Yours **187**

spit out your list of options ordered by my Ranga Scalability Index. Michael Porter called me about using it in his own research. I told him that he can do that if he calls me the sixth force . . . ha-ha-ha . . . the old geezer, I mean he agreed, OK?'

'Oh, that's very impressive, Mr Ranga. Would you like to tell us why you came dressed in *chappals*, shorts and a vest for this interview? I believe most of your peers dressed in suits and ties,' continued Sumant, noticing that Ranjeev was wiping the sweat from his face.

'Oh well . . . I mean, like . . . I'm usually dressed like this. Even when the Dean comes to pay his respects he usually finds me dressed in just the vest. Well, because . . . in those cases, I am usually crapping in the toilet. I mean, that's when I'm most creative. You can also come. Just make sure you let me know in advance. Anyway, I think my peers need the suits to create an impression. Usually I've never had to dress well. Actually . . . you will be surprised to know that I haven't combed my hair since I began my year here. It doesn't affect my grades.'

Impressed, Sumant said, 'Mr Ranga, we would like you to meet our CEO, Mr Jack Welsh.'

'Oh, when did Jack join McKinsey? That's OK, I'll meet him anyway. Send him in.'

The CEO of McKinsey entered and bowed dramatically. He then bent on one knee and said, 'Mr Ranga would you do us the honour of joining McKinsey as VP of Strategy? Please don't disappoint me.'

Ranga leant back and laughed. 'I mean, like . . . yeah, let's see. I also have to think about Goldman Sachs, and the World Bank. My decision will be based not on monetary needs, but simply on who needs the most assistance strategically. I mean, you guys have some talented people. You will do just fine.'

'But Mr Ranga, I will do anything to have you join McKinsey. What do you want?' begged Jack Welsh.

188 *Touching Distance: The Great Indian MBA Dream*

'Don't worry, Jack. I mean, like . . . first let me talk to Porter. He wanted some help completing his new book,' said Ranga, and excusing himself, left the room.

On his way out, he stepped on a banana peel and slipped rather heavily, his head hitting the cold ground.

'Bastard banana skin,' he thundered.

He opened his eyes and saw his *chappals* placed under his bed. The dream was over.

Be that as it may, it was never about the odd dream for the great Ranga. He lived in a world that he had created with a great deal of effort. In this world, things were simple: profits were good, so was revenue; cost was bad. It was ridiculously simple. As he understood it, the MBA was a huge attempt to de-layer this one truth, complicating it with cash flows, RoIs, present value, life-time value, etc., in an attempt to hide the small and simple truth.

In his own mind, Ranga firmly believed that he had stumbled upon a miraculous piece of insight that no one else had. In the cocoon of his reality, he promised himself that he would live by the dictum of strategic thinking, and that he would never worry about the detail.

As well as it worked for him, it would have iconoclastic ramifications for every group member, one of whom was humble me.

His dreams were about to be tested as interview season had begun.

Over tea the next morning, Capt, Ranga and I sat around a table, working out our battle-plan for interviews.

The following things are employed by the ISB students at interview time. It's quite stunning how capable students can be when it comes to bring spontaneous.

1. Resume writing sessions – School-conducted and student-initiated.
2. Resume review – School-conducted and student-initiated.

Strategically Yours **189**

3. Interviewing teams (sized two, three) – student-initiated.
4. One-to-one mock interviews – industry-related.
5. One-to-one mock interviews – non-industry-related.
6. Reading and sharing of relevant Harvard Business Review articles.
7. Reading multiple issues of *The Economist*.
8. Sharing of opinions on pertinent government stances on business licensing issues.
9. Valuation problems faced by industries – high technology, especially in the area of new technology.
10. Interview sessions by students who had worked in target industries. For example, engineers aspiring to enter finance would be interviewed by CAs who had previously held bank jobs.

Knowing that we'd be no good as a team when it came to interviews, we decided to find a bunch of blokes who we didn't know at all, so that we don't end up spending most of our time laughing our arses off.

Working with strangers is the superior option. In fact, that's the perfect simulation, isn't it? You want to start with someone completely unbiased and see what kind of impression you are able to make.

Depending on our aspirations, we picked our interview-partners appropriately. Most teams were formed in a span of two weeks or so, leading to the start of the season.

❖

Her: 'Hello. Hey, before you hang up, please tell me one thing. Did you like the roses?'
Me: 'Roses, really! You girls know what men want, don't you?'
Her: 'Stop being sarcastic.'
Me: 'Look, I know you're trying to make up and everything, but I really think you need to think things through for yourself.'

190 *Touching Distance: The Great Indian MBA Dream*

Her: 'Yeah, I'm really confused . . . I see you and I think, I'd be lucky to be with someone who cares so much. But I think of him and I'm confused as hell. How am I going to blow him off after all this?'

Me: 'I really wish you didn't exist. People like you don't deserve the emotions you evoke.'

Her: '. . . Please . . . don't say that.'

Me: 'I really do. I just hate this . . . this quagmire.'

Her: 'You haven't forgiven me yet?'

Me: 'I haven't forgiven myself for letting myself get carried away. You don't even figure.'

Her: 'Oh God . . . '

Me: 'You know what, I have half a mind to call Rahul and tell him what you're confused about.'

Her: 'You wouldn't do that.'

Me: 'I don't think I would, but I'm beginning to believe that it is about time I did.'

Her: 'You dare not.'

Me: 'Sorry, sweetheart, unbelievable as it may sound, looks like I'm the one with the leverage.'

Click.

20

The Roll of the Dice

So make the best of this question known as Why
It's not a question, but a lesson learned in time
It's something unpredictable, but in the end there's right
I hope you have the time of your life

—GREEN DAY

It was about 9.30 pm. I walked down a long hallway, which was lit, but insufficiently so, given the darkness of the anticipation in my heart. It was February and was already getting warm in Hyderabad. It didn't help that I was wearing a new black suit and tie. Ludicrous, I thought to myself. Who the hell invented suits anyway?

I'd showered and shaved, and dabbed on some after shave. I'd looked at myself in the mirror and had practiced my smile. My polite, non-threatening, affable smile. A smile that evoked a well-researched and specific response from the person at the other end of the handshake – 'What a nice guy. So purposeful, yet so nice. It has to be good *karma* to hire him.'

I looked at my watch. I was ten minutes ahead of my scheduled interview at eGateway, a company that created more

192 *Touching Distance: The Great Indian MBA Dream*

questions than it answered. Their HR manager, the guy who was involved in the process of head-hunting people for interviews, was a guy who liked to call himself 'Jon'. His real name was Gyanesh Perambur. I'd googled him earlier in the day. Jon was on a list of black-listed recruiters accused of 'body-shoppping' people into the United States on H1-B visas obtained on the basis of dressed-up, and sometimes downright false, resumes. Of course, he'd done this while working for an 'IT-Consulting' company. The truth is the company did very little consulting. The best service they sold was by a phantom IT company in the US, who would be able to legally banana-boat people into the shores of the promised land.

What was I doing with them? Good question. March 2003, this was approximately eighteen months after two planes crashed into the WTC. The world was never to be the same again. War, followed by an economic recession, had struck the world. We were reliably informed that placements at Kellogg, Wharton and LBS were bleaker than ever. The MBA dream was slowly becoming a debt-ridden nightmare for most people around the world. All those companies which were regular recruiters at B-Schools – McKinsey, Lehmann Brothers, Goldman Sachs, Citibank, etc., were all either postponing their hiring plans or openly stating their intention to hire fewer numbers. The Placement Cell had worked overtime to convince these companies to show up, but they were dragging their feet. The star-studded ISB board was being asked to rally around to make things happen. A disaster that once seemed unlikely, now stood at our doorstep, axe in hand.

The Placement Cell threw caution to the winds. It didn't help that the people who are responsible for these functions in the early years of a school aren't really the best people for these jobs. Companies that made coconut oil and companies that were trying to make cheap medicines were implored to come by and recruit. The usual suspects from the IT services industry were treated with more respect that they'd ever been given. The latter smelt the coffee

The Roll of the Dice **193**

really quickly. An IT-Services vendor with no particular history in technology made it clear that unless they were allowed to recruit on Day Zero, they would simply not show. Day Zero is the evening before Day One of placements. The truth of the matter was that these people could recruit Arts majors for their jobs, with no difference to their business model. They knew it, and they'd decided this was their best opportunity to go for the broke. They were first in line at the museum sale to buy any Monet they wanted, and they were not going to pass up that opportunity.

And there you had it: the least sought-after IT services company had arrived on Day Zero, before the banks and management consulting companies.

Why should a student care? A student cared because it was eminently possible that the other companies may never arrive. So you had to take your chances.

Of course, there was a catch-22 situation at play here, just like everywhere else in life when you are in a spot and can't go left or right. There was a cap on the number of offers a student could receive. This was to ensure that placements were made available to all students and not to a handful who bagged a bunch of offers they were certain to turn down. Communism was at play in the confines of the sanctum sanctorum of the temple of greed. A catch-22 with some ironic poetry thrown in, how about that? In all fairness, this restriction, or variation of it, applied at every major B-School in the world, so one really couldn't complain. It was just the sequence in which the companies arrived, that was upsetting.

This upper-limit of offers you could be made was 'two'. Read that again. TWO. The moment you were made two offers, you had to exit the system. Classic. Screwed if you're hired, screwed if you're not.

Let's go back in time, to Day Zero of the placements.

❖

194 *Touching Distance: The Great Indian MBA Dream*

DAY ZERO
Part 1

The tone for the student resistance to the oppressive circumstances had been set by Vishal. Vishal came to the ISB with over ten years of consulting experience, a B.E. and a Master's. At thirty-two, he was married and had a child. He was the first one in our batch to begin salary negotiations. The recruiting company was the consulting division of the IT services company mentioned earlier. Let's just call it ITServ for now.

'Ten lakhs is as far as we can go. The economy is bad and we have no idea when things will recover,' they said.

'I'm sorry, given my experience and education, I can't accept that.'

'What is your expected compensation?' came the query.

'I expect to get paid fifteen lakhs plus a variable component.'

'I'm sorry, I don't think we can make that kind of offer. As I said before, the economy is bad and you should be happy you're getting a job.'

'I'm sorry, gentlemen, this conversation is over and I have to leave. Your offer makes no sense and your attitude suggests you are at the wrong bus stop,' said Vishal before leaving.

They looked on flabbergasted. On the campus, the news of this interaction was met with warmth. We were not going to be pushed around by these vultures! Vishal was the icon of the student community. Later that day, the company buckled and met his very reasonable demand. Given his resume, they'd make far more from his overseas billing time. Mind you, this was 2003 and it was a reasonable expectation. It's a salary you would scoff at today.

Earlier that day, another division of ITServ had organised group discussions to separate the wheat from the chaff, so to speak. Never mind the fact that the recruiters from these companies were nowhere near qualified to assess these students. The students certainly had more knowledge, and in some cases, more work experience, than

The Roll of the Dice **195**

those sitting in front of them, trying to make hiring decisions. This was a unique problem at the ISB and continues to be till this day. The ISB is the first B-School in India requiring work experience for admissions. While the spread of work-experience varies, it can be disconcerting for an interviewer to be faced with a candidate who had previously been a manager for several years before he came to the ISB, while the interviewer himself had just become one.

It was humiliating for most students to be part of this charade. Had it not been for the debt sitting on everyone's head and the fact that a couple of planes had flown tragically into a couple of very important buildings in the First World, the tables might have turned. These recruiters may have received a handful of applications, and it was likely that the number of applications might just have been fewer than the number of openings they wanted to fill. Now, they were confronted with the cream of the class trying to outwit each other to grab the rope that hung above the lifeboat, while their Titanic sank in the background.

These group discussions were not pretty. Indian students are competitive at the best of times, and when it came to a zero-sum game such as this one, courtesy was thrown to the winds. There were those who hogged the airtime at the expense of all decency, making complete assess of themselves.

I had one such jackass in my group. The moment the topic was announced, he said something for five minutes, then asked a girl in the group what she thought. No sooner had she opened her mouth and inhaled some air, and no sooner than the air had reached her lungs, and no sooner than her blood vessels had received the oxygen in that air that he stopped her short with a 'No, I disagree with you! I think . . .' blah, blah, blah.

The argumentative Indians, indeed. This continued throughout the group discussion, and was a feature of other group discussions as well. Generally speaking, the students more keen on preserving dignity backed off and kept quiet. It worked. Most of those who kept quiet or said very little, but made sense, were invited to the

196 *Touching Distance: The Great Indian MBA Dream*

second stage – the interview. In case you were wondering, the jackass didn't make it past this group discussion, and several other group discussions in due course of time.

Anyway, the point is, the whole exercise was a nuisance and downright unnecessary at an institute where the students' resumes spoke for themselves. You really don't need a shouting match to know that someone was worth it.

As for the interviews, the standard interviewing procedures did not really work at the ISB from an interviewer's perspective. An interviewer, and now I speak of an average interviewer, expects to probe weaknesses, so he/she can feel better about themselves. This may not be true all the time, but this is certainly true most of the time; I reckon maybe sixty to eighty percent of the time. The whole purpose of interviewing is grossly misunderstood in India. The interviewer feels like he hasn't done his job if he hasn't thrown a few questions that didn't come back unanswered.

The effort seems to be one that probes lacunae, not substance. Between the extremes of finding a fit employee and exposing an unfit one, most Indian interviewers will lean towards the latter. This must be cultural in some sense. We are a suspicious lot here in India; having grown up on so much bad news about people being cheated and duped, on the one hand, while blindly believing in saints and gods, on the other, when we are asked to assess the value of something abstract, like a human being, we just don't know how to do it. We are wary of trusting, simply because interviews are not in a religious context but outside it. We are prone to being suspicious, because spotting a fraud is, after all, a sign of intelligence in our culture, isn't it? You can't blame us. There are so many unscrupulous people around in India, and we don't spend a day without meeting twenty of them. From people selling us things in the street to companies that exist in thin air, to fake watches and bad cars, we have it all.

I was asked a few questions about my resume, no doubt to expose the vagaries therein, but the interviewers failed.

The Roll of the Dice **197**

To the interviewers, I'd like to say – 'Well, you idiots, *I* wrote that resume.'

If I was smart enough to get here and be among the top fifteen percent of a hyper-competitive class, I knew what to say if you asked me questions on what I'd written. Anyway, my panel had four or five people, all attempting to look serious and scholarly like Supreme Court judges attempting to throw a murderer in jail. One of them did most of the questioning.

There were the usual questions that you can count on in these interviews. I have cooked up some honest answers, just so you know what not to say. The 'what you should say' answers, given below, are just politically correct responses; they don't by any means claim to be the best invented, but you should get the drift if such questions are ever thrown at you.

Q: Why did you do an MBA?

Honest Answer (HA): To have this opportunity to look at your priceless face while you ask me the most predictable of questions on a B-School campus, you jackass. Like everyone else, I did it to get rich. At least I thought I'd get rich. And we don't quite know how this story ends, so let's move on, moron. By the way, why are you wasting time asking me this?

What you should say (WYSS): I did it to add value to myself as a professional. I knew I'd be able to contribute more meaningfully if I had knowledge of the multiple functions that are at play in the corporate world. Moreover, I knew that I would benefit from a formal knowledge of subjects such as finance, marketing and strategy.

Q: Why did you do an MBA from the ISB?

HA: Because it's a good school and the GMAT is a more sensible entry-criterion than an exam like the CAT, which disqualifies you if you have to sneeze thrice and end up losing time because you couldn't circle all those black holes on that piece of paper. And also because ISB accepted me . . . and because I was able to get a loan. Besides, where the hell is a working professional going to find the time to do twenty practice-tests a day for a whole year?

198 *Touching Distance: The Great Indian MBA Dream*

WYSS: The ISB is an institute that was founded on the premise that globalisation is an irreversible force in the new economy. Everything the school set out to do, from creating a curriculum, to sourcing international faculty, to inviting people, is aligned with that premise, and I haven't been disappointed.

Q: What was your experience like? What have you learnt?

Q: What has been your biggest learning?

... so on and so forth.

When they'd listened to answers to every single question in their notes, including why I wanted to join their great IT services organisation, they chose a slightly different line of questioning. This is the interviewer grasping for straws:

1. How can you motivate employees who have already resigned?
2. How can you motivate employees who have given up?
3. How can you motivate employees who have not been given raises or hikes for five years?

To their utter amazement, I had answers to these questions as well. My answers simply in the right order, were:

1. You can't.
2. You can remind them they still have a job, i.e., they had something to lose, and that giving up is not an option ever. Moreover, you can move them to a different environment, a new project, to see if that helps.
3. You could ask them if they wanted a transfer to another group or a different location, like the Swiss Alps. After all, you have businesses everywhere, don't you? Lastly, you could remind them they could lose their jobs. If they could leave by themselves, they would have left after five years of a painful wait. That's why GE fires their bottom ten percent every year. You have a lot of people in every company who hate being there, but also cannot get hired

elsewhere, and you can motivate them by reminding them of reality, which you will anyway bring to bear on them when push comes to shove.

I walked out of the room, feeling like I'd done the job I had come to do. Mission accomplished. They'd make their offer.

It's often said that interviews are irrevocably decided in the first thirty seconds. In that time, you have decided that you either want to hire the candidate or not. It is also equally true in my humble opinion that the candidate most certainly knows what the outcome is in the last thirty seconds of the interview. The body language of the interviewer in that period is just a dead giveaway.

❖

DAY ZERO
Part 2: Macrohard

Macrohard Inc. was seeking to fill the positions for program manager, which was a reasonably well-paid role in their company; as in, it was meaningful and sensible. While they paid well, the downside was that such roles had very little marketing or finance exposure. The majority time in this role was spent hassling engineers to do something, and being an engineer, I knew this was not a pleasant job. Engineers, especially those in software, can be a painful bunch. Software is not really a tangible engineering science like cars and bikes and buildings. There are imperfect ways to gauge progress and you don't really know how good something is until you are hit with its failure. Besides, talking to engineers means you have to be familiar with their tools and their language. Which means you were tied to yet another desk in yet another glass cage with yet another Stockholm Syndrome. At least here the kidnapper paid you well for your time. In any case, with all jobs in the IT industry, chances are you would never get to apply all those cool things you learnt at the ISB. Which is a tragedy for both the company and the employee.

200 *Touching Distance: The Great Indian MBA Dream*

I was pretty drained after my group discussions for ITServ, and their interview had taken the better part of an hour. It seemed like each one of the idiots on the panel was super-keen to test their interviewing skills.

The moment I stepped out of the interview room, I was asked to appear for the Macrohard interview. They had short-listed eleven or so students from the large list, and I was one of them. Given their world leading status, I was pretty happy at being shortlisted.

I looked at the coordinator and said, 'Look, I need a break. I just came out of there.'

'Sorry, you have to go in. We can't keep them waiting,' was the reply.

In hindsight, I wish I'd been more stern then.

I walked in, shook hands and sat down.

'Have you just been through an interview?' he asked.

'Yes, I guess it shows,' I replied.

'Okay, let's start with a puzzle,' he said.

Macrohard is legendary for throwing puzzles at you. I have no idea why they do it, but this drives me up the wall. I've always considered myself a right-brained thinker. I can intuit, I can abstract and glean and I can see patterns, but I'm not exactly someone who spends all his spare time working on puzzles.

There were two real problems with this approach. Firstly, not everyone who can solve puzzles is necessarily smart, but I have no idea why Macrohard still persists with this approach! Most modern problems involve synthetic skills, not analytical skills. Yes, there is a way to learn to solve the Rubik's cube, and every other puzzle out there. In fact, most puzzles can be reduced to types, much like movies which finally are slotted into one genre or another. Solutions to bounded problems don't necessarily require inspiration. After all, synthesis or composition is the higher skill. We created computers to break down problems into smaller bits and solve them, didn't we?

The second problem is that the questions which were relevant for hiring programmers or people who needed to have this bare-

The Roll of the Dice **201**

bones problem-solving capability, were being used here. I would rather that he gave me a business problem Macrohard was facing and asked me how I'd go through thinking about that.

Such were the problems with interviewers. They cared very little about understanding the context of the place, time or the person in front of them. They had a bunch of questions that they had been using for eons and they wanted to throw them at you till the cows came home.

He threw me a puzzle about something I don't really remember and despite my tired mind, I made some headway. When I realised it wasn't going particularly well, I decided to come clean.

'Look, I'm not really great at puzzles. I have to be honest about this. Besides, I just walked out of a three-hour process with this other company and I don't think I'm ready for a puzzle at this point,' I said.

He looked at me blankly. What the hell was this? Was I actually turning down an opportunity to solve one of his hallowed puzzles?

He changed tracks and asked me how I'd go about designing an elevator system for a hundred-floor building. A better question.

I responded with a range of requirements, everything from speed and safety, to load-balancing and timing requirements. I also talked about differential priorities for more expensive apartment blocks and the suchlike. I talked about voice activation for the disabled and lower buttons for children to reach. I talked about emergency cameras, power backup and what not. I basically threw everything that came to my mind about elevators in a super-highrise. I could barely get all the thoughts out in time. My brain kept cranking out requirement after requirement for a super-sophisticated elevator and my mouth could barely keep up with the torrent of ideas.

After a few more questions, I was done. I walked out completely sapped. I got to my room, took off my suit, and went in for a shower. I returned to my room, lay back on my bed and gazed at the ceiling. The gravity of the situation began to weigh upon me.

202 *Touching Distance: The Great Indian MBA Dream*

I knew I'd botched up the Macrohard interview. Firstly, I should never have gone in when I was already mentally fatigued. I should have bought time. I would have got it had I pushed really hard or even walked away. Of course Macrohard would have been happy to talk to me whenever I showed. They had enough interest in someone who had worked for a nice, shiny glasscage.

Secondly, even if I'd gone in, I really shouldn't have backed away from the puzzle. These things are weird. Even if you can't recognise the pattern at first, if you look at them long enough, the answer just surfaces. My anger at being asked to solve a puzzle in a B-School interview had got the better of me.

Thirdly, and this was perhaps my biggest error, I had not packaged my answer to the elevator question. I had not applied any formal design principles in answering the elevator question. I should have read his mind. This guy was probably an engineering manager and placed a huge emphasis on someone's formal application of frameworks for design. I should have prefaced my answer by saying:

'All design problems have functional and non-functional aspects. Non-functionally, the design should be:

- Scalable
- Performant
- Available
- Reliable
- Extensible
- Secure

'Then, functionally, the design should serve user-requirements arising out of business and user needs.

Business needs can be those pertaining to profitability and pricing, while user needs can arise out of demographics of the user community.'

I should have led with that. I had just blown it.

The Roll of the Dice **203**

All those days of mock interviewing with fellow classmates, poring over resumes and the stress had got to me. I knew what was going to happen.

I'd come off as personable, confident and excellent at the ITServ interview and had come off as a scatterbrain in the Macrohard one. I knew who would make me that offer, and I knew that I had wasted a decent opportunity, given the economic meltdown.

I closed my eyes and felt nothing but anger and desperation.

❖

It was in this context that on day two of placements, I attended my second interview, with eGateway. Justifiably, I had little or no respect for this company, (it was an opportunistic shop with little pedigree or reputation) but the money was good and this company was hiring people for Business Development roles in the United States. Hiring was still slow, and banks were really not arriving. Those who did, were amazed at the number of chartered accountants with prior experience at the top five accounting and consulting companies. The engineers did not have a chance. The odd engineer who was short-listed and did superbly well in his interviews was still edged out by the weight of prior experience that the CAs brought to the table.

I sat down in the waiting area, and picked up the *Economic Times*. Not that I expected these guys to ask me any questions from there, but I did so nevertheless. I walked in on cue and was faced with a similar panel of four interviewers, all dressed in black suits, all with anglicised versions of their Indian names. Jon was present. With him were Vivek or 'Viv', Sanjay or 'San', Srinivas or 'Srini', and so on. The same questions followed.

Then a few more I didn't expect.

'If we make you an offer, will you join?'

I must confess I wasn't prepared for this one. I know that the right thing to say was 'Of course, that's why I'm here,' but I went with something closer to the truth.

204 *Touching Distance: The Great Indian MBA Dream*

'It depends on the opportunity promised to me and the offer itself,' I said.

They probed more on that line of questioning. I wasn't quite sure what was up.

❖

The next morning, I received a call from Jon.

'Hi, the hiring committee has made a decision to make you an offer,' he said.

Hiring committee indeed, I thought to myself. What the hell was that? A bunch of guys with names that sounded smart? The only other place you'd find this phenomenon is in strip clubs where the girls call themselves 'Candy' or 'Heaven' or 'Eternity', etc.

'We've decided to make you an offer of eight lakhs. How does that sound? This is two lakhs more than you were making at your pre-MBA job,' he said.

Bear in mind that this was a depressed economy and salaries were not as high as they are these days, but I really didn't have a good feeling about this company. I didn't want this to count against one of my two offers. I was pretty certain that ITServ was going to make me an offer and it was going to be a pathetic one. I would rather buy fifty litres of oil, soak myself in it and buy a box of matches with the change.

'I'm sorry, but I can't accept this. I'd really expect something higher,' I said.

'Okay . . . I'm sorry we don't negotiate with candidates. Please call me in case you'd like accepting my first offer,' he said.

'Thank you,' I said, and hung up.

I shot off an email to a few others eGateway had contacted, and asked them if they had been made offers. They hadn't heard from eGateway yet but they had interesting information.

It was rumoured that their CEO was in a turf war with some of his American peers, and that he was planning on launching some kind of coup to get rid of them. He expected their people

The Roll of the Dice **205**

to leave pretty quickly once they'd gone, and he wanted to seed a bunch of his own faithful in those positions. The CEO had been reliably informed that they would be able to hire a set of sales guys from the ISB in India. Anyway, it was too convoluted for us to figure out.

I decided this was crazy. If things went wrong for this CEO, instead of sitting in the US selling IT services to an American over a lap dance in Las Vegas, I might just be sitting in India, either warming their bench or looking for another job at ITServ.

I walked into Capt's room, who had something to tell me.

'Dude, I've been screwed. I sent an email to one of the interviewers from ITServ, asking for a clarification on my designation and location. This is a different division from the one that interviewed you. They want to hire me in their Management Consulting group. Yeah, it sounds strange, but apparently they are creating one now,' he said.

'So, what's the problem?' I urged

'Apparently, that guy didn't like it. He's an ex-army guy and is totally into protocol. He turned out to be the senior director of the group. He's pissed that I wrote to him. He thinks I should have written to the HR folks. Now the HR guy calls me and says I should write an email apologising for my rudeness.'

I was shocked. Some fine company this ITServ was. It was somewhat ironic that an ex-army guy had decided to screw Capt, but being asked to apologise was just bizarre.

Who did these guys think they were?

'Screw them. They interviewed me like they were looking for a witch. This is what happens when you have a tyrannical jerk at the top. Everyone assumes that freaking visage,' I said.

I heard the phone ring and jogged back to my room. Still smarting from what I'd heard.

'Hello, this is Jon from eGatway,' said the voice

'Hi, Jon,' I replied, wondering if he'd dialled the wrong number.

206 *Touching Distance: The Great Indian MBA Dream*

'Well, the hiring committee has reconsidered its decision and decided to increase your salary to ten lakhs. Eight fixed and two variable. Would this work for you?'

I was pretty surprised. Ten minutes ago, this guy was going on and on about a take-it-or-leave-it offer.

I thought quickly and realised this wasn't what I wanted. Who knows what was lurking behind the scenes? And could a company that changed so quickly be trusted in the long run?

'I'm sorry, Jon. It's just not the right kind of offer. There are risks associated with this position and the business itself. Your operating margins have been shrinking and there is a downward pressure on pricing in the industry. Given this situation, it's not wise to count on the variable portion of the pay accruing,'

'No issues. If you change your mind, do call me back,' he said.

'Sure will,' I said and hung up.

I walked back into Capt's room and told him what had happened.

'What's going on with these blokes, *yaar*,' he said.

'Not sure. Any updates on your situation? What did you decide to do?'

'I'm not sure. I have to think about it. I'm finding this hard to swallow,' Capt said, sighing in confusion.

I was a little worried.

'Look, dude. There's a *New York Times* report that suggests things are going to get worse in the US. You should consider playing their game. What does it matter, anyway? It doesn't reflect on you, it reflects on that asshole,' I suggested in all honesty.

'Let me see, *yaar*. I'm not yet sure what to do,' he responded. His face carried the gravity of someone torn between reflex and reflection, of someone wanting to throw a punch, but trying to smile.

I decided to change the topic. 'Hmm . . . what happened to Ranga?' I asked.

The Roll of the Dice **207**

'I don't know. He said he was talking to TechPlant on his own. He didn't make it to the ITServ shortlist. Three days have gone by, and he's getting worried, too,' replied Capt.

'Doesn't matter, right? These are rolling placements. They will continue for the next two months or so,' I said

'That's true, but he's nervous all the same. There's always the danger that companies will start backing off when they know placements have been on for a while and the good people have already accepted offers,' he said.

'Yeah, that's always a danger. Who knows.'

'Exactly,' came the reply.

Ranga had been behaving strangely of late. He'd become more reclusive and carried a perpetual frown. He also had some kind of diarrhoea and was forever in the crapper. At stressful times like this, you notice it even more, especially when you have stress-related diarrhoea yourself and need an open, short, quick and clear path to your safe zone.

'So, what are you going to do about this email?'

'I don't know,' he said.

'OK, let me draft it for you. That might help,' I said and proceeded to key in an email from Capt's computer.

Given that I was not involved, and that tactically Capt needed to do this now, this was the only way this situation could be addressed with the least amount of friction to everyone. Capt could always walk out on them if he got another job.

I wrote an email saying that I was confused about the controversy and its inception, but that I was sorry nevertheless, and that I was keen on strong mentorship and guidance in an organisation I was going to join. Very gently, I aimed at letting the guy see what a dick he was being while appealing to his higher emotion of responsibility.

I turned to Capt and said, 'Read it and see what you think. I don't think you should care about this. If this is their game, play it without attachment. I'm not sure you should be taking a chance.

208 *Touching Distance: The Great Indian MBA Dream*

Look at this frigging economy. Even if there are companies coming in to recruit for finance jobs, we have sixty CAs waiting with an erection to jump on them.'

Capt nodded.

'Also, just think about it. Maybe they'll put you in the US or Europe and a year down the line, this will look like a great decision. Besides, you will probably never come face to face with this prick ever again,' I suggested.

Before Capt opened his mouth to speak, my phone rang again. Who could this possibly be?

'Hello, this is Jon again. The hiring committee has met again and we have decided to offer you nine lakhs in fixed pay and a three lakhs variable component. What would you say to that?' he asked.

'Umm . . . hi, Jon. That's nice of you. Can I get back to you on this one?' I said.

'Err, are you saying you need to think about this?'

'Umm . . . yes, a little. Please bear with me. I shall send you an email as soon as I'm ready.'

'We can't wait very long. I'm having the offers printed today.'

'I understand. I'll take a couple of days. I'm waiting to hear from another company and I'd like to see where things stand before I make up my mind. I hope that's okay.'

I walked back to Capt's room.

'You won't believe what just happened. They want to give me nine plus three,' I said.

'What! What's up with these guys, man? What did you do in the interview? Dance naked on the table or something? Your stock price seems to be going up every twenty minutes!'

'Well, I'm not sure what's going on,' I concluded.

I heard the door open, and Ranga walked in. He had a puzzled look on his face, his laptop bag slung over a shoulder and a few books in his other hand. He wore his cargo shorts and slippers.

He walked straight up to me then looked at Capt.

'I mean, like . . . I think I'm screwed . . . OK?' he said.

The Roll of the Dice **209**

We looked on supportively.

'I mean, like . . . these bastards, OK? They're not shortlisting me. I mean, tomorrow is, like, the third day, and I mean, like . . . TechPlant, they said like, they'd think about it. I mean, I told them I'd like to be the executive assistant to the CEO to get visibility and all that. I mean . . . I don't know. *Faak*, I think this MBA was like, a bad idea.'

'Look Ranga, relax. I'm sure there are going to be so many more opportunities,' I said.

'I don't know. I mean that bastard Bala, OK?, never let anyone talk in the group discussion. Son of a bitch. Who does he think he is? Doesn't he even have basic manners? One job dangling in front, and some people become fucking beasts. I want to fuck his ass with a knife!' yelled Ranga.

Capt and I smiled.

'It's humiliating, OK? Stop smiling. What do these bastards think? They see a chance and they want to walk all over us? Bastards. One guy on that panel. That prick actually applied to TechPlant two years ago and I rejected him. He didn't recognise me. I tell you, OK, this whole IT shit sucks. Unless you're two or three levels below the founders, you are just screwed. All you do is end up working for these losers and begging them to send you abroad. I'm sick of the thought.

'Today my father called, and I couldn't even tell him placements were underway. He asked me if he should sell some ancestral land just in case . . . I . . . I . . . ,' he turned around, his voice tapering to a whimper, as the tears began to roll.

'This whole MBA is a big mistake if the economy is bad, man. Big mistake,' he said in a shaking voice, as he wiped the tears from his face. He turned around and walked to his room, slamming the door shut behind him.

Capt and I were shell-shocked. We had never seen Ranga break down. I walked up to his door and knocked. There was no response. I knocked a few more times, Capt standing behind me. We finally gave up and went back to Capt's room.

210 *Touching Distance: The Great Indian MBA Dream*

'So, this is the river that runs beneath the lake, huh?' I asked.

'Yeah. I've never seen him like this. He's always been so disconnected,' Capt replied.

'What are you going to do about eGateway?' asked Capt, trying to change the topic.

'I don't know. It's too risky. I'm going to turn them down,' I replied.

I turned around and walked back to my room. I opened my mailbox. An offer from ITServ sat in my mailbox. The money was below par, and the acceptance deadline was two weeks away. I shut my laptop and went to sleep. I didn't have the heart to tell Ranga or Capt the news.

I woke up later that evening and went to the cafeteria. Dinner done, I returned to room. I sent an email to eGateway telling them it wasn't going to work for me. I stepped aside and wished them luck. I told them not to make me an offer.

I decided to continue interviewing. I had two weeks to find something else before I accepted ITServ.

❖

As the days rolled by, there was a lot going on. A small number of students tried to sabotage others who were competing at the same interview. Someone made a comment about someone's clothes while the latter was about to step into an interview, denting his confidence. Other students became more aggressive during group discussions, refusing to speak to each other outside the process. A pall of tension and gloom hung over the campus. The squash courts were empty, and people didn't swim as much. There were hurried interview preparations in the library and other meeting rooms. Couples who had received jobs in different cities fought. The fear plague had struck the institute, and all student life had come to a halt.

❖

The Roll of the Dice **211**

The following week, I received another offer from yet another IT services company but it was even lower than what I had already. I decided I was going to accept ITServ and take it from there. They had assured me that they would place me in the UK and they were certain of doing that as soon as my visa could be processed. It was enough for the time being. Having sent the email, I stepped out of my room. Ranga was not around. The door was shut. Strange, this had seldom happened.

I walked into Capt's room. Capt was on instant messenger with some girl. He turned around with a big smile on his face.

'Where's Ranga?' I asked.

'Oh, he's gone to that TCS interview. He's in the final round,' said Capt

'Great. Did you accept your offer?' I asked.

'Yeah, I did. For now, it will have to do. Let's see where things go from here,' he replied.

'Me too. Gosh, I really hope Ranga gets this job,' I said.

'Yeah, same here. I heard the interview coordinator say he's been losing it at the interviews. At times he comes across as being too eager. At other times he seems disinterested. At one interview he apparently told the interviewer that it really didn't matter who they picked for their role. Each person here could do that job with time to spare. At another, he apparently told the interviewer he would be happy to even take a pay cut to get the job.'

'Gosh. He's something, huh? None of that is working, it seems,' I said.

'No, it isn't,' said Capt.

Just then, the door blew open and Ranga came in. From the threshold of Capt's door, I saw him enter, then go straight to his room. His face was red with anger.

Capt stepped out and raised his eyebrows in question. I put a finger on my lips, indicating that all was not well.

212 *Touching Distance: The Great Indian MBA Dream*

We let things be and settled in the living room. We sat talking noiselessly, when Ranga emerged after forty minutes or so. He plonked himself down on the couch.

'It's over guys. I'm kind of . . . like, leaving here without a job. Got fucked again today. All gone . . . ' he said.

'What about TechPlant?' I asked.

'I don't know. I've been calling them and they keep saying they will get back to me. They just never do. There must be something seriously wrong with me if not even my previous employer wants me back,' he said sullenly.

'But you said you'd spoken to your former managers,' I said

'I did. They don't want to help. They say the economy's bad, and that they will do something if things get better. But what do I do till then? I have to start paying back my loan from next month. I can't borrow any more money from my father. I could never do that to him. He's just retired and he's going to have to apply for an extension or look for a job himself,' he said.

'Gosh . . . relax,' said Capt.

'Yeah, let's give it another week, Ranga,' I said.

'Nothing is going to happen, guys. Forget it . . .' he said.

'Come on dude, you're not giving up,' I walked over to his room and brought out his laptop.

'Where do you keep your resume? Did you update it after I told you to?' I asked.

He pulled out the corrected version. He hadn't made the updates I'd told him to. Typical Ranga, always believing he was right.

'Look, dude. Your resume has too much of the crappy tech detail. Just like mine did. We have to tone down the tech stuff,' I said.

'Let me see that,' said Capt.

Of the three of us, Capt was the most resume-savvy. It's amazing how good his resume looked when he was done with it. You'd hire him right off the bat to do anything from flying a rocket to stopping one midair.

The Roll of the Dice **213**

'Ranga, I'm going to work on this with him and I'll send it back to you this evening. We'll post it to the other companies that are to arrive this week and we'll see,' he said.

'Ok, for now, we are going out, dude. Let me call up Prosenjit. We can take his car,' I said.

That evening, we went to Hyderabad City. It was the second or third time we'd been out to the city. Work had been hectic and the only time we left the campus was to go to the railway station to get on a train home. For the hour or two that we were away, Ranga's depression eased a little.

We came back and gathered in Ranga's room, talking about the women on campus. Ranga was in better spirits and Capt went back to the living room to make some tea. Ranga put his legs up on the table and gazed at the ceiling. He was going to survive this, after all.

'I mean, like . . . Capt, if nothing else, you will get a job in a tea shop for sure,' said Ranga.

'Fuck you, asshole!' came the quick reply.

'I mean, like . . . I hope you'll sell me some tea on credit, OK?' said Ranga.

His eyes then veered towards the laptop screen. He swung his legs off the table. I walked over and looked from over his shoulder.

'TechPlant's email,' he whispered.

I felt his spirit soar in the time that the page took to load on the screen.

Dear Ranga,

I spoke to the hiring managers and they have assured me that they are unable to proceed with your candidature at the moment. We wish you good luck in your career.

Thanks,
Shilpa Pai,
Human Resources

214 *Touching Distance: The Great Indian MBA Dream*

Ranga's shoulders dropped and his breathing got quicker. For a minute I thought he was having a stroke. He switched off the laptop and sat down on his bed.

I felt I had to break the silence.

'Ranga, look. Don't despair. We have another week with companies lined up, at least. Something will work out next week,' I said.

Capt walked in with the tea and looked at Ranga.

'TechPlant dinged me,' said Ranga.

We drank the tea in silence. Capt brought his laptop to Ranga's room and sat together on the floor, making changes to his resume. There was a lot to be done. He had underestimated the value of resume quality, and it was probably influencing his interviews. It didn't help that his lack of confidence was combining with that resume to create doubt.

We sat there for hours, asking Ranga for inputs about what he'd done in his prior jobs, as we tried to clean up the text over and over again. Three hours later, at 3.00 am, we had the finished product.

All through, Ranga sat cross-legged, chin supported by his palm, staring vacantly out the window, muttering to himself. The thought of a breakdown in progress crossed my mind. It had happened to two others during the course, and I didn't want to bear witness to the third.

As I left his room that evening, the memory of a friend from yesteryear, who had committed suicide after failing two engineering courses, rushed into my mind. I banished the thought, but walked out furtively with Ranga's room keys in my pocket.

I stayed up for another hour, fighting fatigue, then walked up to his room and quietly unlocked the door. I'd read somewhere that most suicides happen between three and five in the morning. He was fast asleep. Key in hand, I walked back to my room.

❖

The Roll of the Dice **215**

Capt and I kept Ranga company for the next two days, to gauge his mood. He was still very low, but we convinced him that the new resume would change things. Two days later, he was short-listed again for a company in Bangalore, that was working on a new kind of technology product-outsourcing model called Build-Operate-Transfer, for software.

The Fellowship was in motion as we ploughed the internet for interview ideas and then began prepping Ranga.

Two days later was his final interview. Capt and I helped him pick the right shirt and tie. This one had better work, I prayed silently. Placements were close to an end. As Ranga walked out to the interview, Capt and I stepped out to go to our classes.

When we returned, Ranga was nowhere in sight. Worried, Capt reached for the phone.

'Hi, can you connect me to interview lobby, please?'

Then, 'Hi, is Ranga around? He is? Can you put him on?'

As I pushed the speaker button the voice came over the line. It was heavy and sullen.

'Hello.'

'Hey Ranga, all well? How's it going?'

'Going OK. I mean, like . . . it's hard. They were looking for people with finance backgrounds. My first two interviews didn't go so well. Almost like non-starters after the guy saw my credits. Like, no finance courses,' he said.

'OK. Do you have any more interviews?' I asked.

'Just one more. This is with their marketing VP. I mean, I don't have too much hope. Not sure, like . . . seems hard. No fit,' he sputtered.

'Look, Ranga. Just play to your strengths. Make sure you push the material on BOT really hard. All the stuff we've talked about. Lead with that. Don't let the interview lean towards marketing and finance. Assert that you are a strategy major and that you understand nuances of pricing BOT projects,' said Capt.

216 *Touching Distance: The Great Indian MBA Dream*

'Umm . . . I don't know. Like, I was planning to tell him that I don't really know finance,' he said.

'Ranga, tell him what you know. NOT what you don't know,' I urged. It's amazing how loss of confidence immediately shuts down the brain's self-defence, leaving one more vulnerable without even knowing it.

'OK. I have to go now. I think I'm next,' he said.

Capt disconnected the line, and we walked silently to the living room. Gosh, the things lack of confidence does to students! Ranga was a wreck. Here he was, unwilling to even fight the battle. Capt echoed my thoughts.

'Look, this guy is . . . phew . . . I mean . . . . I mean, I've never seen anyone so hopeless. He no longer wants to fight,' he said.

'Yeah, his immunity to difficult interviews has dropped. Can't blame him. This whole process sucks. The notion of hiring just doesn't change. What do they mean to do here if they can't match resumes to jobs. Stupidest thing,' I said.

Silence reigned for a few more minutes. It was close to 6.30 pm now, and I was looking out the windows on yet another sunset, sipping tea, the barren rocks that had stood the test of time coming into focus.

'How long have these rocks been around? Centuries? Longer?' I said. 'What are we after Capt? I mean . . . why did we come here? Money? Fame? Look at us now. We have a huge debt to pay off and we've graduated into a recession. I was planning to do some home renovations that have been long overdue. I was hoping to buy an apartment. I thought I'd find someone here, get married and live with her in that apartment. On my present salary, I won't be able to. My education EMI is nearly sixty percent of my starting pay-cheque. I was planning to find someone here. I haven't. In fact, I've just been heartbroken a few times, that's all. And look at Ranga. He's really in deep shit. This whole MBA stuff is financial suicide if your graduation economy is a damp squib sitting in a pool of fetid recession crap,' I said.

The Roll of the Dice **217**

Capt nodded. 'That's life. How the hell can you control the world? I had this friend who was a spiritual seeker. Went to the Himalayas on an expedition. Wanted to climb Everest. Died in an avalanche. Had a wife and young children. There seems to be this need for adventure in all of us. A need to do something special, even if it comes at great cost. We tempt fate in our own ways,' said Capt.

'All we have to decide is what to do with the time given to us,' I said.

'Huh?' asked Capt.

'From *Lord of the Rings*. Gandalf the Grey says something to that effect to Frodo when Frodo says he wishes the ring never came to him,' I explained.

'Hmm . . . someday you should explain this whole *Lord of the Rings* story to me. This Gandalf guy you keep going on about sounds pretty interesting,' said Capt.

'Yeah, except Gandalf himself would probably struggle to fix this recession or find a job here,' I said.

The door opened and Ranga walked in. He looked dead serious, his eyes brimming with tears. The stress had become permanent. Capt and I looked on in silence.

He walked straight past us and went to his room. He unlocked it and we heard some things shifting.

He came out a little later, dressed in his quad fatigues and flopped down on the couch.

'Capt, tea, *yaar*. Please . . . ' he said numbly.

'First tell me what happened,' asked Capt.

'Yeah, I mean, like . . . interviews done. I don't know. I just came back. Last one was OK. I did exactly what you guys said. Just threw the BOT research at him,' said Ranga.

'Did you say anything at all about finance or marketing or that you weren't sure about these things?' I asked.

'Well, I remembered what you said. I was able to deflect a few things, but in time I got the feeling the interviewer realised what I was up to,' he replied.

218 *Touching Distance: The Great Indian MBA Dream*

'Good. Whatever happens is for the good, man, just remember that. Even if you don't get this one, you will get something else,' said Capt.

'Boss, I can't keep fighting like this. I will join anyone who will hire me as an engineer, man. I can't keep taking interviews and getting rejected,' said Ranga.

As we sipped tea rather quietly, the phone in Ranga's room rang. He walked over to answer it. I turned on the TV and switched to HBO. *Lord of the Rings – The Return of the King*, was on. The scene when Gandalf joins the battle with thousands of reinforcements, riding his white horse, Shadow fax was playing. I explained the scene to Capt and we watched keenly on.

Sixty seconds later, I heard a shuffling behind us. Ranga walked out of his room and stood with his arms thrown up.

'*Faaak faak faak*! Guys . . . got it, man. Got it! Got it! Got. Fucking got it!' he screamed.

We joined in the scream. Sathya took off his glasses and wiped his eyes.

Hugs and high-fives reigned supreme. The Fellowship of the Lost had finally won.

Looking thankfully at us, he began, 'I mean, like . . . thanks, guys,' he said.

'Shut up,' Capt and I echoed.

◈

A month later, we graduated. My mother attended my graduation and it was a special day for her. She carried the biggest smile on her face. I met Capt's and Ranga's parents and we left, following a grand party. ISB really knew how to do things in style.

It really was a magical evening. The party was held outdoors at night, on the lawns surrounding the Atrium. The air smelled sweet and the moon shone brightly. There was a wide smile on everyone's face, and for that evening everything was forgotten.

The Roll of the Dice **219**

Suddenly, suspended in time, there was hope in every heart, the sort that just makes you feel warm deep inside.

I quickly looked around and saw her with her folks. I went over, said a 'Hello' and walked away. As I circulated through the crowd, every face reminded me of an incident, good or not so good, that I had encountered. Emotions never run far too below the surface at times like this. Strangely, I felt enriched. I truly felt I had come a very long way from the person I was sitting in that glass cage, looking out the window, and I'd met some unique, impressive people in a beautiful place that transcended everything else. It really had been an opportunity to be part of something bigger, and live in a realm that had made me so much more different than I'd been.

❖

Me: *'Congratulations on your job.'*

Her: *'Thanks. You too.'*

Me: *'So back to your hometown, eh?'*

Her: *'Yeah. You too, it seems like.'*

Me: *'It's what I wanted at some level. There are too many responsibilities that I need to take care of . . .'*

Her: *'Yeah, you good boy!'*

Me: *'Trust me, no one wants to be a good boy. Circumstances make you so.'*

Her: *'Well, I am going to miss you.'*

Me: *'I have to say the same.'*

Her: *'You'll come to my wedding, won't you?'*

Me: *'As difficult as it may be, I will.'*

Her: *'Good.'*

Me: *'When is it?'*

Her: *'Well, I think it will be in a few months. We've talked it out and it's just up to the parents to meet up now. Hey, remember what I said. Not a peep to anyone. I'm not announcing it till I have the cards printed, okay? One word out of you and I'll come all the way to Bangalore and beat you senseless.'*

220 *Touching Distance: The Great Indian MBA Dream*

Me: 'I get it. I have no interest in announcing your wedding.'

Her: 'Ouch . . . sorry.'

Me: 'Good. Looks like you're leaving with a degree, a job and a husband you are in love with. Every female MBA aspirant's best-case scenario, eh?'

Her: 'Yeah, I'd never imagined things could go so well for me this year.'

Me: 'Yeah.'

Her: 'I mean, I got all this and you . . . someone I love so much now. You're like that soul mate that I never met in time.'

Me: 'Yeah, right. Plan B . . . Stop flattering me. You know you don't believe any of that.'

Her: 'Well, I can't explain it. You're important. But I'm just so sorry; I just can't help the way I feel about Rahul. Known him too long and there's too much history.'

Me: 'Oh God. Enough. Stop stabbing me for kicks. I don't blame anyone. It was my hole to jump into.'

Her: 'Thanks for being so nice.'

Me: 'Hey, I'm a nice guy. What can you say?'

Her: 'You're wonderful. OK, Bye.'

Me: 'Take care.'

Click.

21

The Real World

Well I've heard, there was a secret chord
That David played and it pleased the Lord,
But you don't really care for music do you?
—Leonard Cohen

'Yes, I say. I will get best bonus in this group. What for you? I have worked sixteen years in company. You bloody bet I'll get it,' declared Bala Satish, practice head of the largest consulting division in ITServ, with the thickest of the thick Telugu English accents. He sounded like he was in a street brawl with some poor cyclist bloke who had accidentally scratched his BMW and had the temerity to look him in the eye.

The voice at the other end of the speaker phone lost a tooth filling, given how hard it clenched its jaws together.

'But Bala, I have also been working here for six years. I know my peers are getting more money than me,' cribbed the *desi* voice at the other end of the line.

'Come on, I say. Didn't I send you to UK when you wanted to go? There was lots of people waiting. I sent *you*, I say. Don't forget that. I know how much you are saving in rupees on pound

222 *Touching Distance: The Great Indian MBA Dream*

salary. Don't complain, I say. If you're not happy, tell me, I will bring you back. I can put other people onsite in sales. They will do same job,' said Satish.

'But Satish, please. Just think . . . I have done well. What can I do if those guys are not willing to sign. I cannot make the horse drink.'

'Boss, if you cannot make horse drink, find a donkey that will. Don't give me all these Bible proverbs. Forget it. Ha-ha-ha,' he laughed, and looked at me sternly, as if to send my Allen Solly shirt and Gillete-shaved face a message.

Half an hour ago, I'd walked into his office and he had motioned me to enter. He was in the middle of a conference call on the speaker phone, and for some reason didn't ask me to wait outside. He didn't pick up the receiver either. What was I, after all? A new employee at ITServ. I hadn't yet spent sixteen days on the payroll, leave alone sixteen years.

The conversation seemed to be coming to an end. The guy at the other end of the line wanted more money than he was getting for selling ITServ to unsuspecting IT departments of British companies, and this guy was refusing to re-allocate the money he had in his boot. Welcome to the world of Indian IT Services. Everyone wants more and the guy at the top holds the aces.

'Please exhaust all your options before you consider joining ITServ' was the honest advice I'd received from an ISB senior who had worked there. I had exhausted all my options. I'd given up the eGateway offer – those guys were too weird, and with no other course of action available, I'd joined ITServ, telling myself that they would stay true to their promise of ejecting me from the noise and pollution of India and would place me in the First World.

I was wrong. While there had been a verbal promise to that effect, the person hiring me had simply quit the organisation during the three months between the interview and my joining date. Now I'd been told that I'd be posted in Hyderabad and that I had to suck it up. All protestations involving . . .

The Real World **223**

'Sir, but I'd been told that I'd be placed in the UK,' were met with.

'What do you mean, I say? Who told? What? That person doesn't work here. Who knows what you are saying? If you have problems, meet Practice Head Bala Satish. Thank you.'

So here I was. All options exhausted, facing Bala Satish. I'd looked at his table, his wristwatch, his moustache, his hair, his window, his Sai Baba photo, his little Ganesha idol and his one-week-course completion certificate from IIM-B hanging off the wall. Bala sat in the Bangalore office. I'd returned home after the MBA and had decided that in the two weeks remaining before my joining date, I would do everything I could to have Bala move my position from Hyderabad.

Bala was someone who'd hopped on to ITServ when it was just adding the IT Services business to its old world businesses, and had ridden the wave like every other rich jackass over the age of thirty-five in that place.

'Yes, tell me . . . where you are from? Why you wanted to meet, I say?' he thundered.

I almost felt myself shrink two inches, faced with the power of this Pharaoh.

'Sir, I've been hired from ISB Hyderabad,' I replied.

'So what, I say? ISB, IIM, IIT, whatever. What do you want?' he asked.

'Sir, I was promised a placement in your UK office. Now the person who interview me has quit. I received an email asking me to join the Hyderabad office. I came to talk to you about that. I'm hoping you can allow me to work from here.'

'Who made the offer to you?'

'Sir, it was Mahesh Ram,' I replied

'Oh . . . Ha-ha-ha-ha! Mahesh . . . Yeah, he left,' he said with a twinkle in his eye, suggesting that the circumstances leading to his departure were clandestine enough to warrant his amusement.

224 *Touching Distance: The Great Indian MBA Dream*

'So, why you want to be here in Bangalore?' came the next question.

'Sir, I have my family and home here,' I said blankly.

'See . . . I say, don't come to ITServ with constraints. You will go nowhere in this company. You will not grow. First of all, I don't know why we hire you MBAs. I have always been dead against it. Now you want special treatment, is it?'

'Sir, I don't mean to cause any trouble, but I know most of your practice is based here. Can you please let me work from here?' I implored.

'You please leave now. I will think it over and see. As I said before, I don't know why we hire you people here. We don't need your sort.' He looked at his laptop, signifying that this meeting was over. He didn't bother to look up as I said Thank You and walked out.

I opened the door and walked out with a heavy heart. I felt my Allen Solly shirt stick to my back, wet with perspiration. I wiped the sweat from my brow. I'd come to this meeting expecting to be congratulated for my accomplishment and for showing the prescience of joining ITServ, the Great Indian IT Services Company that was moving every conceivable IT job to India, while still running its other factories and treating people like factory workers. I'd left after being admonished and told that my sort wasn't needed in these parts.

'Fuck him,' I thought to myself as I signed the Visitor's Register on my way out. 'If this son-of-a-bitch makes me go to Hyderabad, I'm just not going,' I said to myself. I was seething with anger as the security guard made me correct the leaving time. I was off by four minutes. This dark lord Sauron at the helm of this ITServ ran a tight ship.

On my way back home I wondered from where I'd cough up the EMI for my educational loan. If I didn't get to stay here and needed to leave, where would the money come from? I needed a

The Real World **225**

job. The fact that I'd done pretty well at the ISB, at the glass cage before that, and throughout my academic life, had no meaning for Bala Satish, alias Emperor of Big Group at ITServ. To him, I was yet another Egyptian slave moving the big rock to his tomb, or moving the next stock option or rupee into his bonus.

The next day, I doubled my efforts: sent out my CV to a few more companies, including my old glass-cage, asking to see if they had jobs for MBAs. There were none. They were happy to re-hire me pushing keys for programs, but there was nothing in sales and marketing or finance. The economy was in the pits and war efforts in Iraq were warming up.

❖

When I joined ITServ, I lived the life that factory workers in the 1970s had come to suffer. Every morning, I had to run to board a bus that would take me to their building several kilometres outside the city. On my way, I'd pass one of the glass cages I'd worked for. I now had to travel much further, had a beast of a boss and was neck-deep in debt and making an extra six-thousand bucks a month more than I did before my MBA. I looked wistfully at the earlier glass cage and thought of all the friends I'd made there and the respect I'd earned.

If anything resembled the desperation and lack of individuality reflected in Orwell's *1984*, this bus was it. Bodies slammed together, in a bus that employees coughed up a lot of money for. Transport wasn't even free. A bus that strategically got people in at 8.30 am and plied with very low frequency thereafter to discourage late coming. Women hung from the footboard and men hung from the side rails like beggars on the last bus out of hell. It was filled with people in their twenties and thirties, mostly males, too frustrated to observe niceties and some too uncouth for me to suffer. It amazes me. India is supposed to be the centre of the developing world, but the people in the bus still behaved like they were in a cave. Sneezes

226 *Touching Distance: The Great Indian MBA Dream*

were meant for public consumption, women remained standing while young, fit men looked absently out the windows and other yawned straight into whatever was in the firing line. All this in contrast to their fashionable outfits and shoes. These people were part of the services industry, for Christ's sake. I guess social niceties are just something that our education seems to ignore altogether, among a horde of other things.

A few trips later, I decided to drive to the factory at more than three times what the bus cost me. I just couldn't live like an ITServ factory worker anymore.

I didn't really have anything to do. I was given a chair and a desk and all I did was sit there, looking at a screen. I walked up to Bala regularly, telling him I was available to be assigned to something sensible, and he said they had nothing at the moment. They didn't need me unless I was able to crank out computer programs like engineers. Their 'business analyst' opportunities were fully staffed, apparently. A business analyst was a glorified documentation guy, someone who knew English and could type out what the customer wanted built. These jobs should never be touched by MBAs unless they are being paid abnormally large sums in foreign currencies of countries which have strong economies and allow immigration.

I sat at my desk and ruminated at my existence and progress. Had I made progress? I didn't think so. Whenever I went to the water cooler, I marvelled at the frugality of this sweatshop. There were no glasses or paper cups, and one was expected to either carry one's own, or join palms in the traditional rural salute to the 'elixir of life'. There was *one* steel tumbler at the end of a steel chain that was attached to the concrete in the wall, dirty and rusted, reminding one of such tumblers at the city's bus terminus. Apparently, ITServ had been a blood-sucking company in all their other businesses, by design.

When I went into the restrooms there were no paper towels to dry my hands with. I looked for a electric blow drier. No luck

The Real World **227**

there, either. I ended up using my handkerchief. I didn't dare to go into the pots to see what they were like.

Of course, the customers who came to visit the facilities saw none of these things. They just saw honest, young Indians bent over computer screens, saving precious IT dollars that went straight into the year-end bonuses of the IT directors and CIOs who came visiting.

One fine day, towards the end of my first month of doing nothing, I was summoned by Bala. I walked in with my winning smile, expecting to be assigned to a project in Switzerland or Sweden, helping Paris Hilton with her latest venture.

He looked up at me and said, 'Oh, come. Sit.'

I sat.

'See, you are not billable. You are appearing on the monthly non-billable employee report for my group. You are going to get into trouble and you are going to get us all in trouble.'

'I don't understand, sir. I haven't been assigned any work since I got here. Not sure what I am supposed to do about that,' I replied as neutrally as I could, while mentally picturing my shoe slamming his groin flat.

'Well, yes, what you can do? You said you can't do any database administration work. You also said you can't do any programming,' he mocked me.

'I don't remember the programming languages. I used to, but that was over a year ago. Besides, I got myself an MBA. Could you not use me in a role more appropriate to my education?' I asked, as neutrally, but not picturing his eyes popping out.

'Boss, what you want, huh? I can't give any onsite role. There are no openings. And you will just sit here, is it? Go meet Arjun Pemmaraju. He has some work. Maybe you can help him and at least I can say you are doing pre-sales,' he said.

This time I just got up and walked out. I refused to thank him or be polite. He was back to looking at his screen. He was enjoying

228 *Touching Distance: The Great Indian MBA Dream*

this. He belonged on the have-not side of the MBA spectrum and this gave him a great high, I could tell.

I walked out towards Arjun Pemmaraju's office, and then went right past it. I kept walking for a while till I reached the main gate. I then kept walking, till I reached the main road, feeling like I wanted to punch something. My thoughts ranged from the utter ludicrousness of the moment to my participation in it. What had happened? Until that time, I'd never know what it was like to work in an Indian company where a manager just assumed he was a feudal lord. I'd just learnt how bad it was for the millions of employees stuck in jobs in the manufacturing companies which didn't bear the MNC tag. I'd just learnt what it was like to be a cog in the wheel of an Indian company. I decided I was going to double my efforts to leave.

Later that afternoon, having blown off steam and having reconciled to the situation at hand, I returned and found Arjun Pemmaraju and asked him what he wanted me to do. I'll remember his assignment till I hang up my boots, blackberry and laptop.

'Hello. OK, I need some work done. We have some common information which goes into every proposal we make. I need it to be organised so we can copy-paste it into our proposals easily.'

'What information is that?' I asked.

'Oh, some common information – building address of our headquarters, phone number of the company, number of employees, etc.,' he replied.

'You mean you don't know these things?' I was stunned to say the least.

'We have to look for it. Either on our website or from other proposals. It would be easier if we could simply copy paste it from a single word file,' came the response.

'So you are telling me to create a word file with some addresses and phone numbers which appear on our website?'

He nodded earnestly.

The Real World **229**

I have to say that I prepared that word file, as much as it burnt a hole in my soul. It had the company's corporate address and phone number, and had other pieces to information from their own website.

I found a job in the meantime and wasted less than a second before I walked into Bala's office and told him I was leaving. He smiled, the bastard.

Bala: 1, me: 0. Damn.

❖

My next job was worse. This was at a Supply Chain software products company that was moving jobs to India in order to save costs. The company itself had been profitable and successful in the past, and had a number of good people from IITs and IIMs, but having lost its way, was now floundering, and trying hard to save its existing businesses.

My designation was a glorified 'product manager'. I ended up helping engineers fix problems at implementations. I'd just jumped from the frying pan into the fire.

Worse still, I had a boss who didn't want MBAs any more than Bala Satish did. One fine day, I'd decided I had had enough. I walked into my manager's office and said, 'Aman, I'd like to have a quick chat. I'm not sure what whether you really want me to be doing setups for engineers to test software issues.'

'What's the problem? Is there an issue?' he wondered.

'I mean, I just . . . we never talked about these duties during my interview. I though I was being hired to interface with customers and help product evolution.'

'Well, yes, but we need to keep our current accounts. We can't afford to mess up our implementations,' he said.

'I appreciate that. But this is something that I'd get an engineer or someone else to work on. Why do you need an MBA to run four Linux terminals to test software?' I asked, trying to sound as civil as I could.

230 *Touching Distance: The Great Indian MBA Dream*

'Well, what's the problem? You need to learn the product to sell it or to discuss it with customers, don't you?' he asked, his voice getting colder.

'Aman, I've been doing these setups for five months now. I know the product. I just shouldn't have to do software testing . . . I wasn't hired for this. It's a lot cheaper to hire someone else for that skill set. Do you really need me to do that?' I was on the ledge of my boss-employee building here.

'Well, we all get paid to do what we are asked to do. I don't know what else to say. This is what I want you to do,' he said defiantly.

'What does that mean, Aman?' I asked, one foot off the ledge now.

He sized up the situation and realised that I wasn't going to buckle.

'I need you to do this now. It's that simple. When your role may change, I cannot say.'

'Thanks,' I said, and walked out. My face was red with anger and I'd put my feet back on the ledge.

I walked to my computer, determined to update my resume and float it for when my day just got worse.

Just as I sat down and looked at the screen, I had one unread message. It was hers. A wedding invitation. I opened it, hating myself for doing so. I read it, closed the message and deleted it.

It's funny where the energy arrives from when one's pride is hurt. For the next few weeks, I carpet-bombed companies with my resume, called ex-managers and lined up interviews. If Aman thought he could pull the salary threat over me, he was about to find out how quickly my uppercut landed on his chin.

I prepared for interviews like an assassin. I rehearsed my story, and got really good at it. In time, I had a few offers and I chose one. It was the glass-cage I had escaped from to do my MBA in the first place! They had just created product management roles and they were keen on having me back. More importantly, I had

The Real World **231**

a manager who wasn't even in my time-zone. He was miles away on the other side of the planet.

It was a virtual homecoming of sorts. Ramesh was still around, and he'd been promoted to the position of manager, in the year that I was away. Things were better than they'd been at my previous two companies. The money was good, and so were the hours. The work wasn't great, but I'd made my peace with what was available in the technology sector. I'd accepted fate.

❖

22

A Soul Insured

Beyond the horizon of the place we lived when we were young
In a world of magnets and miracles
Our thoughts strayed constantly and without boundary
The ringing of the division bell had begun
—Pink Floyd

𝓐 few years after our graduation, I heard that Capt had moved back to Bangalore from his assignment in the UK. Things had gone well for him. He'd made a lot of money, lived outside the *karmabhoomi* for a couple of years, and had returned to India in a terrific role, working for an international insurance giant which was setting up shop in India. Yes, he'd been made a terrific offer, one that you would not believe. Capt had become what every MBA student wanted to be. The ISB had made great strides in the meantime and that had helped Capt and indeed all of us immensely.

❖

Since he was back in Bangalore, I made the time to meet him immediately. I walked into his office, a corner office, and there

A Soul Insured **233**

sat Capt, in his blue suit, expensive shirt and embarrassed smile. I had walked through a sea of cubicles, mostly filled with people looking at hard copies of insurance claims. Almost everyone until then was dressed modestly, as was I. They earnestly pushed ball-point pens across paper, and sometimes diligently entered claims into computers, replete with the most creative spelling mistakes. Capt, in his attire that probably cost more than the monthly pay cheque of a few ball-point pushers, simply looked either out of place or distinguished, depending on who was looking – the guy in the cubicle or the guy who hired Capt.

His expensive desk phone was on, and a sweating interviewee at the other end of the line was cooking up answers about the insurance business in India. Capt was trying to hire someone to do something for him in the company. Capt, rather inimitably, told me to come in and meet him since all he was doing today was interviews. I think Capt was quite happy that I walked in while the interview was in progress. It was like being invited to watch a 'fixed' game of chess. Capt could win whenever he wanted; he gave me a broad smile as he marked his territory on the phone line with the pungent odour of his intellectual ammonia.

The candidate at the other end of the line oscillated between bouts of anxiety and stress, revealing unmistakable and deadly correlation between his bladder and brain functions. At a karmic level, and almost with a divine intuition, he probably knew he could not ask for a rest-room break. Capt would ding him just for that. I mean, what kind of soldier cannot hold his bladder in the course of an attack. I was quite positive Capt had a few stories up his sleeve about the time he held his bladder, bowels, uterus, eggs, bacon and what not for three days, while he resolved which way the missiles should be pointing, during his past life in the army.

Capt held the *swamis* who could effortlessly control their bodies, in the highest regard. As a well-read Hindu philosopher, Capt firmly believed what we all know – that the body is just a vehicle and should be controlled by the mind-soul complex. I

234 *Touching Distance: The Great Indian MBA Dream*

remembered the time he would go on and on about Ranga's inability to prevent matter in all forms escaping a few overworked apertures in Ranga's otherwise underused body. Capt always had a smile of superiority when he sent me chat messages in class, such as 'four minutes to explosion, care to wager?' He was right on occasion, as Ranga would slowly get up with intense concentration and walk in a straight line to the door.

As I watched Capt continue the interview, I marvelled at his ability to make up questions about an industry he joined less than a year ago. 'Are you aware of any industry standards for actuarial processes in eventualities?'

Silence.

'What industry statistics are you aware of that relate revenues and cost structures to market sizes and profitability?'

Silence.

I wondered if the interviewee had simply let his bladder go in response to the void that echoed in his mind. Maybe his brain was finally stretched to the point of breaking its own sphincter muscle.

Capt hit the 'mute' button and smiled in satisfaction.

'I need his company's numbers, dude,' he said, glint in his eye and mischief in his soul.

I nodded gravely, as I often did, with a smile of the most practical existentialism on my face. One man's bladder is another man's bullet on a power-point presentation.

◈

As the interview continued, I gazed at the squirrels and crows that perched from time to time on Capt's window. Every time Capt asked an impossible-to-answer question, the crows pooped. Impressed at the bird's sense of timing, I gazed even more hypnotically. Capt, with his back to the crows, smiled at me. In his own mind, he was putting on a terrific performance.

My expression was a mix of delight, amusement and irony, given that there were so many things wrong with the picture unfolding

A Soul Insured **235**

before me. I was also somewhat pleased – usually, all is well with the world when Capt is feeling this way.

The picture was remarkable. Capt, who once froze his rear-end on the cold rocks of Rishikesh, when in meditation, standing at a stone's throw from the door of enlightenment, was now dressed in the ways of the world, playing to galleries or at least to cubicles filled with people processing insurance claims. Capt was sitting in a corner office with large windows, against the backdrop of a setting sun – a far cry from sitting at something resembling a barber's saloon when he worked at his first post-MBA job at ITServ. ITServ claimed to be doing 'high-end IT consulting', but the interiors in that office were dingy to say the least. Rows of employees sat at a desk, facing the wall as blank as their collective futures. Sometimes, they'd lean back, touch or smell the Parachute coconut oil in the hair of the guy sitting behind them. I sometimes wondered if they actually put up mirrors on weekends and rented it out to the cheapest barber in the area. Nothing epitomised 'Save money at all costs' like that office. I was convinced that Capt deserved so much better for all his abilities, and for the fact that he was genuinely a good guy.

I turned my attention to the interviewee, who was probably now on the verge of having to buy new pants. He was manufacturing answers on that holy subject of all MBA students, professors and graduates – 'strategy'. He believed, perhaps, like all interviewees, that unless he sounded convincing about the existence of his ability to 'think strategically', the interview shall be over because nobody wants to hire a donkey to push ball-point pens on paper, even if that's exactly what he was being hired to do. This is the irony of being part of a billion-strong workforce in a culture that's over five thousand years old. You must be a philosopher even if you are powdering stones.

I pulled out my cell phone and turned on the video recording, wanting to preserve this oh-so-Dilbertish moment for posterity. Someday when Capt would be famous, I would play this to the world on YouTube. Make no mistake about that – Capt will be

236 *Touching Distance: The Great Indian MBA Dream*

famous; and I will be rich, on account of my presence of mind. Capt had too much good *karma* going for him to miss the pot of gold and recognition in this lifetime.

A while later, the interview ended. Captain's flunky came in and asked me if I wanted tea or coffee. I was honestly embarrassed since I was used to standing in line in front of a noisy machine, but I asked for tea, as I continued to record on my phone.

My thoughts raced back to ITServ. Capt had been a soldier indeed to have lasted the years that he did. The good news, however, was that he had neither lost his wit nor whereabouts, despite spending time in those circumstances. He had hung around till they sent him to the UK on an assignment, and had isolated himself somewhat from the reality of the hole. Never discount the intelligence or fortitude of someone I respect.

But even before that, Capt had done something even more unbelievable. He had married! Every renunciant monk has his day. Capt had his, and then some.

◈

Unbelievable as Capt's stories are, they are not false. He once described to me how he waited at a bus stop in Bangalore, and deliberately considered taking the wrong bus so that he would miss his engagement, which was to be held the following day in Coimbatore. He considered boarding the bus to Chennai, in the hope that he would be evicted somewhere along the way, and would then find an old *swami* who would be the spiritual guru that Capt had craved his whole life.

Capt took the right bus anyway and got married to a very, very patient girl who put up with all his spiritual protestations leading up to the time that his nuptials were complete. She patiently listened to him and came up with the right answers.

Capt: 'I might renounce the world and take off to the Himalayas after I'm married.'

A Soul Insured **237**

Capt's wife-to-be: 'That's fine. I'll come along and do the same.'

There were other protestations like these, which Capt came up with from time to time. These protestations magically vanished soon after the '*taali*' was tied.

I asked Mrs Capt, the same question I ask of all my married friends' wives, 'Have you realised the enormity of the mistake you have made?'

She said nothing but smiled. I knew she'd make Capt happy. I was relieved. Only someone fairly enlightened could respond in a manner such as that.

Capt soon shelved his spiritual ambitions and went the family way. How much things change over four or five years! Capt is now a package deal and comes with his entourage: wife, first daughter and a newborn babydaughter, one of the cutest and smartest things you'd see.

❖

Following his wedding, the shit-hole company finally worked out for Capt, depositing him in the UK. As Capt stepped off Heathrow and observed the discipline and order all around him, he smiled in satisfaction. Here was a country which looked and behaved like the army Capt was so proud of. He watched in amazement as passers-by nodded and smiled as he walked past them knocking his luggage on the pavement.

'Will India ever get to this state?' Capt asked himself.

'Maybe in two-hundred years,' he thought.

As the man upstairs would have it, Capt was then shown a sight which quashed his thinking. An impeccably dressed lady walked past, with her dog on a leash. They both smiled and nodded at Capt. Capt stopped short of patting the dog's behind in salutation. They walked past Capt with the greatest dignity as he looked in admiration.

'What a cultured dog! I'm sure he listens to Beethoven during his siesta,' Capt thought.

238 *Touching Distance: The Great Indian MBA Dream*

The dog then slowed down, stopped, and emptied its bowels. As Capt watched in amazement, the lady produced a poop-picker, and then proceeded to remove the refuse from the street and deposit it in a poop box.

Capt thought, 'No, I guess India's not going to get here after all.'

Capt began his new innings in the UK. He was posted in the IT operations of one of the largest insurers in the country, where he floored local employees with his diligence, moustache and attempts at trying to be funny.

One afternoon in Wales, when his phone rang, the call emanating from a call centre in India, Capt, in his loudest voice and in a pronounced fake British accent, said, 'No, I don't want your long-distance service. Don't call me again . . . you and your stupid Indian accent!'

Capt looked around as he saw huge smiles pasted on the faces of all his colleagues – Caucasians, Indians, Asians, Martians. There was laughter. I've often thought that this incident described Capt better than any other. Only someone like him can pull off something like that.

Mrs Capt joined him soon in the UK, and found him having long conversations with a Liz, Emily or Helen, but Capt insisted that their interests in him were only spiritual. She looked at me blankly, recounting these incidents, and was appalled when I laughed. Trust me, Capt was not the philandering type; his notion of *swami*-hood would not allow that, but he'd like to believe he could philander if he wanted. As long as Capt believed something was possible, he would do nothing to destroy that belief. What's the saying? . . . It is better to remain silent and be thought a fool than to speak up and remove all doubt. Mrs Capt knew he would never 'speak up'.

◈

Anyway, to cut a long story short, it's been five years since I began writing this book, and everything changes. I'm happy that things

A Soul Insured 239

worked out for Capt. For someone who wanted to insure his soul by committing to a life of self-inquiry, Capt had transformed into someone who sat in material surroundings, interrogating others in an insurance company. Life, it seems, is not without a sense of irony. Either way, if you are to believe karma and dharma, Capt had done enough to insure his soul. '*Hari om*'!

❖

As I walked back from Capt's office that day, I received a very strange call. It was a blast from the past, something I'd never expected.
Her: 'Hi.'
Me: 'Hello . . . '
Her: 'It's me!'
Me: 'I know, I can't believe it. It's been so long. What is it . . . four, five years?'
Her: 'Yes, it has. How have you been?'
Me: 'I've been okay. And you?'
Her: 'I've been fine.'
Me: 'How's Rahul? How's married life treating you?'
    After a long pause she said, 'We've separated.'
Me: 'What! Why? . . . '
Her: 'It didn't work. I guess I've just stopped being in love and I hated how little he cared.'
Me: 'I don't understand any of it.'
Her: 'I can't understand it either. We had differences. With him it was all about work. It wasn't the life I had imagined. Slowly, it rubbed off on me as well. I felt nothing after a while. I didn't feel adored, and I didn't feel loved. . . . I don't really want to get into the gory details if that's OK with you.'
Me: 'You two have been together forever. How can it just happen?'
Her: 'I don't know. I guess it just happens. It's the way you feel. You can't control it, can you'
Me: 'Yeah, I've heard that before.'
Her: 'What are your plans?'

240 *Touching Distance: The Great Indian MBA Dream*

Me: 'About what?'

Her: 'Marriage.'

Me: 'Well, I don't know. I haven't had a chance to think about it.'

Her: 'Are you seeing anyone?'

Me: 'No, I just guess I haven't met anyone I feel strongly about.'

Her: 'OK . . . Well, don't worry too much; it will happen.'

Me: 'Yeah, I hope so.'

Her: 'Just make sure you get this one right. It's really important.'

Me: 'I'm sorry . . . for you. Are you okay?'

Her: 'I've come to terms with it. Besides, work keeps me busy. By the way, I haven't told anyone yet. It's not like a wedding, right? There's no need to shout it from the rooftops.'

Me: 'Don't worry about it.'

Her: 'Anyway, I called you because I was looking at the alumni directory online and found your number there. Over the years, I always wondered what your life might turn out to be. You were so intense, so idealistic. Are you still like that?'

Me: 'I guess idealism is a luxury that leaves you when it finds someone who can treat it better.'

Her: 'Still the convoluted talker. Nice . . .'

Me: 'I'm really sorry to hear this. How did your parents take all this? Are you staying with them now?'

Her: 'Yes, they were shocked. It doesn't help that they got to hear this at their age. They spend all day looking through matrimonial websites and the classifieds.'

Me: 'Okay. And you?'

Her: 'I . . . haven't recovered yet. I thought I had, but there are . . . severe bouts of depression. I should be okay, though . . .'

Me: 'It will all get better, I promise.'

Her: 'Thank you. You're as sweet as ever. Anyway, I have to run to a meeting in half an hour and I need to get my act together. I don't think I want to look like a mess after this chat raking my nerves.'

Me: 'OK. Take care.'
Her: 'You too.'
  Click.
Me: 'Phew . . .'

23

The Da Ranga Code

I have legalized robbery, called it belief,
I have run with the money, I have hid like a thief,
Rewritten history with my armies of my crooks,
Invented memories, I did burn all the books
—DIRE STRAITS

'*Ashte naa?*' (Is that all?), Ranga thought while picking his nose, as he gazed at Mona Lisa at the Louvre. He looked around, hoping to find the curator or a guide.

An old Frenchman dressed in a black suit walked by, and Ranga decided he looked desperate enough to have worked in a museum all his life.

Pulling his finger out of his nose, in respect to the old man and da Vinci, he asked, 'I mean, like... is this the original?... I mean, like size and paint and all?'

The old man looked quizzically at Ranga and muttered, '*Je ne sais pas*,' and walked on as his xenophobic bias strengthened. What was this? Another Indian digging his nose at da Vinci's temple? What was this guy doing anyway dressed in shorts, floaters and a t-shirt that had the French flag on it and looked like it was something

The Da Ranga Code **243**

that had seen D-day at Normandy? What did this *desi* care if it was the original or the reproduction? Could he tell the difference? Also, the sight of Dan Brown's book in his hand caused the old man a great deal of revulsion. Suddenly, every *desi* visiting the Louvre had been pointing at the 'M' in 'The Last Supper' and yelping in joy. He walked on hurriedly, hoping Ranga wouldn't follow him like other *desis* often did with repeat questions.

Ranga wondered what he'd said. He wasn't about to ask again. 'What's the big deal? She's not even sexy. No boobs also,' concluded Ranga.

In rumination, and somewhat absentmindedly, he reached for his navel to have a dig, but found his camera resting on his belly.

Paris had ceased to be interesting after his walks along the promenades, his visits to the museums, the wine-tasting sessions paid for by his employer, and the endless analysis-talk that he had been flown in to deliver. Also, Ranga nursed a feeling that his French counterparts were wary of the number of times he quoted Michael Porter and his six forces of competitive strategy . . . or was it five? Never mind. It was a Sunday afternoon. Tomorrow, he would call his wife in Bangalore and talk to his baby son.

❖

A little over a year ago, Ranga had stood in his bright brown suit, yellow tie, hair on end, beaming at all and sundry as he stood on the dais next to his wife, who displayed a look of cautious apprehension. After all, she was told that she was marrying an ISB graduate with plenty of prospects. All true.

Ranga smiled over and over again, reassured that all his pent-up frustration in the days spent at the ISB was coming to an end. Mostly, he was relieved that his bachelor imagination would finally find form and expression.

I had often heard that people were unsuccessful in consummating their marriages on their wedding night, for a variety of reasons.

244 *Touching Distance: The Great Indian MBA Dream*

When I conveyed the observation to Ranga on the day following his wedding, he shot back.

'*Yaaar heliddu?*' (Who told you that?) I apologised for doubting his carnality and desperation.

'No problem. There's nothing to it. I mean, like . . . I thought I was great,' he replied.

This guy baffled me. Things seemed to fall in place like clockwork. I'd seen people struggle like hell to change functional areas from product development in IT to financial services. Stories of struggle became the norm the year after ISB. I'd then seen CAs trying like hell to get jobs in corporate finance departments of companies, and they'd failed too.

Ranga had done it somewhat effortlessly. He'd joined Metaphony Services, a Build-Operate-Transfer products vendor as a program manager. They were a hot company who'd created a new business model that enabled outsourced operations of US companies to be run in India, with the option of the units being acquired at a later point of time, by the outsourcing company. Instead of hiring employees one by one and develop scale, Metaphony had resorted to acquiring smaller IT sweatshops in Bangalore by the half-dozen. They saw the requirement for a small Bangalore-based M&A group that needed a few people with IT services knowledge and valuation skills. The group was to be headed by the owner's man in Bangalore, an old faithful of the founder.

When Ranga heard of this opportunity, he walked into the man's office, and reeled off names of every Wharton-based finance professor who would help with valuations since he was an alumnus of the ISB. You had to hand it to this guy. He had initiative and the ability to lie through his teeth.

The man had bought it and entrusted Ranga with getting this done.

Ranga was now in France at the conclusion of his second acquisition. He was here to meet with the founder, who was rather pleased that small companies were getting added to the facility

The Da Ranga Code **245**

in Bangalore at a pretty decent pace. Ranga was to meet him the next day and for now, he was soaking up the culture in the middle of Paris.

◆

'Hello, I mean, like . . . Hi, Mr Sambvani,' said Ranga, trying to sound as cheery and as Web 2.0 as his now tightfitting suit would allow him. Spending his time on a company expense account, he'd stuffed himself with every dessert available on the menu. The buttons holding his jacket together seemed ready to dislodge and fly through the air and pop into one of the many available cleavage crevices on view at the upmarket restaurant buffet.

Mr Sambvani smiled profusely and shook hands with Ranga. What a sloppy, brilliant guy, he thought as he reached for his handkerchief to wipe off the soufflé transferred from Ranga's palm.

'So, Ranga, tell me, how are things back home?' he asked.

'Oh, I mean, fine. Like, with oil prices going up so quickly, I mean India had better watch its deficit,' he replied.

'Oh, no, I mean, at Metaphony.'

'Oh, yeah . . . that. OK, things are OK. Pretty cool. I mean, like . . . I just finished my second acquisition – Beta Services. Pretty good guys. I mean, like . . . we paid a small premium because some of their guys actually had a fair bit of experience.'

'Yeah, I was a little concerned about that. We paid almost fifty percent more than we usually do for a thirty-man company.'

'Oh, come on. Don't worry. I mean, like . . . I'll tell pre-sales to change the billing rates on that unit to be two times what it usually is.'

'OK. I'll watch that closely. How's Mohan treating you?'

'He's a good guy, I mean. Speaks highly of you and all. Not sure how long he's been around. Might help to send him for a short-term executive MBA. He only has a B.Com.'

'Really? And why MBA?'

246 *Touching Distance: The Great Indian MBA Dream*

'I mean, like . . . he doesn't really understand the stuff I talk about. Kind of there's a gap between his skills and mine.'

'Really? I thought he was very talented. He's run my business in India for such a long time without any glitches.'

'Ha-ha . . . I mean, like . . . there's not much to do, right? All these years . . . he just . . . like, had to print offer letters and sign them.'

'I thought so too. The really high-skill stuff is coming in now. That's why I was happy to learn that we had an MBA in our own backyard to do this stuff for us.'

'Yeah. I mean, like valuation is more strategy than finance, I think.'

'Well, learn the ropes quickly. You paid a lot for this acquisition. Was this your first? I thought Mohan was teaching you how to value these companies.'

'Yeah, I mean, like . . . he helped me with the first one, and this was one I did all by myself. Like I said, I think we can charge higher rates for these guys we acquired.'

'OK. Sounds good. I'm going to keep an eye on you, so don't let me down.'

'Not a problem. When you interviewed me, I told you about all the finance courses I took, right? I'm more up-to-date on valuation than all these management consulting companies.'

'Well, I'm pleased to hear that. I'll tell Mohan to discuss some stock options with you.'

'He-he. Thanks. I'm going to get some soufflé; would you like some?'

❖

On the flight back home, drunk on four glasses of wine, Ranga wondered what kind of options Mohan was told to give him. Were they going to be discounted and back-dated? Were they going to be stock awards? Were they going to vest tomorrow?

It was so silly, guys like Mohan. Poor thing had been slogging his arse off all these years and had never amounted to anything.

The Da Ranga Code **247**

He'd learnt that his salary was pretty close to what Mohan was making two or three years ago. He really had arrived.

It was all about talent. His roomies were in different boats. Capt has a huge slice of luck to make it into insurance. As for the other guy who lived across him? He was just thinking hard, not thinking out of the box. Some guys have brains, but no talent. Not street smart. Not thinking-out-of-the-box. Ranga laughed and spilled some wine on his shirt. He wiped it with his hands and licked his finger. Tasted good.

Ranga ruminated on his own accomplishments. A year out of B-School, where he free-rode on his teams and on the stupid slogger from across the shared bathroom who had complained about his hygiene.

Now it was his turn to call the shots. He'd been a lateral entry into M&A. Sure he had to push his way in, and sure it was a tech company, but he'd made it. So what if he didn't have all the answers to the questions his job threw at him? He'd got his ISB CA friends at other finance companies to send him prepared spreadsheets for valuation.

In fact, so scared was Mr Mohan at the sight of all these fancy spreadsheets that he'd backed off completely and let Ranga do the valuations. He'd in fact dropped into the background, doing research and cowering in fear every time Ranga passed him on the way to the loo. The roles had been reversed.

Ranga thought Mohan had done a good job of research. For Beta Software, the price was a little high, sure, but Mohan had done the due diligence, got all the thirty resumes from the target company, and they were indeed excellent people. Typical Indians, he thought. Such smart guys sitting in a company like Beta Software. Some guys have no enterprise. Ranga hadn't visited their office and met those people, but Mr Mohan with his lowly education could do all that grunt work. Even at the higher price, Ranga thought the company was a steal.

248 *Touching Distance: The Great Indian MBA Dream*

He really felt like a CEO – an acquisition, where he'd put his name on the price. Ranga had eventually assumed all responsibility, and even his CEO Mr Sambvani was pleased. This is how guys move up. Work smart, not hard. Identify the right people, get them to deliver, and take credit. That's what a CEO's job is.

◆

Back in Bangalore, the next morning, Ranga decided he'd accost Mr Mohan and talk about stock options. He'd spent the last twenty minutes thinking of what he could push for. He'd now arrived at the number and the time was right to ram home the deal. He stood up and opened the door. He walked out, then returned and flushed the toilet where he'd spent all the time doing math in the throes of relief. That arse from across the shared bathroom had sure got to him over the year, making him do things he'd never worried about before.

He went straight to Mohan's office, who wasn't around. He checked with his secretary.

'Where's Mohan?'

'Oh, don't you know? Where were you last week? I thought you returned to India two weeks ago.'

'Yeah, I did. I was like, taking some time off. I mean like, the acquisition got to me. I needed to like, relax and blow off some steam.'

'OK. I'm surprised he didn't say anything to you. Mr Mohan announced that he was quitting the company when you were about to return.'

'Oh. Where was he going?'

'He didn't say. Some people say he's decided to retire.'

'Oh . . . OK. I mean, I should like, call him. I needed to go to Beta Services with him this week to talk to the people there and make arrangements for consolidation.'

'OK. I haven't been able to reach him. I heard he's gone back to his home town. Maybe he has retired.'

'OK. If you hear from him, let me know.'

24

The Cookie Crumbles

So high above, the world tonight,
The angels watch us sleeping
And underneath a bridge of stars,
We dream in safety's keeping.
But perhaps the dream, is dreaming us
Soaring with the seagulls
Perhaps the dream, is dreaming us
Astride the backs of eagles

—STING

Ranga picked his nose, and then took a swig from his cappuccino. He began to speak, utterly oblivious to the big frothy tapestry of coffee and milk froth on his upper lip.

'I mean, like ... fucking Metaphony, OK?'

Mid-sentence, he licked his lips and continued, '... assholes. Screwed up my life!'

Capt looked at him with a disgusted frown. Army table-manners die hard. I'd once seen him eat a perfectly good banana picked off the tree with a fork and a knife. Yes, it can be eaten with a fork and a knife in about the same amount of time that it takes for the

250 *Touching Distance: The Great Indian MBA Dream*

tree to grow – a little less if you don't use your napkin to touch your lips after every bite.

'Boss, what happened? Will you tell us already or do you need two more coffees?'

We were at a Cafe Coffee Day in Bangalore. Capt was supposed to be on a business trip down South, and Ranga had called us up, saying he had amazing news. So far, he'd lingered on and hadn't said anything concrete.

'I mean, like . . . as you guys know. I mean, I got a great offer. CFO's office and all, thanks to my experience in TechPlant and my aptitude for finance . . .

'I mean, like . . . a large part of Metaphony's new business involves like, acquisitions and all. They were looking for someone to do valuation for smaller IT services shops. I mean, like I hounded them, man. Showcased my skills, told them about professors. Like, told them how much material I had. I reeled off all this like some experienced waiter at an SLV restaurant in Bangalore for a few months, man.'

He paused to take another sip.

'I mean, I made presentations about valuation, and the work I'd done before at ISB, I mean, like . . . courses and all. I told them about what I wanted to do. Local country head was impressed. He gave me some assignments.'

'Did you end up working on something live?' Capt asked. Companies were notorious for throwing presentation assignments at freshly minted MBAs who would never do anything where the rubber met the road.

'No, I mean, like . . . same new-guy syndrome, *yaar*. I was only given some crap to do for the first few months. Then I was formally moved into the M&A team. Then helped them with two acquisitions. Basically, I got dumber doing some basic models and all,' he said.

'Ranga, what the hell do you know about valuation at all?' I asked, exasperated.

The Cookie Crumbles **251**

Ranga hadn't taken too many finance courses and had audited a few classes. After those classes, he'd come back and slept soundly, and for much longer than usual, which told me his brain had been exhausted. I'd taught him most of the finance he knew, and he'd borrowed freely when it came to assignments. His gift of the gab, coupled with his earthly behaviour, led people to believe this guy was a misunderstood genius.

'Look, *yaar*. I mean . . . you don't need to know anything, OK? MBA is about being creative and applying things as and when they make sense. I mean, I'm not a finance PhD. You buggers always think we have to be like PhDs or something. That's your problem. Asshole. That's why you're stuck in a job twenty levels below your potential,' he said, now visibly red, angry and sputtering coffee.

'Apologies, your highness,' I said. 'Go on.'

'I mean, like . . . I don't know finance, *yaar*. I was hoping to learn something on the job. Isn't that what people do? I mean, like I'm an engineer, OK?' he remonstrated, getting a little dramatic.

'Get to the point, genius. What happened after that?' interjected Capt. Capt was sick of my frustration with the injustice of the world where I hadn't got my due and was even sicker of reliving Ranga's vague monologues, which really had no point so far.

'I mean, like . . . at first, I obviously didn't know how to do valuation, OK? So I like, asked some guys from our batch to help me out.'

'Who?' I wondered. We had sixty chartered accountants, most of whom had cooked every number possible before they set foot in the institute. Any of them was capable of seeing the truth and dressing up estimates in exactly the manner you needed. They really knew how to create a Mona Lisa from a Dilbert doodle.

'I mean, like . . . I asked the good ones. The toppers. Like Subbu, Arun, Pranav.'

Capt smiled. Ranga may have been lazy, but he knew who the hardworking people were. The people he'd named had slaved for a year at the ISB and had all found jobs in M&A divisions of large

252 *Touching Distance: The Great Indian MBA Dream*

companies, or were working in management consulting, their dream jobs. They'd got these jobs the hard way, interviewing off-campus more than a year after their ISB stint. To them, helping Ranga out with this task was more pencil sharpening and more interview content, not to mention a possible CFO job in due course, should they ever interview with Ranga's company or its competition. It's amazing how far-sighted newly-minted MBAs want to be in their first year. To them, anything is still possible. Indeed, in some cases the faith is not misplaced. It's amazing how many ISB grads end up being interviewed on these business news channels in their first year of graduation. The talent levels are truly stunning in general.

'What did they say?' I couldn't wait much longer to know what was so damaging about this whole exercise.

'Gosh. I mean like, they were awesome, OK? They sent me all the stuff they had. I used that to make a case for more autonomy. Like, it worked, OK? I finally did a deal all by myself. Like, numbers were watertight. Even the country head guy, like . . . he himself had suggested the target. Like, Beta Services or something.'

He stopped midway and caught me laughing.

'Dude, who calls a company Beta Services?' I asked.

'Fuck you. You want to listen or not?' he threatened.

'Sorry, *dorai*,' (king) I deferred.

'So, I mean, like . . . I do the numbers and like that guy, HR prick Mohan even sent the resumes and all. So basically I took like, responsibility for it because he made me sign on the valuation and the deal. Like, I mean he stayed away.'

Capt and I let this sink in for a minute. Anyone entrusting Ranga with this much should brace like saints doused in petrol trying to walk on a coal bed. It was a test of faith where science would win.

'Why you?' Capt and I said together.

'Yeah, I wondered that too. But I thought at first that it was because that guy like didn't understand valuation and all. Anyway, he was only fit for sourcing and reading resumes. HR prick. In the

The Cookie Crumbles **253**

meantime, I went to Paris, I mean, he had sent me on like, a trip to Paris to meet the CEO of Metaphony, some family businessman dude who had come into IT during the gold rush. No MBA or anything. It was like some slow-motion shining-moment crap. Like a reward for closing this deal.'

'So what happened, then?' Capt wondered as Ranga stopped to finish his coffee.

'I mean . . . I came back and this guy Mohan had quit.'

'Nice . . . ' I said.

'OK, so like, I had to do the integration, and I found like all those resumes were like, fake, and that company was worth nowhere near what they suggested,' he closed.

'Huh?' Capt and I chorused.

'Fucking, I just got like, *scroood*. I mean, like . . . I almost had a heart attack.'

'So, Mohan screwed you?' I finished.

'Yeah, some insider deal. Apparently, he was sick of working for that asshole. Wanted to make some money and quit clean. Also, he was upset that I was going to be offered some good options. Now everyone thinks it's my fault. No one believes that Mohan did the due diligence for something I closed,' he finished.

'So what happens now?'

'I mean, for one, like . . . I mean, I've quit. I would have been fired anyway, you know. And two, I hope that asshole buys my story and doesn't sue me.'

Flabbergasted, Capt and I asked, 'What are the chances of your getting sued?'

'I mean, like . . . last week I explained everything to him. He came down. Told him I knew jack shit about anything that was going on. He finally bought it. It helps that Mohan's departure was somewhat sudden. If he wants to sue someone it would be Mohan, but Mohan has too much dope on him. Something like he knows all the malpractices in that place for a while. So, nothing. Just stalemate, OK? Oh yeah, but I sure needed to quit.'

254 *Touching Distance: The Great Indian MBA Dream*

'If he knew you were innocent, why did he have you quit?' asked Capt.

'Because he said, "Ranga, if you don't quit, I'm going to fire your fucking arse!"' he said, picking up his *samosa*.

Capt and I exchange blank glances, letting it sink it.

Finally, I said, 'OK, so what about your loan and stuff. Are your payments okay?'

'Yeah, should be fine. My father-in-law owns two petrol pumps,' he said.

Capt and I gasped.

'You told them!'

'Yeah, like not the whole truth, but I told them the company was closing shop.'

'So what now?' I wondered.

'I mean, like . . . can you guys look for anything in your company? Like, no finance jobs please, any safe job in IT will do. I want to just fly under the radar till the economy turns around.'

'And what then?'

'I mean, like . . . I'm thinking of a PhD or another exec MBA at INSEAD.'

'How are you going to pay for that?'

'I mean, like . . . I don't know, OK? But maybe I could do it part-time. Especially if my job sends me onsite.'

'Dude, first of all, are you OK? You sound like you've been through a lot,' I said.

'Yeah, I mean, like . . . it used to suck before. But I kept asking them why the fuck that guy quit so suddenly after all these years. Also, they just wanted to make sure that I was not working like, hand-in-glove with Mohan. So, I assured them. Showed them my phone, my bank-account statements, everything. It took a long time, but that's over now. That CEO Sambvani got his revenge, I'm leaving with no severance. Like I've been fired, but without any hit to the company,' he explained.

The Cookie Crumbles **255**

'Look, Ranga. You know where I work. There's nothing there. All I do is talk to engineers. I don't even know what a customer looks like, leave alone go onsite. . . . Have you found something else?' I said.

'I'm talking to TechPlant. They are okay to give me something in pre-sales. But I'm trying to push hard on entering their M&A group,' he replied.

'Amazing, we both end up going back to where we came from. I busted my ass, did all the running, got the grades, had zero luck. You sacked out, rode some crazy luck, ran out of it and we both end up at square one,' I summarised.

'Yeah, I mean, like . . . this whole tech stuff sucks, man,' he replied.

Capt sighed and we both stopped talking.

'Come on, *yaar*. Everything sucks. Look at me: I've spent all this time doing strategy and marketing for insurance. I never get to sleep, don't get to see my kids, my wife. My boss—son of a bitch—forced me to move to a north Indian city. I make a lot of money now and I spend even more. I'm in constant fear of being waylaid by some jackass in Gurgaon or Noida. Security sucks there, man, I tell you.'

'What's your problem, dude?' I asked resentfully.

'My problem is very simple, *yaar*. The whole MBA thing worked for me, right? I had all this experience, went to ISB, made a shift to finance, got this job paying over a hundred thousand USD in India, did the TV interviews for my company, rose to head of strategy, and yet I'm no happier for it. I hate being scared about losing it and I hate the fact that my fucking boss thinks he owns me. Once these bastards start paying you a high salary, they realise they've defined your consumption and spending, and they know they have the leverage,' he said.

'So, what are you going to do?' I wondered.

'I don't know. That's what kills me. At least back at the ISB I wanted to make a difference. I wanted to be spiritually enlightened.

256 *Touching Distance: The Great Indian MBA Dream*

Now all I can think of is how I'm going to pay for that piece of land I've booked in Coimbatore without this job. And I don't know how long my job is going to last, honestly. I can't deal with living in the North, and I can't deal with that aggressive culture on the streets.'

'What are you going to do?'

'No idea . . . damn it. I have enough money saved to not work for three years, at least. I think I'll come back here. My Bangalore apartment is ready and it's all been paid for already. I'm at a point where I really can afford not to work for a couple of years.'

'Your ISB loan? Your land purchase?'

'If I sell some equity I should be able to pay for it. It will make a dent but I should be good for another three years. I did get paid awfully well.'

'Great. What are you going to do?'

'I've been talking to some friends in the non-profit space. I really am going to do something in education. I was talking to some folks from an NGO that does good work. Also, I'm going to reconnect to my spiritual side. I'm thinking of taking an intense three-month yoga course and start my own yoga school in due course,' he said.

❖

Two years later . . .

Capt started ventures in primary education and solar lanterns for villages in South India. He recently sent me a picture of himself surrounded by fifty smiling kids outside a building that had a school board on it. With him was his wife. They were smiling from ear to ear. He looked blissful. Not just happy, blissful.

Ranga rejoined TechPlant and works in pre-sales. He's currently in Paris on an assignment. He posted a picture of himself in front of the Louvre on Facebook. He wore the same t-shirt with the French flag printed on it. His hair stood on end and his camera rested safely on his bulging stomach. He had a huge smile, one I'd only seen on the faces of Zen-monks who know life does not matter.

My life went on as usual. I finally settled into the glass cage, and became a great Stockholm victim. Soon, I began to take my own prisoners and grow my organisation as success began to arrive. I performed my own perfect kidnappings. I had my own team and my people loved me. I never once saw my team members looking out the window. If nothing else, I'd learnt what to say to people in the workplace after all the rubbish I'd heard after finishing my MBA.

One morning, I walked into the building, mentally prepared for another hostage day. There was something strange in the air that day and I'd felt ebullient right from the start. As I walked into the lobby, my eyes caught sight of something that made me stop in my tracks. It was a girl, seated with her back to me, but there was something about her that was so familiar. I wondered if I should walk around unobtrusively to see who she was.

I didn't have to. The receptionist called out her name and said, 'You can go in for your interview now.'

I stood there, somewhat frozen, feeling a storm of memories and emotions hurricane their way through my senses.

She nodded at the receptionist, stood up, picked up her things with a grace that had been so innate to her. It was a grace borne out of determination, now somehow coloured by a vulnerability which was new to her, but it only added to her elf-like fragility. She turned around and stopped, staring at me, her face an avalanche of emotion.

As I walked up to her, she turned red and began to mumble with increasing speed, embarrassed and shocked.

'I wasn't sure if you were still here in Bangalore ... I'm so embarrassed. I should have called. I've been looking for jobs outside my city to get away from everything ... I ...' She stopped, overwhelmed, to catch her breath, the pressure of an impending interview and meeting someone who knew too much plunging

258 *Touching Distance: The Great Indian MBA Dream*

her down to drowning point. She reached for her handkerchief to quickly wipe away tears, in a manner which suggested that the lachrymal reflex was all too familiar these days.

She stopped talking as I hugged her and whispered, 'Good luck.'

16 | 11 | 13

100 Pw
70 R.
= ~
20 DAYS